SINS OF THE FLESH

SINS OF THE FLESH

DEVYN QUINN

KENSINGTON BOOKS
http://www.kensingtonbooks.com

APHRODISIA BOOKS are published by

Kensington Publishing Corp.
850 Third Avenue
New York, NY 10022

All Kensington Titles, Imprints, and Distributed Lines are available at special quantity discounts for bulk purchases for sales promotions, premiums, fund-raising, and educational or institutional use.

Special book excerpts or customized printings can also be created to fit specific needs. For details, write or phone the office of the Kensington special sales manager: Kensington Publishing Corp., 850 Third Avenue, New York, NY 10022, attn: Special Sales Department, Phone: 1-800-221-2647.

ISBN-13: 978-0-7582-2017-2
ISBN-10: 0-7582-2017-0

First Kensington Trade Paperback Printing: October 2007

10 9 8 7 6 5 4 3 2 1

Printed in the United States of America

This book is dedicated with love to Stephanie Kelsey.
Friend, advisor, and diva wrangler.
She said, "Yes, you can." And believed it.

Acknowledgments:

Once again, a big thanks goes to my fabulous editor, Hilary Sares, for taking a chance on a little novella and helping me turn it into a full-length book. Without her encouragement and vision, this story wouldn't have been written. More thanks goes to my fabulous agent, Roberta Brown, who got the "Kynn" stories on Hilary's desk. Both ladies are very important, and I couldn't do what I do without their expertise and generous support.

A big hug goes to my friend Tammy Batchelor. Ha, ha. Gotcha in early! Surprise!

Not to be left out are my kick-butt cohorts at Wild Authors! Stop by and say hello at http://www.wildauthors.com.

Prologue

Warwickshire, England, 1895

Immortality was within his grasp, if only he'd reach for it.

Devon Carnavorn stared at the two naked women sprawled across his bed. The soft flicker from nearby candles caressed their bodies, lending a warm sensuous glow to their skin. Throughout the chamber light and shadow drifted together, an indolent waltz driven by periodic flashes of lightning from the storm outside.

Mesmerized by the sight, Devon smiled. Anticipation thickened the air. Appetite whetted, all basic primal urges rose inside him.

To be. To become.

The previous night his eyes had closed to the world around him. His heart ceased to beat, his lungs had drawn no air, and his mortal life had come to its end. The breath of an immortal had awakened him from his brief slumber, the blood drawn from his sire's veins and the taste of her unholy kiss erasing the last traces of his mortality.

No longer did he walk as a human among humans. No. That shell, that damning shawl of decay he'd cast aside, just as the earthbound caterpillar cast away its chrysalis to become a jewel of the air.

The storm suddenly wrapped around the manor, shutting out the rest of the world. A strange, almost glacial chill persisted in lingering around the edges of the bedchamber, untouched by the heat of the fires lit inside the twin hearths. The wind outside kicked up a notch, a voiceless phantom echoing the tempest about to be unleashed inside his soul.

Skin prickling, Devon reached up and pressed a palm to his clammy forehead. His hand shook from the struggle of awakening from death's iron grip. Tension in his shoulders, rigidness in his spine, he couldn't relax. Seconds ticked away, melding into minutes. Awakened, he'd known he'd have to feed, replace the energies reemergence had sapped from his body.

Ariel's voice pulled him back to awareness. "We're waiting, darling."

Devon drew a steadying breath, his tight muscles automatically relaxing. Ariel had promised to bring him his first victim, and she had delivered. The sight of the women sparked little flickers of nerves just beneath his skin.

Hunger rose. His cock stirred inside the confines of his trousers. *I'll feed well tonight.*

Ariel smiled at him. Glittering silvery blue eyes locked with his. The impact of her penetrating gaze caused Devon's heart to skip a beat. Thick black hair framed her heart-shaped face. A bluish sheen emanated from the soft curls, further enhancing her otherworldly aura. Full breasts, a tiny waist, and slender legs. The face of an angel. The body of a vixen.

The soul of a succubus.

"This is Hannah." Pleased, Ariel lazily stroked the girl's blond hair in an intimate and familiar way. "She is to be your first."

Devon's gaze raked over the girl. Very young. No older than eighteen, nineteen at the most. Eyes closed, delicate lashes fanned across rosy cheeks. Damp lips slightly parted. The pale roundness of pert breasts topped with enticing pink nipples beckoned. In a light trance, she'd remember little of the experience.

The impact of her lush, full body caused Devon's mouth to go dry. Carnal demand knifed at gut level, a double-edged blade slicing through his guts. His cock was so rigid he ached. He wanted to taste the girl. No. He *needed* to taste her. "Where did you find her?"

Ariel laughed low in her throat, intimate and amused. "No one will miss her, if that's what concerns you, Lord Carnavorn." She drew the last two words out as if she mocked his title. Such an esteemed position meant nothing to her. Trusting the allure of her femininity, she gave no thought to anything save her own wants and desires. Others would provide.

Devon's blood pulsed beneath his skin, the low, steady beat of his heart driven by adrenaline layered over alert hormones and emotions stretched taut by his crossing. Most likely the girl had been culled from the East End opium dens Ariel so loved to haunt. "Forgive my prying, my lady. I have trusted you this far."

As he spoke a twinge of pressure surged through his head. The beast had awakened. Fingers pressing his temples, he stood, half swaying.

Offering a small pout of forgiveness, Ariel lovingly slid her palm across Hannah's flat belly. "Take her, darling. She is for you." Her voice persuaded.

Conscience tugged at morality, one immediately cast aside. Guilt was a habit he found no difficulty in avoiding. Right now he felt incomplete.

To be. To become.

Burying virtue under a dose of contempt, Devon began to undress. Erection throbbing and straining, shaking hands hurriedly unfastened awkward buttons. Somehow he worked free of his vest and shirt, dropping them to the floor in his hurry. Boots and trousers followed.

Ariel's mercenary gaze devoured his lean, muscular frame. "I knew you belonged among us." Her eyes darkened with invitation. "Come to us, Devon."

Devon slipped onto the bed, stretching out on his side. The silk of soft sheets whispered against his hungry flesh. From ceiling to floor, every item bespoke luxury and decadence to the extreme. Walls were covered in richly woven ivory fabric wallpaper, edged with a crimson-tinged wood trim. Deep pile carpeting spread from wall to wall, a slightly richer shade of scarlet.

Hannah's pliant body melted naturally into his, fitting in that way only a woman's could. His erection pressed against her thigh. He could have taken her immediately, but an invisible hand squeezed his lungs. It took every last ounce of his restraint to keep hunger at bay.

Slow down, he reminded himself. *That is not the way it is done.*

Ariel smiled. "Touch her."

His hand crept to Hannah's hip, his fingers flexing into the soft flesh under his palm. Feeling his touch, Hannah's lashes fluttered, and she smiled vacantly. "My lord," came her half-slurred Cockney murmur.

Beneath the surface of her skin he felt a low, steady hum. Touching her, he felt electric tension spark between Hannah's skin and his.

Pure human energy.

Devon pressed more firmly. A vibrant force throbbed. The tension grew. Somehow his touch seemed to be tapping into her body's most dynamic reserves. The sensations were awesome. Amazing.

Devon closed his eyes, immersing himself in the exhilarating sensations. The effect spread through his system like a virus, invading and restructuring. As a mortal he'd barely been aware of it. As Kynn, his body naturally recognized its nourishment from the energies generated by humans. Desire teasing his senses, his cock surged again in demand.

"Do you feel it?" Ariel's words were a whisper, holding a wonderful secret shared only between them.

All tense muscle and trembling need, Devon nodded. "This," he murmured in return, "was worth the pain."

A feminine laugh of sheer power. "The price we pay to defy God allows us to walk as gods."

Ariel nudged aside Hannah's long hair and gave her slender throat a soft kiss. She stroked Hannah's bare shoulder, then down her belly just above the small triangle of delicate curls.

Ariel had a taste for both sexes and indulged her desires liberally and without restraint. "You were taken many times before your crossing. Do what comes naturally with a beautiful woman." She slid her hand lower, and Hannah's legs parted without instruction, revealing her delicious sex.

The dampness of Hannah's pubic mons indicated she'd already been well prepared. She moved to Ariel's caresses with lazy, sated movements, clearly enjoying the hand working her wet flesh. Her breath caught on a sweet moan, long and low. Her skin glowed from the scented oils she'd bathed in.

Ariel met Devon's gaze as she lifted her cream-soaked fingers to his mouth, smearing his lips with the musky juices. "She's so moist . . . and tight. Take her . . . taste her."

Shifting his weight so that he was half on top of Hannah, he cupped the back of her head with a palm. His mouth searched for and found hers. Hannah accepted his kiss, her tongue darting out to tangle with his. Whatever she might be, she wasn't protesting. Their lips smashed together, doing a heated dance that soon left both panting with craving.

Devon's hands explored her body, slender and strong under his touch. She quivered with tension, a fine flush rising up over her throat to heighten the blueness of her eyes, eyes that held an expression of naked vulnerability.

A moan of pleasure rippled from Hannah's throat. "Touch me." She writhed beneath him, nuzzling her cheek against his shoulder. "All over my body."

Devon maneuvered one hand through the silky curls, then lightly slid his fingers between her legs and gently caressed her. The moist evidence of her pleasure stoked his own. The muscles of his thighs tightened, hips tense.

Hannah grasped the railing above her head and spread her legs wider, every delicious inch of her sex open and ready to be filled.

Devon stroked up and down her labia, enjoying the soft mewling sounds spilling from Hannah's lips. Her body shuddered, and she pushed back against the mattress. He dipped his head, his mouth covering a nipple. He flicked his tongue over the hard little nub and sucked harder, drawing humid circles around the peak. Each dart of his tongue, coupled with the sizzle beneath her skin, sent shock waves of need through his system. The sensations of more than mere lust arrowed toward his groin, making him dizzy from the ache. Body shaking with the need of his new craving, a sheen of perspiration slicked his skin.

Cock tightening, a red haze floated across Devon's vision. He wanted to be inside her cunt, buried to the hilt; feel her every tremor of pleasure as his body absorbed the energy of hers. Excited, frustrated, he wanted more. Now. "I need this."

Ariel smiled, fingering the odd piece of jewelry around her neck, a silver charm fashioned in the shape of a Celtic triquetra, a series of interlocking triangles symbolizing the triple aspects of the Kynn dominion, the communion of flesh, blood and sex.

The edges of the charm were sharp enough to cut human flesh, and often had. A jerk of her hand snapped the thin chain. She offered the charm with a satisfied smile.

Control slipping away, Devon accepted the charm. For a moment he froze, doubt and apprehension warring. To make the connection with his victim, he'd have to take her blood.

He glanced down. A series of small scars were scattered across his abdomen. A cold, tight feeling of dread tightened his chest. A lump rose in the back of his throat. Thorns of his abandoned religion pricked. The Kynn must take communion of their victim. He'd known this when he'd chosen to accept Ariel's invitation to join her forbidden world. Fallen from heaven, denied entry into hell, the Kynn walked as outcasts from both worlds.

Ariel noted his hesitation. "Be quick with the edge." Her lips curved in amusement. "It won't be so painful."

Shedding doubt, Devon clenched his jaw and swallowed down the lump. His hand shook not more than a little when he pressed one sharp edge to the softness of Hannah's left breast, then drew it sharply downward. Her skin parted, the intimate invasion causing her to gasp with shock. Blood welled from the thin red slice.

Bending close to her ear, Ariel stilled Hannah's writhing with soft words of reassurance and even softer kisses. Their mouths soon joined, devouring each other's lips.

The charm slid from lax fingers. Sensing blood, the beast hovering at the edges of Devon's mind took over. Shoving his thoughts aside, an ancient and primeval beast took control. Instinct, fiercely animalistic, surged. A hunger forbidden by God and scorned by Satan flooded through him, an invisible pulsing of power flaring into vibrant control.

Devon felt it in his head, felt it tearing down his spine, vibrating to his bones as if to rip him asunder and scatter the pieces to the four winds. Searing, uncontrollable, the entity he'd unleashed became unstoppable. To deny it would be fatal.

Trembling with the strength of his craving, Devon pressed his lips to the wound. Warm blood covered his tongue, the taste not as unpleasant as he'd anticipated. He drank, reveling in the coppery sweetness flowing smoothly down his throat. Its taste was like sun-warm honey fresh from the bee's hive.

"Just a bit is all you need for the psi connection," Ariel warned. "Now you can take from her body the energies that will sustain yours."

Devon rose to his knees, positioning himself between Hannah's spread legs. Hardly daring to breathe, he slid his hands up her legs, inside her thighs. Touching her intoxicated, its effect filling him like a shot of fine whiskey on a cold winter's night. There was instant satisfaction in the sensation. Looking down at her beautiful sex, his cock arched up against his stomach, a beast eager for the feed.

Like a conductor guiding her orchestra, Ariel shifted her position, moving behind him. He felt her reach around from behind him, teasing his dusky nipples with slow circles. Her fine-boned hands felt cool against his burning skin. The contrast between heat and ice maddened. "You are doing well, my love. Take her, possess her."

Devon groaned, his features drawing into a grimace as though he were in great pain. "Oh God, I can feel it inside me."

A tiny whisper caressed his ear. "Let it guide you. Your body knows what to do."

Devon gritted his teeth. He needed this with a fierce burning desire, a thing he had never felt before.

Gripping Hannah's hips, he pulled her forward, entering her in a single hard thrust. Her naked thighs were sleek and smooth against his naked hips. A deep moan escaped him at the same time Hannah let out a little cry. Silken bindings gripped him, and held.

His erection pulsed. *Not yet.* The single savage thought was more instinctive than conscious.

Devon closed his eyes. Pulling out with torturous slowness, he stroked back in, watching her depth swallow his entire length. His senses fractured a little.

He drew out. Another thrust.

Sensation ratcheted up tenfold. Rippling inner muscles gripped him like a fist encased in a velvet glove, liquid and warm.

Oh. My. God.

Tempo quickening, Devon's control threatened to slip away. Shedding all restraint, he raised Hannah's hips, cupped her ass, then impaled her again. A hot fist punched in his groin, expanding with each stroke into her creamy depth.

Time ceased to exist, spinning out of his reach. New strength surged through him. With each entry of his body into hers, his body sapped at the core of energy sustaining each and every life.

Devon could barely make out Hannah's form as his penis shuttled in and out. Her desperate whimpers flogged his passion toward fever pitch.

Hannah moaned, faltered, then lost control of the pace. Shock, then pleasure, turned her sighs into primeval guttural cries. The reach for climax was building, sure and strong.

Breath scorching his lungs, hips an unstoppable piston, Devon pulled back, then rammed in until seated to the hilt. This time he felt the physical results of their friction, the crackle of pure energy leaving her and entering him. The pulse of her very core filled him to the brim.

The air around him quivered, a strange prickling crawling over his skin to shimmy down his spine. He felt rather than saw strange distortions begin to creep along the outlines of the familiar room. Inside his mind, the disfigurement sparked and flared, spinning around and closing in on him with alarming speed. A distant roar filled his ears, a sensation so swiftly dizzying that his vision blurred, then blackened. The immense weight of eternity threatened to crush him and resurrect him all in the same instant. Mind-shattering power mingling with everlasting pleasure tormented, pure energy moving through him until he was sure he'd splinter from the overload.

Glowing red and brilliant orange, the sizzling light exploded. The energy of all life, of all creation, washed through him. In that moment time and space existed as a single entity of pure power and majesty. He'd joined the beginning, the end, and all in between.

Breasts heaving, throat arching, Hannah jerked and shuddered. Her pulse raced in her throat, beating against her pale skin like the fluttering of a bird's wings. She groaned, low in her throat. Panting hard, her eyes burned with the heat of their connection.

Body shuddering, Devon's cock surged. White-hot pleasure imploded in his belly, running like rivers of fire from the top of his head to his toes. A starburst of sensation riddled his brain, tearing his thoughts into tiny pieces. He couldn't think, couldn't breathe, but didn't care. The bed beneath him quaked and shook, then all became quiet.

Willpower alone slowed his breathing.

Little by little, Devon felt his body relax, muscles uncoiling. The strange lethargy holding him in its terrible grip had lessened.

Limp and worn with the aftermath of being claimed, Hannah drew a shaky breath. The color that had drained from her face slowly returned. Releasing a soft groan from between pale lips, her eyes fluttered shut.

Pleased with her lover, Ariel spread a soft mantle of kisses across Devon's shoulders. "You did well, my love." Her arms circled his waist, palms pressed possessively against his chest. Knowing and eager, she nibbled on his damp flesh.

Terrible fever quenched, Devon could savor the sensations

setting his blood to quickening and his senses to humming with renewed vitality. He felt light, buoyant. What was new, what completely stunned him, was the knowledge that such a primal act would spin him into a long and lovely eternity.

Amazing.

1

Warren, CA, Present Day

Once again, the night had come to its end. Dawn's grasping fingers had seized the earth's horizon, refusing to let the darkness have one more hour than necessary. Pale pink lashings began to illuminate the edges of the night's sky. All too soon the merciless sun would rule again.

Sprawled across a chaise lounge, Devon Carnavorn swirled the last of the sherry in his glass. "Another night gone," he muttered under his breath. "Wasted."

Clothing askew, reeking of sexual musk, he glanced around his den. A proliferation of naked bodies filled the space around him. The odor of bodies in motion fused with the cloying scent of sandalwood incense, burned in such quantity the air hazed. The sexes not only seemed mingle, but merge. Though no music played, several danced together in rhythmic slow motion. Others more engrossed in pleasure had commandeered sofas, chairs, even the floor to engage in heated lovemaking. Locked in intimate embrace, hands and mouths explored every inch.

Devon signed, frowning in displeasure. "It's getting to where I can't tell one night from the last." His life had turned into a big blur. He wasn't even really living. He simply existed.

Disgusted, he stood up, nearly tripping over the naked woman sprawled on the rug at his feet. Vague recognition registered. He'd fucked her. More than once, anally, orally, and in every other position he could think of.

Closing his eyes on a memory he didn't care to recall, his mouth twisted into a grimace of displeasure. The sight of her nude body did nothing to arouse him. He wondered what he'd seen in her beyond a tool to sate his hunger.

A low growl broke from his lips. "Nothing, damn it. Nothing." Instead of feeling satisfied, all he felt was hollow. The woman meant nothing, had made no impression. He didn't even know her name. In a few hours he wouldn't even remember her face. "God forgive me." A mean, grating laugh escaped him. "I never thought I'd be bored with immortality."

A bitter utterance, but true.

Devon's lips flattened into a hard line. Everything that should have been right in his life was wrong. Seriously wrong.

Feeling the closing of the walls around him, the pressure of too many living, breathing bodies, he needed to get out. If he didn't he'd start screaming. And never stop.

Pausing only to refill a glass emptied with alarming regularity nowadays, Devon wove his way toward the French doors leading into the back gardens.

Stepping outside, cool air scented with a fine morning's dew filled his nostrils. His head cleared a bit. Only the smallest of headaches remained.

Sipping his sherry, Devon watched the day begin its advance, wiping away shadows with a cruel hand. The quiet hours before the rest of the world awakened were the times he felt the loneliest, felt the emptiness inside the soul he'd pledged to the darkness. Soon, he'd have to seek shelter. During the day, his energies and paranormal abilities waned. As long as he stayed shielded he could move around with a fair amount of freedom, dashing from car to building unscathed should he have to venture out.

Lately, though, he'd toyed with the idea of not seeking sanctuary from the day.

Suicide tempted, but he'd always held back. Not because he wasn't strong enough. He didn't have to be strong to walk into the sun's light. He'd just walk, until the flesh had burned from his bones and his skin crumbled to dust. Such a death would be painful. Perhaps even a well-deserved penance.

Ariel had died, and he had survived.

Devon took a step forward, then a second. He couldn't take a third.

He stopped. Shaking the idea of self-immolation loose from its moorings, he stored it instead in that secret place in the recesses of his mind. The Kynn were few and far between. The *Amhais,* the shadow stalkers, operated effectively. Driven by religious fanaticism, the vampire-hunters simply wouldn't let up or back off. He'd had one too many close calls himself. The human assassins were expert and all too willing to die for their cause.

To the Amhais, a vampire was a vampire. *And vampires must be slain.*

Air vanishing from his lungs, Devon felt his throat tighten. An icy shiver slid down his spine. Almost a century had passed since he'd lost Ariel to those ignorant fools.

Though hardly a man to weep and gnash his teeth in grief, he was given to days of deep depression, often seeing only futility in the long existence he now considered to be a curse. Immortality meant nothing when the time was spent alone, making his sire's loss no easier to bear. He thought he'd moved on since that time. He hadn't.

Devon closed his eyes. Just thinking of how Ariel had died

made his head throb, the glass in his hand tremble. Fearing he'd faint, he lifted ice-cold fingers to his eyes, pressing hard against his lids. He and Ariel hadn't been together long, but the mark she'd left on him was indelibly etched on his brain like acid on glass.

Ariel had been his sire. His lover. She'd been everything.

They'd planned an eternity together. They'd had less than a decade. He'd never found another female who even came close to replacing her. The women who came into his life nowadays were just faces—bodies really. Drifting through, leaving no impression on his mind or his heart.

Once a hedonist in the fullest sense, there had been a time in his life when he couldn't restrain himself from seeking out sin. It was his nature. Life was meant to be enjoyed, the temptations of this earth too many.

Time had passed, though. Times had changed. Humans aged, grew old, died around him. Technology had changed, geography had shifted, cultures met and merged. Keeping up had never been a problem.

Until now.

At some point Devon couldn't quite identify, entropy had set in. The rot had wound around his senses and woven its poisonous vines around the very fibers of his being. The twin beasts of lust and greed had finally turned on him. Too much of a good thing didn't enhance. It decayed. Thirty-four when he'd ceased aging, he was barely through the first half of his second century. The life he'd once vowed to seize now bored him stiff.

Well, hell. Everything seemed wrong and nothing felt right. Were immortals supposed to have a mid-century life's crisis? Somehow he didn't think gold chains and a Lamborghini would solve this one.

Devon eyed the dangerous sun. His stomach suddenly felt queasy, his knees weak. So hot a moment ago, he now felt stone cold. Perspiration soaked his shirt, dotting his forehead. "You and I may yet be meeting again."

A voice from behind broke through. "Sir?"

Devon turned. Simpson, his manservant and closest confidant, stood behind him. Discrete and utterly reliable, Simpson could be counted on to do his job, his eyes open, his mouth shut.

Devon swallowed hard. Whether in relief or disappointment he couldn't be sure. His meeting with the glowing golden eye wouldn't come today. Tomorrow, perhaps. But not today.

"Have they gone?"

Grim faced and unsmiling, Simpson nodded briskly. "I've cleared them out."

Devon nodded. He hated nothing more than a house full of deadbeats hanging around. Orgy over, he wanted to be left alone. "And the young lady?" he asked, meaning his own recent fuck.

Simpson frowned. "Has been paid and sent on her way." His words simmered disapproval.

Devon sipped his sherry, hating what he had to say. "Suppose I shouldn't be dragging in all these strays." Not a question.

Simpson's lip dropped lower. "If I may say so, sir, it's dangerous to keep exposing yourself to the riffraff. Your reputation isn't highly regarded. One of these days—"

Tension knotting his shoulders, Devon cut him off. "I'm going to stumble, I know." Discretion had come to mean little lately.

Simpson snorted, eyeing him with more than a little annoyance. "A little more, ah, restraint on your part would go a long way toward salvaging your reputation. Word does get around about the goings-on here."

Brow wrinkling, Devon shrugged, unable to protest. Truth, all truth. Attempting to salvage his reputation would probably prove futile at this point. As one of the Kynn, he'd chosen not to limit his proclivities for sexual adventure. Quite the opposite. He'd exploited the vampire mythologies by founding a string of successful Goth-themed nightclubs. In doing so, he'd remade his fortune several times over. If problems arose, he employed a rich-man's solution: money.

One thing money couldn't buy was his peace of mind.

Or love.

Something I haven't truly had since Ariel was alive. He'd begun to doubt he'd ever have another chance at finding a second mate.

Thrusting the idea from his mind, Devon emptied his glass. The emptiness was eating him up inside. "I don't want to hear any more right now." His words ended the conversation then and there.

"Of course, Lord Carnavorn." Simpson only used Devon's title when displeased.

Lips pressing tightly, Devon pawed at his pounding temple. Oh hell. Let the old bugger be pissed off. Better pissed off than pissed on. His headache had taken on fresh strength, banging behind his eyes, which felt like they'd pop out of his skull. He'd drank too much, fucked too much, and felt like shit. Exhaustion had crept up on him, and he hadn't even realized it. Instead of feeling invigorated from his recent feed, he felt like concrete. Heavy, dull, and lifeless.

A touch of the sun on his skin sent him back into soothing shadows. Simpson followed. As if aware of his master's earlier thoughts, Simpson drew the blinds. They closed with a brisk snap, shielding him from the outside world but not his thoughts.

Devon wished he could simply close his eyes and go on to no particular destination, just quietly exist in limbo forever.

Simpson stood across from him, keeping his distance deliberate. "Are you all right, sir?"

A ridge of muscle tightened Devon's jaw. A painful sensation began to work its way through his neck and shoulders. "I'll be fine."

At least he hoped he would be.

Feeling the pressure of the night's exertions, Devon pressed the heels of his hands into his eyes. Perhaps if he rubbed hard enough he could obliterate every brain cell in his head. Stop thinking. Stop breathing. Stop being.

Thinking of the empty bed waiting for him only depressed him more. He'd slept very little lately, mostly because he hated facing that desolate expanse of cold sheets. Despite the bevy of beautiful women he'd recently had at hand, he'd be going to bed alone.

Again.

2

The saleswoman turned the sign from OPEN to CLOSED. "I can't believe this is the last time we'll be doing this."

Rachel Marks glanced up from the day's receipts. "We tried, Ginny. There's just not enough business to stay open." She frowned. "We're just not located in the new additions being built on the other side of town."

The old lady nodded. "It's a shame too. The mall just sucked business away from Main Street."

Rachel frowned. Because of the new mall, she was out on her ass, unable to compete with the huge new chain store installed there. She would've loved to move to a more desirable location, but she simply couldn't afford the outrageous rent charged for the spaces. No matter how many specials she ran, no matter how much she slashed prices, the new bookstore was always one step ahead of her.

Moreover, the new store had a coffee and snack bar, something she just couldn't compete with. Why come to her small shop when a cornucopia awaited across town?

Ginny wiped away her tears. "I did so like working here."

She cast a final look over barren shelves. "It's such a cozy little store."

"*Was* such a cozy little store," Rachel grumbled, writing down the day's numbers on the sheet of paper by her register. This last month of "Going Out of Business" had secured barely enough to cover the rent on the building and Ginny's salary. Zilch left for her. Depressing. Unless she got a job quickly, she wouldn't be able to meet the rent on her own apartment.

Rachel quickly counted out a week's pay for Ginny. "Here you go. I'm sorry it's not more."

Ginny shook her head. "I don't want to take the money."

Rachel smiled despite her sadness. Ginny Smithers never wanted to take her money. A sixty-year-old widow, Ginny lived on a limited income from Social Security, barely making enough to get by.

Though Ginny would protest she didn't need the money, Rachel would have to insist the old woman take it. Ginny had been the only one she was able to keep on these last couple of months. The rest of the staff had been slowly let go as business decreased from a flow to barely a trickle.

Rachel sighed tiredly. "Please, Ginny, not today. You've worked hard this week. Take your money and go home and relax. It's been a long day."

Ginny tucked the money into her purse. "Do you need some help closing up?"

Rachel shook her head. "No. I just need to get those last few boxes of unsold books out, and I'm done."

Ginny hesitated, dragging out her exit. "If you're sure . . ."

"I'm sure." Rachel came around the counter. "Just give me a hug, and promise me you'll take care of yourself." She gave the tiny woman a gentle squeeze.

Ginny reached up and patted her cheek. "You'll come by and see me sometime?"

Rachel smiled, even though she wasn't feeling very cheery

inside. "Of course I will, and I expect to have one of your delicious chocolate muffins just waiting for me."

An easy smile crossed Ginny's face, lighting her eyes. "I'll bake up a big batch."

"You do that." Rachel walked the old woman to the door. "Now you get home before it gets too dark outside."

She glanced up. A storm was brewing. Already the sky was leaden with clouds: heavy, pregnant, threatening a violent storm. The wind was picking up, coming from the North, bringing in a chill. Hanging on with cold hands, winter was refusing to go easily.

In like a lion, out like a lamb, they always say. March is coming in like a lion. So much for sunny, summery California.

Truth be told, though, she liked the weather. Rainy days made one think of a warm fire, a mug of hot chocolate, and a good book to read; of a day lost in a world not one's own.

Arms wrapped around her body, Rachel watched Ginny shuffle up the sidewalk. Five o'clock, and the rest of the businesses on Main Street were also closing. This part of town usually rolled up the sidewalks by sundown.

Sighing, Rachel shut the door and locked it behind her. Turning, she cast her gaze around the store, once filled to the brim with books. New Releases. Fiction. Nonfiction. Biography. Travel. Self-Help. Children's. She'd tried to stock a little bit of everything, keep customers happy by always ordering the latest bestsellers or tracking down that hard-to-find title. She simply couldn't win the war with the online booksellers.

She wasn't alone. A lot of the little Main Street businesses couldn't compete. Didn't make her feel any better. She had still failed. She'd had to sell most of her stock at rock-bottom prices just to get people to come in and take it off her hands. What went unsold would be returned to the booksellers for future credit. Not that she needed credit now. She was out of business.

For good.

No use standing around thinking about it.

Rachel hurried to the back of the store and propped open the rear exit, then opened the trunk of her car. The wind had picked up, bringing in a blast that went straight up her skirt. No thunder yet, but the insistent flicker of lightning warned of the coming storm.

Catching her hem before she gave the world a fine view of her panties, she hurried back inside and picked up a box of books. Hefting it, she carried it out to the car and packed it away. Two more trips followed, and that was all.

She slammed down the trunk. Twelve years down the drain. People were driving straight past Main and heading down to the larger shopping area.

"To the mall." *That goddamned mall.*

A short, heavyset woman with glaring red hair and apple-red cheeks stepped out of the rear exit of the building adjacent to hers. Dressed in one of her wild gypsy outfits guaranteed to blind the fashion conscious, Frannie Sutter hurried over. The charms around her neck clinked as she walked, making her sound like some sort of medieval wind chime in the hustling breeze. The wind did little damage to her hair. That red mess always looked as if she'd fixed it with an egg beater, then sprayed on cooking oil to set it. Jewelry, some expensive, most gaudy, crusted every finger of her hand. Even her thumbs. A self-proclaimed white witch and fortune teller, Frannie ran a magic shop. She'd often have Rachel order the latest titles on witchcraft and the supernatural.

"You going already, dear?"

"Yes, all packed up to go."

Looking at Rachel's old wreck that had more rust than actual paint left, Frannie released a sigh. "I'm sorry, hon. I worked every spell I could." Looking a little sheepish, she shrugged. "Guess my power failed me this time."

Rachel's lips quirked down in a frown. "No biggie. I knew it was coming. Truth be told, I should have closed the store a year ago." *Might still have a little credit left to my name*. As it stood, she didn't have a dime's worth left.

Frannie folded Rachel into a bear hug. The scent of gardenias clung to her skin. "It won't be the same without you."

Rachel blinked away her tears. "I hate this," she whispered. "Losing everything."

Frannie also had tear tracks on her face, but she tried to smile. "I know." She sniffed, wiping her eyes. "Anything I can do?"

Rachel felt a lump rising in her throat. She hesitated a long, nerve-racking minute. "Light a candle for me."

Pleased with the idea, Frannie gave a devilish look and waggled her eyebrows. "And pray for tall, dark, and handsome to come your way."

The idea went all over her like a dash of icy cold water. A definite no. *And get fucked again? Never.*

Rachel drew herself up straighter. "I'd prefer a winning lotto ticket, please."

Frannie winked. "Even better. Then you can buy all the toy boys you want."

Lightning cracked, giving a taste of the storm to come.

Giving a final hug to her friend, Frannie waved and hurried back inside her shop. She had a job, a place to go. Customers to wait on.

Vision blurring again from unwelcome tears, Rachel slid in behind the wheel just as fat droplets of water began to pound the hood. The rain struck with fury, punishing the earth. Crinkling her nose, she wiped a few stray droplets off her face. She didn't want to go home. Not yet. No hurry anyway. No one waited for her except Sleek, her cat. And it wasn't like he'd miss her as long as his food and water dishes were full.

Feeling like a complete loser, Rachel sank down in her seat. Closing the store, she'd lost not only an income but every last cent she had in the world. What did they call young, busted business owners who didn't have a pot to piss in?

Yubbies?

Failures.

"Failure, indeed," she sniffed. "I might be out of business, but I still have a degree. People will be dying to snap me up. I can make a living anywhere."

Brave words. In the back of her mind she was scared shitless. Bitter bile churned in her stomach, filled her throat. Once again she was left on the outside looking in, her nose pressed against fortune's window. She felt as if life had given her the boot. She'd been evicted. Again!

Tears prickled. She blinked and one escaped, trekking down her cheek. Another followed. Swiping them away, she pounded her palms against the steering wheel. "Damn it, I'm thirty-three. I'm too old to start over."

The stack of bills occupying the passenger seat caught her eye. She winced, mentally ticked off each one.

Rent, utilities, phone, car insurance. Visa to the max. MasterCard, ditto. Almost a thousand dollars in bills, not including the extra three months she still owed on her bookstore's rental space. She'd stupidly signed a lease that required her to finish any given semiannual calendar period, whether open or closed. She owed on the damned building until June. Almost twelve hundred dollars.

A cold chill swept over her. *I don't have enough money.*

Digging in her purse, she flipped open her checkbook. The balance discouraged. Two hundred in checking, another eight hundred in savings. Pay nine hundred on the lease, and she'd have a grand total of one hundred dollars to her name. And that wouldn't even come close to clearing the debt on the store.

"Brilliant." She tossed her checkbook aside. "You are a fucking genius with money." Depression kicked in. The rain pattered harder against the windshield, echoing the thoughts beating through her mind like ominous black wings.

Rachel rubbed her tired eyes. Right now she wished she could evaporate, cease to exist. Life hadn't really been lovely or interesting anyway. Certainly no one would miss her. Her parents were deceased, years ago. She had a few distant aunts and uncles, some cousins. People she barely knew and hadn't seen in years. If she vanished tomorrow, would anyone come looking for her?

Nope.

The thought brought a frown.

Alone. That's how she'd gone through life.

She did for herself. Period. And right now taking care of herself meant getting another job. Fast.

"That's just the way it is." Her words ground out from between clenched teeth. "All for one and one for me."

3

Sitting with the paper open to the classifieds, Rachel sipped her afternoon treat, a double mocha latte with whipped cream. She might be nearly broke and not have food in the fridge, but she damn sure wasn't about to give up her single joy in life. She'd forego eating for the happiness of knocking back a too-small, overpriced coffee drink in a fancy cup.

Pen in hand, she'd circled several possible jobs to go out and apply for. Most of them were minimum wage, a lot of rungs lower than what she was accustomed to working for. She'd already applied for every management, secretarial, and clerking position that paid a decent wage, even swallowing her pride and putting in for assistant manager at the bookstore at the mall. But with the economy on the downslide and the unemployment rate skyrocketing, she wasn't the only person pounding the pavement for a job. Employers could pick and choose.

Rachel didn't have months to wait for the job she wanted. She'd take anything to keep ahead of the bill collectors until something better came along. Well, almost anything. No matter how low she hit, some things were off limits. Fast food was a definite no, as was washing cars or working as a janitor or nursing-home aide. She hadn't fallen that far. Yet.

She crinkled her nose, leaving the clerking section and skimming over to food services. Just when she was about to give up, her gaze fell on an ad.

HOSTESS WANTED, it read. MYSTIQUE NIGHTCLUB. ALSO HIRING WAITRESSES AND KITCHEN STAFF. EXPERIENCED ONLY NEED APPLY.

She read no further, beating the pen against her chin, holding off on circling the ad.

Mystique was the hot spot to party at. A Goth-themed nightclub that had opened about a year ago, it attracted an interesting mélange of people—from the normal ones looking for a drink and dance, to the psychos who seemed to have a problem with reality. Like the underground gay community, Warren also harbored a huge pagan community. By day, they worked jobs like everyone else. By night, they ghosted around in indigo robes, fancying themselves to be supernatural beings.

Do I really want to work in a place like that?

Rachel tapped the ad with her pen, marking it with tiny red dots. Something about the ad beckoned her. Go to work in a nightclub? She wasn't the type who fancied bodies packed like sardines in a can. Mystique was loud and wild, and it attracted the type of crowd she just didn't run with. However, from miscellaneous conversations that she'd overheard at the unemployment center, the girls who worked the floor there made good money. A waitress could rack up a few hundred dollars in tips a night. That certainly wouldn't hurt her feelings.

Using the figures bandied about in the women's conversation, she did some quick addition at the edge of the paper under the doodles she'd already drawn there. That kind of cash would help bail her out of debt faster. She flicked the end of the pen against her chin again. She supposed she could put up with the crowds if it meant making decent money. She'd waited tables in college. It wouldn't be hard to deliver drinks from point A to point B.

One hurdle hobbled her.

Mystique's owner always hired certain types of women. Only real knockouts got past the management's discerning eye. The girls were all beautiful, with huge tits, firm asses, miles of permed waves, and perfectly capped white teeth—actresses on their way to Hollywood. The sad reality was that most of them had no true talent. Some actually made porn stars seem intelligent. Most of them usually ended up working as hookers.

Okay. So she didn't have a shitload of bleached-blond hair. So she didn't have double-D tits. She did have a B-cup rack on her chest and long killer legs, part of the glory that came from being a giraffe standing five foot ten inches tall. Since she wasn't looking to be the next Oscar-winning actress, perhaps working at Mystique would help make ends meet until she could land a more stable position.

The hostess position wouldn't be half bad. Those girls just drifted around, shaking hands with the customers, making sure everyone was happy, well taken care of, seeing that no one swiped tips off the tables, arranging seating for groups. That shouldn't take a lot of brainpower.

Drawing several small circles around the ad, Rachel quickly finished her coffee, tossing the cup and napkin into the trash.

Why not?

Mystique stood on the outskirts of Warren, one of the last sights people saw when leaving the city. Built from the ground up, the two-story club had been designed to resemble a medieval castle, complete with turrets and a drawbridge. Instead of going over water, though, the bridge connected with the concrete parking lot.

Checking her makeup and smoothing her tresses into place, Rachel got out of her car. She didn't bother to lock it. Nothing to steal but a newspaper and a lot of empty coffee cups. Hitching her purse strap higher up on her shoulder, she walked to the front entrance of the nightclub. Even in broad daylight, the club was impressive. Surrounded by an acre of trees, manicured hedges, and evergreen grass, it was one of the best sights in town. The owner had spared no expense.

At ten in the morning, the parking lot was nearly empty. The place didn't open its doors to the public before noon. Enough cars were scattered around to let Rachel know that some employees had already arrived to start their workday.

Taking a deep breath and readying herself to paste on her "public" face, she reached out and pulled on one of the twin doors that would take her inside.

Butterflies filled her stomach. She was used to being on the other side of the desk doing the interviewing, not being interviewed. That still stung, and she doubted she would ever get over the profound sense of loss she felt. Truth be told, she didn't like the idea of punching someone else's time clock. She'd enjoyed being a business owner, being her own boss; had liked working in the quiet, slow pace of her bookstore.

Walking inside, she was immediately struck by the immensity of the nightclub. The panorama greeting her took her breath away. It was a massive space with several levels. It had not one, or even two, but three dance floors. Dark, decorated in a neo-Gothic style reminiscent of a medieval age gone hard punk. The walls were covered with huge, custom-made tapestries that revealed scenes of hellish brutality when lit by the overhanging black lights.

In the Mystique world, evil triumphed over good, night overcame day, and death ruled over life. As if echoing Torquemada's dungeons, faux instruments of torture decorated shadowy corners. Cages the girls danced in hung from the ceiling. There was a balcony with a huge disco booth so the DJ could see the dance floors. The balcony ran all the way around the nightclub, allowing a view from every angle. Overhead, a wall of mirrors spanned one complete side. When the place was in full swing, an elaborate lighting system flashed multicolored strobes in sync with the music. The perfect place to party.

Quiet and motionless, the bar was eerie without people packing it, music thudding. Rachel could imagine she was walking through one of the seven levels of hell itself, deeper into the bowels of a purgatory from which none returned.

A silly thought, but Rachel had a big imagination.

In reality, the bar was well lit at the present time. People worked throughout—restocking the booze behind the bars, putting down chairs, getting ready for the night ahead. She reasoned that the waitresses would probably not be straggling in until around eleven.

A voice behind her caught her ear. "Can I help you, Miss?"

Rachel pivoted on her heel.

Standing behind the backup bar was a young man dressed casually in a Mystique T-shirt and blue jeans. The design was of a vampiric sorceress sucking the life out of a half-naked man.

She smiled. Girl power, indeed.

"I'd like to see the manager, please."

"Are you here to apply for a job?"

She nodded, flashing her best toothy grin. "Yes, I am."

"I'll need you to fill out an application." After reaching under the counter, the young man came around the bar and handed her one. He put down a chair and motioned for her to take a seat. "Fill it out here, and when you're done, let me know."

Rachel didn't fail to notice his striking gray eyes and the way his cowlick fell casually over his forehead. A good-looking fellow. But young, oh, too young for her, a puppy of twenty-one or twenty-two. She sighed. It had been a long time since she'd had a man in her life. Too damn long.

Digging in her purse for a pen, she set to filling out the application with the appropriate information. She wrote slowly but precisely, careful not to make any mistakes that would cause her to have to strike through what she'd written.

Done, Rachel stood up, pushing the chair into place. "Now what?"

He looked at her with bored eyes. "Finished?"

Duh. Beauty, but no brains. Why else would she be bothering him? Rachel smiled. "Yes."

The hunk motioned for her to follow.

Rachel trotted across the dance floor behind him, heels clicking on the polished wood. He led her toward the rear of the building, through a door, and into a rabbit warren of intersecting hallways. People passed them without looking twice, not caring that an outsider was trying to penetrate their clique. They had jobs there. She didn't. She was no threat.

A nearby door read MANAGER. The young man knocked on it, opening it and sticking his head in.

"Rosalie," he called. "Someone needs to see you."

A woman's tart voice answered. "Who?"

"Dunno. Some lady looking for a job. She's filled out an application."

The bite lessened. "Send her in."

The young man stepped aside, allowing Rachel into the office. Windowless, it was well lit. Her eyes flicked over the desk, filing cabinets, a couple of chairs, some innocuous framed prints on the wall. All in all, quite normal décor.

A woman sat behind the desk, tapping at her keyboard, squinting from behind her glasses at the monitor. Giving her head a little shake at whatever she was working on, Rosalie took off her glasses and stood up, offering her hand. "I'm Rosalie Dayton. And you're . . ."

Rachel offered her own hand, covertly looking her over. Rosalie Dayton was an imposing-looking woman. Fat as a tick on a hound, she had the face of a brindle bulldog and hard, tiny eyes that seemed to bash through everything she set them on. It was clear that beauty was not hers, past or present. With her wrinkled skin and shock of white hair, it was hard to tell if she was fifty or seventy.

A tough old bird. Not easily impressed or bowled over by charm. Best to be straight and talk tough back.

"Rachel Marks."

Silence. The old lady clearly wasn't impressed.

Rachel handed over her application. Rosalie's desk was already literally papered with more of the same. Many of the applications looked scrawled by half-wits and idiots. Hopefully, her neat, letter-perfect penmanship would win her a few points.

"I'm here to apply for the hostess position advertised in the paper," she prompted helpfully.

Rosalie flashed her a small, grim smile. "Mister Carnavorn has already filled that position."

No deterrent. "Well, too bad for me." More bright smiling. "What else have you got open?"

"Waitress is all we have open," the old lady said. "We need to hire at least two more girls to replace the ones who quit without notice."

A little relief. "I'm interested."

"Really?" Rosalie's gaze raked her body. "You don't look the type."

Spine stiffening, shoulders going back, Rachel drew herself up to her full height. Even in flats, she was taller than average. Time to use that height to her advantage. "As in, I don't look like a whore?" she countered coolly.

To her surprise, the old battle-ax smiled and nodded. "Exactly."

"What do I look like?"

"You look like a nice woman who doesn't work in a place like this."

Rachel sighed, disappointed. Damn. What was it about her? Not a single position she'd interviewed for thus far had called her back and made a firm offer of employment. Did she look too eager, too stupid, too desperate? "Then you're not going to hire me?"

"I didn't say that. That decision is entirely up to Mister Carnavorn." The way Rosalie Dayton slanted her tone made it sound as if Rachel was wasting her time.

"Will I be allowed to meet him, or are you going to hustle me out the door for not coming in dressed like a tramp?" Rachel asked in a crisp voice, hinting that she would not have her time wasted either.

A small smile touched the old woman's lips. "Very well." She fiddled with the glasses hung on the chain around her neck. "If you insist."

A small victory. Hammer it in. "I insist."

"Then follow me."

4

Devon Carnavorn's private offices were on the second floor. To say they were huge was an understatement. He occupied an absolutely massive suite that allowed him to look down upon the first level through the two-way mirrors that made up nearly an entire wall. No filing cabinets or any other business accoutrements at all, for that matter. Two visitor's chairs were positioned in front of the desk. Huge oriental-style carpets in lovely shades of gold, blue, and red were spread across the expanse of the polished wood floor.

Carnavorn himself held the prime position behind an enormous desk, fashioned of rich, dark, exotic wood with ivory insets at the corners. Chair tilted back, his feet were propped up on one corner. Putting aside the paperwork he was reading, he waited for the two women to make the trek toward the Holy Grail his presence implied.

Rosalie Dayton didn't waste a minute. "Devon, this young lady wishes to speak with you about a job." She pushed Rachel's application across the wide desk.

Rising gracefully, Devon Carnavorn reached out and claimed

it. His eyes flicked to the paper and then up to Rachel. "Miss Marks, thank you for coming today." Lightly tinged with an English accent, his voice harkened images of warm toffee and rich, dark chocolate. Delicious.

Rachel nodded, feeling slightly uncomfortable. "Thank you."

Oddly, he didn't offer his hand and only the barest trace of a smile. His gaze, however, went all over. From the top of her head to the tip of her toes, his steel gray eyes practically peeled away her clothing.

What's he looking at?

Then it hit her. Maybe she wasn't pretty enough. She'd dressed simply in a white blouse, a navy skirt, taupe hose and low navy heels.

Rachel caught her breath. Determined not to be overwhelmed by his blatantly sexual stare, she returned the assessment.

Pretending to brush a piece of lint off her skirt, she sidled a few looks his way. Fashionably styled brown hair swept away from his high forehead. His eyes were most striking. Stormy gray, like a misty evening's sky a few moments before the sun set. His strong jaw wore just a hint of fashionable stubble. He had a mouth made for kissing, for devouring.

He was tall, at least six foot four. Rachel had no doubt this man could span her waist with both hands and still have a few inches left over. His body appeared sleek and solid under his tailored Italian suit.

Eyes crinkling at the corners, his gaze locked with hers. "I don't get many women in here that look like you, Miss Marks."

Feeling an immediate hot tug deep within her body Rachel sucked in a breath. Her nipples came to instant attention, the hard little nubs raking uncomfortably against the soft silk of her bra. A series of lusty images flooded her mind—images of Carnavorn holding her hips while he plunged deep into her sex.

Reluctantly pulling her mind out of her crotch, Rachel managed to choke out an answer. "Is that an insult, Mister Carnavorn?"

A wry smile worked its way into his devilish gaze. "A compliment."

Rachel's cheeks heated. She took a shallow breath and made herself meet his unblinking stare. She couldn't let his personal magnetism distract her. She needed work. If being ogled by the owner was par for the course, then so be it. If he must look, fine. That didn't mean he could touch.

"Thank you for allowing me to see you," she said, adding a formal tone to her words. "I understand you have a few waitress positions open, and I'd like to interview for one of them."

"Fair enough." Breaking his eye lock on her, he glanced toward Rosalie. "Could we offer the lady something to drink?"

Slightly annoyed to be tapped as a flunky, Rosalie looked to Rachel. "Coffee or tea?"

Relaxing ever so slightly, Rachel shook her head. The tension in her bones eased to a manageable level. "Nothing. Thank you."

"Your usual, Devon?" Rosalie asked her boss.

"Please." He smiled absent thanks. He obviously took his manager's good graces for granted.

Rosalie bustled off across the office where a small but well-stocked kitchenette ruled. This man apparently spared himself no luxury, even when at work. A family of four could be comfortable in the space his office occupied.

"Sit." Carnavorn indicated a chair. "Please have a seat while I look over your application."

Rachel sat, glad to have a reason to duck her head. Fighting the need to fidget, she laced her hands together and waited for him to make the first move. At this point, she'd make the man use dynamite to get her out of his office. No reason to let him rattle her, either. She had more important matters to think about than this strange man stripping her naked with his eyes.

Taking his seat, he began to skim Rachel's application. After a few silent minutes, he lowered it. "It says here you have owned your own business. Tell me about it."

Rachel pasted on a diplomatic smile. "Yes. The Book Nook. On Main Street." The name seemed to have no effect on him. Apparently he didn't frequent tiny bookstores clear on the other side of town.

Rosalie returned to the fray. Handing over a delicate china cup perched on a saucer, she put in her two cents. "I've noticed that a lot of businesses are closing on that end," she commented, tone going flat.

A little miffed at her intrusion, Rachel stiffened. Her smile vanished. She'd hoped Rosalie would leave. Clearly the old biddy didn't intend to budge. "Mine included," she countered. "The mall sank me."

Sipping his tea, Carnavorn offered no words of sympathy. "I see you have some experience in food services . . ."

Rachel shifted uncomfortably. The song and dance to sell herself felt more than a little tawdry. "That's right. In college, I waited tables. A long time ago, I admit, but I think I can handle the work."

A critical scowl cut across Rosalie's face. Giving Rachel a ferocious frown, a slight negative shake of head followed. "Waiting tables in a nightclub today is different from waiting tables in a diner a decade ago."

Her crisply spoken words struck the wind from Rachel's sails. Her confidence vanished.

Rachel shrugged. "That's true." Her chin trembled slightly until she clenched her teeth. "I have very little experience waiting tables."

Christ. She felt like a fool. Another job had slipped through her fingers. If she left now, she could get on with her job search.

Placing her hands on the arms of the chair, she started to rise. "I'm very sorry for wasting your time, then."

A sharp glance from Carnavorn pinned her in her place. "Hold on a minute."

Hope blossomed.

Rachel sat back down.

A frown warped his lips. "It says here you have an associate's degree in business administration. First and foremost, I'd think you'd be overqualified for this type of work."

Rachel winced. Did he think she didn't know that? He spoke like she'd just cleaned out the till, not graduated at the top of her class. She resisted the urge to glare back. "I do know what bar work entails. I haven't been hiding under a rock these last few years. I'm aware Mystique is the hottest nightclub in town—and the busiest."

"And you think you can handle the crowds?"

Anxiety knotted though her. She wasn't sure, but why admit it?

She forced a competent smile. "Although this isn't my chosen career path, at this time I am looking at other options that will allow me to support myself. In that capacity, I am not overqualified. I'm just trying to seek out work so I can pay my bills."

His left eyebrow rose into an arch. "I can certainly understand that sentiment." Picking up a pen, elegant and expensive, he made a few notations on her application. "I really do need at least two girls today, and the applicants coming through lately have left a lot to be desired."

Relief filled her. "Thank you."

The cutoff came swiftly. "But let me set you straight. If you were to take this job on, I would warn you that you've got an uncontrolled crowd of people wired on alcohol and whatever else they've put in their bodies."

Rachel nodded. "I understand."

Shaking his head, Carnavorn raked strong fingers through his stylishly clipped mane. His hair settled back into place as if untouched. "I don't think you do. People push and shove, with no mind that a waitress has a tray full of drinks. The men—and some women—grope any part of a girl's body they can get their hands on."

Rosalie cut her no slack. "Some girls don't last an hour," she said. "And most don't last more than six months. We need reliable people who will show up."

Having sat through the lecture, Rachel decided to give as good as she got. If they thought they could deter her, she'd show them they were dead damned wrong. No doubt these two would safely make the rent this month. She might not. Still in the red, it would be a long time before she'd be free of debt.

"I'll take the job."

Rosalie Dayton made a sound of disgust. Not good enough. "Until a cushy nine-to-five desk job comes along?"

Face paling, Rachel shook her head. "I wouldn't be here if I didn't want to work." A lie. A damn lie. If she had better prospects, she wouldn't have set foot in this tacky place.

The harangue continued. "You're not fooling me, Miss Marks. You're better dressed and better qualified than the usual women who parade through my office. Frankly, I just don't see you as one who would be a long-term employee."

Exasperation and near panic filled her. Back against the wall, there was only one way out.

Rachel leaned forward. Ignoring Rosalie, she pressed her palms on the obviously expensive desk. "Back off your dog," she snarled. "An interview is one thing. An interrogation another. If she's trying to scare me off, insults won't work."

Brows raising in surprise, Devon Carnavorn leaned forward and propped his elbows on his desk. "Do you really want to be here?"

"I beg your pardon?"

"Just how many days do you think you'll last before you throw in the towel and walk out the door?"

Rachel shook her head. "I don't understand."

"I don't think you have what it takes to work here." Blunt and to the point. At least he didn't insult her.

Rachel refused to back down. She forced herself to stay calm so he wouldn't know how close she was to tears. "Look, I'll be honest. This isn't the most desirable type of work. You know for every mall opening up, ten little businesses like mine curl up and die. People are out of work and scared. I'm scared. All I'm asking for is a chance to make an honest living."

Her simple words seemed to impress.

A long silence followed. Too long.

Carnavorn finally nodded in satisfaction. "If nothing else, you seem to have determination." He turned slightly in his chair and gestured to Rosalie Dayton. One would imagine he wanted to snap his fingers, but refrained.

"Please put Miss Marks into the system. Have Gina put her on the schedule to start tomorrow, six sharp."

Rachel sighed in silent relief, glad she wouldn't be starting that same day. At least she'd have a day to psyche herself up.

Still, she needed the job. Had practically begged for it. No turning back now. "Thank you."

The older woman pursed her lips, but kept her thoughts to herself. Rachel was sure Devon Carnavorn would soon get an earful of her opinion of his latest hire.

I'll just have to prove them both wrong.

After hearing a description of the conditions, she had a sneaking suspicion that working at Mystique was like being thrown into the lion's den with a cadre of hungry animals. If she didn't watch out for herself, they'd eat her alive.

"Go with Rosalie, Miss Marks. She'll take care of your employee file and give you your uniform."

"Certainly." Rachel nodded her acquiescence at her new boss. Her very sexy new boss. She pushed that thought aside.

Sexual enticement across a desk meant nothing when she and the man in question were entering into an employee/employer relationship. Bitter experience had taught her not to dally with males who held the upper hand financially.

Don't shit where you eat, she reminded herself. "Thank you, Mister Carnavorn."

A smooth return. "Call me Devon, please."

Rachel smiled. "Thank you, Devon." Sounded strange to hear his name crossing her lips, but she liked the sound of it. "You won't regret hiring me."

"I'm sure I won't." In return his metal gray gaze raked her body, probing and dissecting every visible inch. A spark lit the depths of his eyes, suggesting all sorts of primal appetites lurking in his mind. A look more intimate than any corporeal caress, the feel of it seemed to penetrate all the way to her core.

An intense sensation of awareness flooded her veins. Something about Devon, something so ferociously male, aroused the female animal in her all over again. Ignoring his silent call was impossible.

Rachel locked her jaw against the carnal images filling her brain. No luck. She had to wonder what his muscles would feel like under her fingers, what his heated cock would taste like to her hungry mouth. How his hard body would feel over hers, his hips parting her thighs in intense sexual demand.

As if he could read her mind, a small smile curved Devon's lips. Despite the space separating them, a strange sizzling connection had been made.

Devon's gaze turned hot and sultry. Pressure built as their invisible intimacy deepened.

Feeling as though he'd stroked her bare skin with hungry hands, Rachel's clit pulsed harder, dampening her panties. Heat rose in her body, impossible to ignore. Her clothing suddenly felt too heavy, binding and constricting. Beneath the surface of her skin, a strange glow permeated.

Rachel's mind spun. Swirling spirals of sheer energy seemed to envelope her entire body. Vision clouding, her lips parted as she panted for breath. She trembled, feeling her spine melt. Heat poured into her engorged clit. Teeth clenched, thighs tensed, it took all her control not to moan when climax washed through her with all the intensity of an avalanche.

The seconds vanished, lost.

Devon spoke again. "Are you all right, Miss Marks?"

Rachel scrambled to recover some semblance of her scattered sanity. Her eyes, half unfocused, blinked back into sharp reality. Drawing a steadying breath, she felt as if she'd been drugged, as if her own body didn't even belong to her. "I'm fine, thanks." Despite her words, her blood banged wildly behind her temples. Holy shit! That man could give an eye-fuck and then some! Her cunt practically wept.

Rachel stood, brushing her skirt into place. "Guess I need another caffeine kick to get myself going." She shook all over, so badly that her purse had dropped from her lap and she hadn't even noticed. She bent, groping, glad for a few minutes' respite to hide her embarrassment. Oh God. She couldn't believe she'd climaxed just looking at him!

Devon rose and rounded his desk with the sure steps of a man comfortable in his control. "Of course." He extended his hand. "Welcome to Mystique, Miss Marks."

Rachel hesitated. The spark in the depth of his eyes said he hadn't missed a moment of her delicious pleasure. If he touched her, she'd melt into a puddle. Still, it would be rude to refuse.

"Please call me Rachel," she said, returning the favor. Tamping down sexual desire, she accepted his offering.

Strong fingers closed around hers like a glove, the size of his hand practically swallowing hers. Like a barbarian conqueror, the strength behind his casual touch weakened her knees and set her stomach to roiling all over again. "Rachel it is, then." The sound of her name came out like a silken purr.

Composure threatened to take a hike. Time to get out while the getting was good. "Thank you for giving me a chance." Her voice sounded huskier than usual.

He smiled. "The pleasure, my lady, is all mine. I look forward to having you around a long time." His words were easy and assured, but his lingering intimate gaze still seared.

Rachel's heart slammed into her ribs. She made a point of drawing away her hand, slipping the strap of her purse onto her shoulder. That physical barrier helped shield her from his incredible magnetism.

Taking her unspoken hint, his hand dropped. If he felt any disappointment, he didn't show it. He turned to Rosalie Dayton. "Make sure you don't lose this one."

Rosalie's face puckered in a sour grimace. "Certainly, Devon."

Rachel had a feeling that if the old woman could get away with rolling her eyes and snorting in derision, she would. No way Rosalie could have missed Devon's ogling. He'd practically stripped her naked and fucked her all through the interview.

Well, it wasn't the first time a man had undressed her with his eyes. In the back of her mind she held the sneaking suspicion that Devon Carnavorn ogled women the way an alcoholic would pop the tab on another can of ice cold beer. Automatically and without thought.

Of course, she wasn't interested in Devon, either. At the employment agency, she'd already heard more than one disparaging remark about his sexual proclivities. Rumor had it the man burned through women the way an elephant devoured peanuts. She probably wasn't the first who'd been treated to a visual stripping, and she probably wouldn't be the last.

Turning away, Rachel scowled at herself. Attraction aside—

and the attraction was definitely there—she didn't intend to be another notch on his bedpost. She'd work for him, give him the respect due to him as her employer. Nothing more.

As for the idea that they'd become lovers?

Ridiculous!

5

Rachel examined the black dress Rosalie Dayton had given her.

Picking up the confection, she pressed it against her shoulders and stood before the full-length mirror hung on her closet door. "There's barely anything to it," she muttered under her breath, holding it up to the light.

The dress was short, the sort of costume that would attract Elvira, whom she supposed it was supposed to be modeled on. Examining it more closely, she saw it wasn't wholly a dress but more like a cheerleader's outfit, with a crotch that snapped together between the legs. Good. She'd worried about bending over in the frilly skirt: without shorts, a girl would give everyone a prime view of her pussy.

The silky material was embroidered with the Mystique logo over the left breast in crimson, the *M* and the *t* of the word elongated to resemble a set of vampire fangs. Clever, but hardly original. The tag sewn into it said MEDIUM, but she was sure it must be a SMALL instead. She'd also been given an apron, much-needed pockets for a waitress, and a name tag. If she stayed for more than a month, Rosalie had promised she'd be given additional uniforms.

For now, though, she'd have to make do with one. The rest of the uniform she had to provide: her hose and shoes. Pumps, the higher the heel the better. That made no sense. How the hell did they expect a woman to spend all those hours on her feet, running across a bar in high heels? Fortunately, the bartender had told her to choose comfort over looks and wear a low, half-heeled flat. Because she had long legs, Rachel felt she didn't need the extra sexy height four inches would add.

Deciding to try it on, she tossed the cocktail dress on her bed and began to strip down to bra and pantyhose. She wriggled into the outfit, tugging it into place over her body, smoothing out the wrinkles with the flat of her palms. The damn thing was tight, fitting her like a second skin. It allowed not an ounce of spare fat, showing every curve of her body. The neckline plunged deep between her breasts. Making a face, she cupped them. She was a perfect B-cup, not too big but not too small. Because her frame was a long one, she had been blessed with a small waist, flat stomach, and slender thighs.

The uniform didn't look terrible on her at all.

In front of the mirror, Rachel turned every which way. Thank God her ass didn't look like a freight train.

"Not bad for a thirty-three-year-old woman."

Pleased, she pivoted right and left, giving the skirt a sexy little flip. She liked the way the uniform looked on her.

Until she caught sight of the mark on her left thigh. The costume was slit up each side of the skirt, giving a perfect view of the ugly blotch.

Nose crinkling, Rachel grimaced. "Shit. I hate that damn thing."

That damn thing was a birthmark about the size of a fifty-cent piece. The color of burgundy wine against her pale skin, it seemed to vaguely resemble a broken pentagram. She called it her mark of Cain, the thing that set her apart from other people. When she was younger she'd considered having it tattooed over, but had never gotten around to having it done. Really, it wasn't a problem, as she rarely wore skirts or shorts that let it show. Only lovers knew it was there, and most had said nothing, being interested in other parts of her body.

She tried to tug the skirt down over it. Of course, the second she moved, the skirt flicked open to reveal it. Maybe she could cover it with a flesh-colored foundation. Getting out a cover stick in a light shade that matched her skin tone, she quickly pulled down her pantyhose and daubed some of the makeup on the mark. That somewhat concealed the mark, but the experiment was doomed to failure. The material of her hose quickly rubbed the makeup off her skin when she walked around.

Okay. So much for that.

I guess if I want the job, I live with the damn thing. Hell, it's a dark bar. No one will notice it. People aren't going to be gawking at my legs. They're going to be dancing and drinking, not thinking about a blotch on my thigh.

Feeling somewhat better about the birthmark, she took off the uniform and laid it aside. Tomorrow she'd begin work. Since she didn't have to go in until six in the evening, she could stay up late and celebrate. She decided to have a quick shower, then settle down with a glass of wine and a good book.

Stripping off the rest of her clothes, she shook her head and ran her fingers through her hair. She'd recently chopped her waist-length mane down into a cute, chin-length shag. The stress of watching her business go down the drain had set her nerves on edge, and she was getting tired of struggling to fix it. The layers framed her face, giving her a fresh modern style. She could easily pass for twenty-five on a good day.

She liked the cut. The best decision she'd made in a long time.

Turning on the tap, she adjusted the water to a comfortable

temperature and slipped into the water. Relishing the warmth lapping against her skin, she lathered up and began to wash herself. Starting at her shoulders, she worked her way down, pausing when her hands came to her breasts. She cupped their fullness, giving both a long, soapy caress. Desire unexpectedly swamped her.

Rachel traced the tips of her nipples with her fingertips, feeling delicious little shocks. Her nipples puckered, then hardened, as she gave each a gentle twist. The contact electrified. A moan escaped her lips. Her clit ached with carnal hunger.

She had a little itch that still needed to be scratched. Devon had definitely lit her fire this afternoon, and the flames weren't going to be easily banked. That is, unless she took matters into her own hands.

Settling back against the tub, her fingertips brushed over the aching peaks. She pinched lightly. Nothing she loved more than a little hard nipple-play. The feel of a man's teeth scraping over the pink softness was guaranteed to drive her wild.

Rachel pinched again, relishing the electric spark shimmying down her spine. Her nipples were large, puckering tightly under the tips of her fingers. Trembling, needy sounds of desire escaped her.

Her breathing grew deeper, more ragged as she slid her hands down her belly, caressing the planes of her flat stomach and the flare of her hips.

Catching her heels on the edges of the porcelain tub, she spread her legs. Perfect. After today's mental fuck with Devon, she needed something closer to the real thing. Sadly, her hand was the only thing she had for satisfaction at the moment. She made a mental note to stock up on batteries for her vibrator. She'd probably really be needing them. Soon.

Cupping a hand over her mound, she worked a single finger through her soft labia. Swollen flesh greeted her touch, wet and slippery even through the warm water. Her clit was the kind needing a lot of slow persuasion. Clumsy strokes and jabbing caresses just wouldn't do the job right. To reach orgasm, she required long, slow strokes, followed by quick flicks.

Closing her eyes, she pressed the tip of her index finger to the small hooded organ. A rush of pleasure lit up all her nerve endings. Definitely on track.

Rachel moaned, stroking herself with a light, soft pressure. Feeling wonderfully wanton and fierce, she traced the lips of her labia, rolling the tender flesh between her fingers.

Her free hand worked her left nipple, pulling and twisting. She trembled, feeling her vaginal muscles sharply flex and contract. Her sex craved a long, hard cock.

She'd just have to use a little substitute. Her lids flitted down over her eyes. Reality faded to black.

Easily recalling Devon's intense gaze, she imagined what might have happened if they had been alone. Had he undressed her in his office, he'd have been in for a treat, finding full breasts cupped in a beautiful lacy white push-up bra. Lifting her skirt would have revealed a pair of panties cut to enhance every inch of her long legs.

That desk of his would be perfect for a racy fuck. Easy to imagine him lifting her atop its polished surface and stepping between her spread thighs. Zipper coming down, he'd free his cock, long and rigid.

Parting her lips, Rachel could almost feel the press of his erection, the crown of his penis throbbing against her clit. She'd never felt so aroused.

Fantasy unfolding in her mind, Rachel penetrated her depth with two fingers, then pulled out and inserted three. Light rhythmic stokes quickly turned into harder, more demanding ones. Only it wasn't her own hands working her breast and pussy so intently. Devon was the one she wanted. The only one.

Wanton need suddenly splintered into a ferocious craving. Nearing climax, Rachel pressed her fingers deeper into her sex.

Her flesh throbbed with a sweet quiver. She stroked again; an intimate convulsion, and her legs began to tremble.

Passion peaked in a rush of molten heat. The darkness behind her eyelids exploded into exquisite bands of shimmering color as her orgasm flooded through her. Breasts heaving, her head arched back against the porcelain as a low harsh moan broke from the depths of her throat.

Coming back to earth seemed to take hours.

"Holy shit." Rachel gasped, running her tongue over her dry lips. Her throat was parched and her lips were rasped raw by her heavy breath. Body still tingling, she snagged a towel off the rack and wrapped it around her body, taking another to dry her arms and legs. "I haven't felt that good in years."

She smiled.

Working at Mystique might prove to have a few unexpected benefits.

6

Thirty minutes before she was due to start work, Rachel parked her car in the employee section of the parking lot, then made her way around to the back, staff entrance. She wore a long sweater over her uniform, since she was a bit embarrassed to be seen in it in public.

Inside, she was greeted by Rosalie Dayton, who gave her a quick tour behind the scenes, showing her the employee break room, explaining the scheduling, and introducing her to the bartenders, busboys, and other waitresses. She got a quick lesson in how she would carry her money. Given a working till of a hundred dollars, she would pay for the drinks at the bar when she picked them up, then collect the money from the customers at the table.

Six p.m. Showtime.

And no sign of Devon.

Rachel hit the floor behind her trainer, Lucille, the one who would keep an eye on her and help her out if needed. The nightclub was divided into sections among the girls, giving each a bank of tables.

Though the night was just getting started and wouldn't really wind up until about nine, the nightclub was already full. There was a strange odor in the air, a mixture of sweat, perfumes, alcohol, incense, and cigarette smoke. It overpowered her. The music was pumping, wall shaking, with multicolored lights flashing in sync with the music, a strange, oddly appealing Goth-techno remix of a familiar classical number. Not bad at all, if you liked that sort of thing.

"Here's where you'll work." Shouting above the music and chatter, Lucille gestured toward a shadowy row of booths.

Rachel's eyes skimmed over the girl. A pretty redhead who couldn't be more than barely legal, she had green eyes and the palest of skin.

Lucille continued, "That's your bar, and Alan's your bartender."

Rachel nodded again. What was there to say? She was petrified about plunging into a new job, working among strange people in a strange environment. She was used to a quiet, closed-in workspace. Here she was now, trying to make her way through a place where bodies were packed together like sardines.

Lucille noticed her discomfort and smiled, giving a knowing wink. "You'll get used to it." She gave Rachel a reassuring pat on the arm.

Rachel wasn't sure. Already a headache threatened. "It's so loud. I can barely think."

Lucille nodded in sympathy. "You tune it out after a while. Just keep your head up, smile, and get the drinks to the table. That's all you have to do."

With those words, she sent Rachel off to work.

Four hours later Rachel limped into the break room, smiling weakly at her coworkers, too damn tired to do anything more than nod and murmur a few words. A little after ten p.m., and she was ready for a chance to sit down and rest a little.

Putting down her iced tea, she flopped into a metal folding chair; she lifted a foot and slipped off her shoe, rubbing her aching toes.

Oh God, but her feet were killing her! How did these girls do it, day in and day out? She'd worn flats with the barest hint of a heel, and both her feet felt like painful lead weights. Tomorrow she was going to go to the drugstore and buy some gel pad inserts for her shoes. Those who dared to totter around in heels higher than an inch must have feet of steel, or else they would be crippled by the time they were thirty.

It hadn't escaped notice that she was one of the older girls on staff. She felt positively ancient compared to these young chicks, most barely old enough to be serving liquor. So far, though, no one had pinched her ass or fondled her as she bent over to put the drinks on the table. She had no doubt that it would soon happen. It was just a matter of time.

A couple of other girls, name tags reading TAMMY and DEBBIE respectively, wandered in and sat down. Both were blonde and chesty and gave new meaning to the word sexy in those little outfits. She'd already noticed that some of the girls had a certain way they bent over the customers, giving men a prime view of their breasts or asses. Those girls invariably walked away with the big tips, later pocketing the twenties or fifties that the men would slide down their cleavage.

Lighting a cigarette, Tammy offered her one. "Smoke?" Debbie took the one Rachel refused, using Tammy's cheap plastic lighter.

Rachel put her shoe back on, shaking her head. "Thanks, but I don't smoke."

Tammy's gaze raked over her. "So you're one of the new girls?"

Rachel nodded. "Yes."

Tammy exhaled through brightly painted crimson lips. "Like it?"

A shrug. No, she didn't like it. But no way she'd admit it out loud. Things had a way of filtering up to the boss. "It's different. Going to take some getting used to."

Breaking out of her self-imposed stupor, Debbie piped up. "I'm starving. I had better get something to eat before my break is over." She got up and headed out.

Tammy eyed Rachel. "You having anything?"

Rachel shook her head. A meal and soft drinks were offered to the staff. "Too nervous to take a bite." She took a sip of her tea. Later on, she'd take advantage of that. A free meal would cut down on her grocery bill.

Tammy stubbed out her cigarette. "I vomited for hours my first night. You're lucky. At least you're getting an easy break."

A disbelieving laugh escaped Rachel's throat. "This is an easy night?" she asked incredulously.

Tammy nodded. "Oh yeah."

Rachel slumped down in her chair, covering her face. She moaned. "Oh great."

Tammy gave her a friendly pat. "It gets easier. You learn to ignore the people and take the money."

Rachel sighed. "That's why I'm here." Money. That thing making the free trade system a viable thing. It would keep a roof over her head and food in her mouth. She hadn't had time to count her tips, but there was already a nice wad of bills in her apron, along with lots of change, mostly quarters. No one counted their tips where the others could see. If she were lucky, perhaps she'd go home with a hundred or more.

7

Break over, Rachel got up and headed back. Spurred on by need, she pasted her best smile onto her face, determined to stroll away with a few big tips herself.

When she walked out onto the floor again, she saw her new employer heading straight for her. She watched him glide through the crowd, seeming to float more than walk. People reached out to shake his hand. If he offered his own, you were in favor. If not, you were shit out of luck. A life like his was to be envied. He had money, power, beauty. Everything.

For a few tense minutes she was afraid she'd done something wrong, but the easy smile on his face belied any anger. He paused only to shake hands with favored customers, gradually making his way to where she stood.

To look busy, she grabbed a tray from a passing busboy and began to clear one of her tables. She was more than a little pleased to see a twenty-dollar bill had been left as a tip among the debris of empty glasses and overflowing ashtrays. The group had been a large one, ten people in all, and they had kept her running for almost two hours.

Just as she was pocketing her money, Rachel felt a light hand on her shoulder. An electric current seemed to shoot through her entire body, causing the fine hairs on the back of her neck to rise.

Empty glasses in hand, she whirled, clutching them tightly, her heart hammering wildly in her chest.

Her gaze skimmed every inch. A fresh rush of sexual warmth unfurled in her belly as she visually measured the way the form-fitting design of his vest enhanced his trim waist. The way his slacks hugged his narrow hips left nothing to the imagination. She noted with envy that not an ounce of fat troubled his lean frame.

"Rachel," he greeted over the pounding music, bending close so she heard his words. "I just wanted to see how you're doing this evening."

Rachel struggled to gather her wits about her, fumbling for words. "Fine, thanks," she finally managed to spit out, trying not to shout out too terribly loudly.

"Good." Devon's gaze flicked over her, intimate, more than a little curious. Finally his eyes settled on the glasses in her hands, and a slight smile lifted one corner of his mouth. "Let the busboys clean the tables. That's what they are paid for. Your job is to keep the drinks coming." He snapped his fingers, catching the eye of one of the hostesses drifting among the customers. "Get someone over here to clean these tables. Now."

The hostess nodded, hurrying off to make his words a command.

Gulping, Rachel set the dirty glasses down. Everything about him tantalized. His presence, so very close, seared her from head to toe. "I was just trying to keep busy," she stammered.

He smiled down at her. "You'll have plenty of chances to be busy, Rachel. Enjoy the slow moments. Sometimes they are few and far between in this place."

Rachel resisted the urge to fan herself with her hand. My, but she was suddenly so hot. "I'll remember that."

Devon briefly glanced around, then brought his unsettlingly direct gaze back down to rest on her face. "So now that you've done it a few hours, how do you think you'll like working here?"

His words played through her mind in the most suggestive manner. *Done it*? Oh yeah. She'd love to do it with him.

Head swimming, Rachel shifted and leaned back against a chair. Oh God, how she'd love to take his hand and guide it between her thighs, feel those long fingers of his stroking her wet heat. "I think I'll survive."

Devon tipped his head to one side, reaching out and giving her left cheek a soft touch. "Good. I'd like to keep you around for a long time."

His hand stayed in place. Rachel felt the warmth of his body, way too close and intimate. A corresponding rush of warmth headed into her cheeks. "Thank you." She stammered out her reply.

Dazzling sparks lit the depths of his eyes. Everything in the background faded around them. Through silent communication, his touch vibrated desire. "I wouldn't want anyone else to take you away from me." His deep throaty voice suggested a lot of pleasant possibilities.

Heart leaping into her throat, Rachel felt the oxygen drain from her lungs. Her muscles threatened to turn to liquid at the wondrous feel of his caress. Surely he wasn't putting the moves on her, right in the middle of a crowded bar. A single look into his eyes confirmed her suspicion.

He was!

Gaze drifting to his crotch, she wondered what he'd look like aroused. Lord, but she would love to unzip his pants and explore every inch of his cock with her tongue. She could imagine her hand seeking, finding, squeezing, drawing a moan from him as she pleasured him. Forbidden fruit was the sweetest.

Just. One. Taste.

Muscles tensing anew with treacherous need, the image of his erect cock pressing against her belly flooded her mind. Lust hazed her senses. Imagining their bodies entwined in the passion of lovemaking, she swallowed hard. The juncture between her thighs ached, her clit ripe and pulsing with moist heat. Biting back a moan, she pressed her legs together. The need he created just by standing there threatened to drive her crazy.

This can't be happening, Rachel insisted to herself. Resentment conflicted with the growing tension his presence engendered.

She should get back to work. Standing around wasn't earning any tips. She was paid a measly three dollars an hour, and her need to supplement those earnings with tips was vital. No tips, and she'd be taking home a very tiny paycheck.

Shaking off his touch, she pushed away from the chair. The heel of her shoe caught a snag in the carpeting and pulled her off balance. Losing her balance, she stumbled.

Right into Devon's arms.

His hands wrapped around her hips, breaking her fall. The press of his wide palms and splayed fingers burned through the thin material of her uniform.

"Careful," he murmured, setting her back on her feet. The weight of her body hadn't even thrown him off balance. He was that damn solid and massively built.

They stood just inches apart.

Everything stopped. Her heart. Her breathing. Her thinking. Caught between the urge to lean into the hard planes of his chest or run like hell, Rachel couldn't do either. Confusion swamped her. It had been such a long time since anyone bigger and stronger than herself had embraced her. She was turned on, to the point where she couldn't seem to stop trembling, stop desiring . . .

Devon must have felt it too. He leaned in. Bending forward, his head dipped as he—Oh God! He actually intended to kiss her. Right in front of the whole damn nightclub!

A small breathy moan broke from Rachel's trembling lips. "Please—" she started to say. Then, seeming to catch herself faltering, she finished. "Don't."

Pale gray eyes flaring with dismay, he immediately drew back. The heat of his penetrating gaze caressed. "Why not?"

Brain threatening to burst, Rachel couldn't think why not. Except that mixing work and play would be a mistake. A *huge* mistake. With complete honesty, she said, "I don't fuck the boss." Her voice was a rasp, half fear, half carnal greed.

One sculpted brow arched. A smile curved his fine mouth. His eyes, glittering bright, held hers. "Is that all that would stop you?"

A heavy drum of silence passed.

"No." Resolve close to melting, Rachel's legs trembled. Her entire body trembled. A lie, but he didn't need to know that. No man had ever done this to her before. Made her feel so good. Desired. Conflicting emotions bombarded her. Lust tore at her libido, the music throbbing in the background seeming to keep time with the blood in her veins.

It wouldn't be hard to fall in love with Devon. Not at all. The man had the most sinfully seductive eyes she'd ever looked into. Just looking into the cool gray depths softened her, lowered the wall of resistance she'd struggled to build around her emotions. She was tired of life's battles, tired of being alone. It was easy to wish he'd be her knight in shining armor. He had everything to offer.

She had . . . zilch. Out on her ass and in debt up to her ears, she owned only her car, clothes, and scrawny black cat. Everything else was mortgaged to the hilt. Were she to lose her apartment, she'd be homeless. Disaster hung over her head like an ominous pendulum.

A second glance at Devon made him less attractive. What he'd want from a woman like her became glaringly obvious.

Just sex.

Scowling at her own näiveté, her fingernails reflexively dug into her palms. Nausea rolled in her gut as shame clawed at her senses. Talk about being ripe for picking. Waitresses were a dime a dozen, coming and going as if through a revolving door. She was nothing special in Devon's world, nothing new. Just a pair of tits and a shapely ass. Nothing more.

Her eyes narrowed. It took only seconds to compute the obvious reason he'd come to see her tonight. Had he hoped a few hard hours on her feet would enhance her desire to drop her panties and spread her legs?

A wave of rage struck her squarely in the solar plexus. How could she be so easily tempted? Devon could have any woman he wanted. A waitress working in his bar would be nothing more than a dalliance. Wrong, all wrong. As much as she desired Devon, she did have some morals and scruples about her.

Don't be an idiot. He's just looking for a quick fuck.

The crowd returned to her consciousness, suddenly pressing in and demanding attention. Tittering voices, the clink of glasses, the stink of bodies packed too tightly together. The entire place reeked of decadence. The grime of it all made her feel tawdry and cheap. Nausea rising, the sensation of so many people around her became unbearable. She couldn't believe she and Devon were playing out a private moment in such a public venue. Apparently he didn't care who saw him harass the help.

Giving herself a dash of mental cold water, Rachel stepped back, putting an arm's length of distance between them. Hardly enough, but it would suffice. "I'm not cheap, or easy, Mister Carnavorn," she said, making a point to drop familiar use of his given name. "Just because you gave me a job doesn't mean you can take any personal liberties with me."

Caught off guard, Devon frowned. His steel gray eyes weren't warm now. Her reaction obviously surprised him. "You think that's what I was thinking?"

Rachel squared her shoulders. Hands curling into fists, distrust propelled her frown. "Isn't it?" Summoning all her willpower, she gave him an arctic glance guaranteed to wither testicles. "Unless you'd like a sexual harassment lawsuit, I do suggest you keep your goddamn hands to yourself."

Devon stood, speechless. He couldn't have looked more floored if she'd punted his balls up between his shoulder blades.

Rachel gave him no chance to gather his wits and launch a counterattack. "I'm taking a break," she curtly informed him. "Please be gone when I come back."

Marching off, she wondered if she'd have a job by the time she reached the employees' break room. Never a violent or aggressive woman, she'd surprised herself at her outburst. She had a feeling very few people ever said *no* to Devon.

Entering the break room, Rachel took a deep breath to calm her racing heart. Holy shit! She couldn't believe what she'd just done. Losing the bookstore had put her into the frying pan. Telling Devon to stick it would most likely put her right into the fire. She could practically feel the heat toasting her ass.

Tears pricked at her eyes. She refused to cry.

Pride goeth before a fall.

Hardly a comforting thought. Walking a tightrope between barely making ends meet and not making the rent terrified her.

Her scowl returned. So did that unsettling ripple of fear. "I'll think about telling people to fuck off when I'm sitting on the sidewalk with my stuff in a cardboard box."

8

She must think I'm a jerk. The thought made Devon wince.

In his office high above the crowd, he stood with his hands locked behind his back, looking down on the scene below. Though the place was by no means filled to capacity, there was a decent crowd present. Behind the wall of two-way mirrors he could see every corner of the club. Just the way he liked it. Nothing escaped his notice. Nothing.

Especially Rachel Marks.

Watching her work, an edge of keen anticipation stole away his breath. Spellbound, he couldn't seem to pull his gaze away from her. In her revealing uniform nothing was left to the imagination. The silky material glittered with sequins that sparkled as she moved, drawing attention to her full breasts, slender hips, and long, sleekly muscled legs. She looked enticing and tempting, a woman with a sexier-than-sin body and a mouth made for sucking.

A rag, a bone, and a hank of hair . . . God no. Kipling had it all wrong. Women were full, moist, and succulent. And Devon believed he'd sell his soul for one night of Rachel's willing favors.

Lips parting, his breath came faster. Reaching up to loosen his collar, Devon heaved a sigh of longing. An image of those beautiful thighs parting to welcome his cock sent a spur of heat straight to his groin. The idea of her naked and willing made him break out in a cold sweat.

Strategic body parts hitched up a notch. Then two.

Moaning softly, his head dropped forward as if his neck had lost the strength to keep it erect. Since she'd walked into his office, she'd occupied every moment of his time—waking and sleeping. Dare he think why?

No. It's impossible.

Swiping at his perspiring brow, Devon tried to thrust the niggling thought from his mind. It wouldn't tear loose, hanging on, all ten claws unshakable in their penetration. His loss of control was almost disgusting in its intensity. He hadn't felt this way about a woman since . . .

A single word escaped his lips, a name so precious he hesitated to speak it aloud. "Ariel."

The resemblance between the two women was eerie, right down to their raven's-wing black hair and odd, silver-blue eyes. One look at Rachel Marks, and the air had vanished from his lungs. Almost spellbound, he'd been unable to take his eyes off her.

An instant and magnetic attraction had sizzled between them. He'd felt it penetrate all the way to his bones, and then some.

Devon had no doubt that Rachel had felt it too. Her passionate physical reaction to his psychic probe electrified. Her body had responded to his phantom caresses as surely as she would to a physical touch. Make no mistake. Beneath the surface of her detached demeanor lay the soul of a vixen begging to be unleashed.

Tempting, mysterious, and erotic, Rachel beckoned to him like a shadowy dream of luscious appeal. Her face and body were jarring enough, but her obstinacy went under his skin, touching a raw nerve. He'd had a taste of her.

And wanted more.

Desire reared up with a vengeance. Once he'd set his sights on a woman, he wouldn't take no for an answer. That was a jolt to his ego, not a pleasant sensation at all.

He drew a deep breath, trying to tamp down his simmering sexual frustration. Erotic fantasies better saved for the bedroom began to unfurl across his mind's screen. His erection threatened to burst through the seams of his trousers. Need simmered under the surface of his calm.

Devon slipped a hand into one pocket, stroking his throbbing length. Easy to imagine peeling Rachel out of her uniform, parting her slender legs, dipping his head to take in her scent. Would she taste ripe, like a melon? Or would she taste sweet, like dark rich chocolate?

Just as he considered stepping into the restroom to give his fantasies free rein, the door of his office opened. The unwelcome pad of footsteps sounded on the carpeting behind him. Hardly the time to have his most carnal thoughts interrupted.

Busted! He'd just been caught masturbating, right out in the open of his office. One good stoke down his erect shaft and an eruption would break loose.

Rosalie Dayton stepped up to the mirrored wall. A big, burly-looking woman with an unbending air and the intense control of a frigid Joan Crawford, she was all business and no nonsense. Some swore the earth trembled when she walked. Stone faced and stern, many were convinced she pissed ice water and ate gravel for lunch.

Devon quickly shifted, attempting to hide the embarrassing evidence of his carnal greed. No luck. His erection ruled, front and center. A raw curse broke from his lips. "Bloody hell, woman. Won't you ever learn to knock?" Humiliation sliced like a blade.

Arms folded across her chest, the old lady glanced down. A single eyebrow lifted in hearty disapproval. "You do remember the rule," she reminded him tartly. "No menacing the help."

Caught with his hand in the forbidden nookie jar, Devon's recalcitrant cock deflated with great haste. Rachel's verbal scalpel had already sliced a few inches off his manhood. Rosalie might as well snip off the rest. "I'm not bothering the girls." Deep and throaty, his voice hardly sounded like his own.

Rosalie's tongue lodged firmly in her cheek. "Ah so. Then tell me I didn't see you out on the floor with Rachel." Eyebrow quirking a little higher, she tilted her head down to peer over the thick rims of her bifocals. "Seemed to me you were getting a little hands-on with her, Devon." She frowned like a frustrated spinster. "That's a definite no-no, and you know it."

Devon silently grumbled. Rosalie might be nigh on seventy, but time hadn't dulled her mental faculties one little bit. Like a bloodhound sniffing out a trail, she missed nothing. "I was just checking on her, to see how she's doing on her first night." He grabbed the explanation, hoping it sounded logical.

Nope. Lame as could be.

The old lady snorted. "That's bullshit, and you know it. I know when you get the craving for one of the girls." Her gaze sought out the source of his immediate discomfort. She frowned. "You can smell a hot young cunt through a concrete wall."

Grim amusement curved his mouth. His cheeks felt stiff, unnaturally stretched. Pulse still elevated from his recent arousal, his skin seemed too small to fit his bones. "Amazing how you always know exactly what's on my mind."

Hardly in the mood, Rosalie waved one crooked finger in the air. "What amazes me is how many times I have to remind you not to mix work and play. It's one thing to troll among the smutty riffraff for your pussy. No one cares how many whores you hire to screw. But business is business. You should know that."

Devon nodded without speaking. It might give the impression he was paying attention.

Determined not to be ignored, Rosalie continued without pause. "Mystique keeps you respectable—and barely. How many do you fuck a week? Four? Five? More?"

Devon didn't bother to argue the numbers. One of his few confidants, Rosalie knew he was a sexual hedonist who indulged his every carnal whim even when he didn't have to. He licked dry lips. "You're right. I know the rules."

Rosalie cleared the annoyance from her throat. "Then act like you remember them." Readjusting her glasses on her nose, she looked through the opaque glass to the nightclub below. "She's good, that one. Hard worker. I didn't think she'd last an hour."

Devon watched too. He easily picked Rachel's figure out of the crowd. Carrying a tray of drinks, she glided around the dance floor, never losing her balance when an errant body jostled hers. His eyes narrowed when a man ran his hands over her thighs as she bent over to deliver the drinks.

Jealousy knotted the pit of his stomach. Seeing the male patrons drool over her ate him up inside. Men could smell fresh meat. Like pack animals at the hunt, every male in there would probably try and talk her out of her tight uniform and into bed. For the offense, he thought about going downstairs and breaking each finger in the man's hand.

Totally unnecessary. Rachel smiled, giving the offending hand a swat. Her indication was crystal clear. Ogle, fine. Hands strictly off.

"She's got class." Sounding immensely pleased with her observation, Rosalie absently nodded her approval. "It'd be stupid to lose this one. She handles the mashers just fine. The customer's not offended, and her reaction will most likely earn her a hefty tip."

Discontent gnawed inside his rib cage. Devon didn't agree one whit. "She doesn't belong down there, mauled by common trash."

Rosalie nodded. "I agree. She's leagues above most of the bimbos we get in here. I checked her references, by the way. She really needs the work. Losing her business cost her everything."

Pressing a hand against the glass, Devon leaned in closer. The demanding throb inside his chest refused to lessen. "I can change her whole life," he murmured softly. "Give her things she's never dreamt of."

Resembling a dog guarding its prized bone, Rosalie eyed him suspiciously. "You're having some dangerous thoughts. I'm warning you now, whatever you're thinking—don't!" She glared, daring him to defy her edict. A loyal and fierce sentinel, her business was all about minding his.

A long pause, then he said softly, "I would never do anything to hurt her."

Rosale sighed in resignation. "Why her, Devon? Why her, and why now?"

Another pause.

How to explain his attraction? He couldn't. Even if he went down to the nth degree in details, he doubted Rosalie would understand. Humans might know of the Kynn, but they didn't truly *know* the Kynn. Until he'd entered the realm of the occult, he hadn't completely understood the invisible world himself. No one could. No explanations could suffice. Only experience would.

"All you need to know is that I will have her. Nothing else you might say matters."

Her lips pursed grimly. "I was afraid you'd say that."

Devon released a short, annoyed laugh. "You make it sound as if I plan to tie her down and rape her," he said half under his breath.

A deep silence ensued.

Rosalie finally placed a gentle hand on his arm. Although crusty on the outside, most of her brittle countenance was bluster. "I know you wouldn't hurt her, Devon." Her grip tightened as if to emphasize her words. "But I sometimes think you forget that your world demands a lot from us poor humans. Open Rachel's eyes to what you really are, and she may not welcome the sight." A gentle warning shaded her words.

With a shuddering breath, Devon's hand covered hers. Paper-thin skin covered her blue-veined hands. His gaze focused on her face. He could recall a time when not a single wrinkle had marred Rosalie's peach-firm cheeks. Time's hourglass had drained away, and he hadn't even noticed.

Depression and despair washed over him. Like a prisoner counting off the days to freedom, he realized he hadn't been living. Only existing. "I was human once." His voice grew husky. Emotion threatened to clog his throat. He swallowed it down. "Not so long ago as you'd think."

Rosalie's gentle smile wavered. "Then remember what it's like. Please, think twice before you drag Rachel into something she might hate you for. She doesn't deserve living hell . . ."

Before he could reply, Rosalie pulled her hand away. Leaving him behind, she exited without looking back. The door shut behind her, softly but firmly.

Devon squeezed his eyes shut, rubbing ferociously at his eyelids. He felt raw, every nerve exposed. "Damn it." He truly didn't want to hurt Rachel. Ever. He'd just as soon cut off his right arm than cause her one minute's heartache.

But even more than that, he didn't want to walk away and leave her. No. Keeping an emotional distance would be impossible. Not when he ached to gather her in his arms, hold her body close to his, and make long, languorous love to her while he immersed himself in her enchanting eyes.

Exhaustion crept in.

Devon hadn't slept in days, had eaten even less. He could use a hearty meal, but later. At the moment his appetite had deserted him.

Shrugging off his jacket, Devon tossed it over one of the visitor's chairs in front of his desk. A ton of paperwork piled there needed attention. Sitting down, he pushed it aside. Tough shit. It would have to wait.

Leaning back, he propped his feet up on the edge of his desk. He undid the top button of his shirt, pulling away the constricting collar and tie. He pressed his fingers to his throat. The ridge was still there, a small scar across his jugular. Hardly a deadly cut, just enough to mark him.

Even after all this time I can still find it.

There were more scars under his clothing, all evidence of Ariel's feedings. Having her draw his blood into her body even as he'd been inside her was an incredibly spiritual experience. When they had become handfasted in the mating bond, he'd believed it would last forever.

Forever hadn't lasted a decade. "You've been alone a long time," he murmured to himself. "For a Kynn, that's unnatural."

To be with a human served only one purpose: to feed the hunger for a body's energies. With a Kynn female, the sensations were far different. He'd be able to make love, giving as well as receiving pleasure.

Devon exhaled a trembling sigh. The memory of Ariel's touch still haunted. After her murder, he believed he'd grown used to being alone, that he could accept living without a bloodmate. Seeing Rachel not only widened the hole in his heart, it reaffirmed a hard truth. Without his *she-shaey*, his bloodmate, he was as useless as a one-armed paperhanger.

Devon unbuttoned his shirt. Tugging it open he bared his

chest. There, just above his left nipple was a birthmark. Rachel Marks had one just like it. On her left thigh. Coincidence?

He didn't believe so. Just as he didn't believe Arial had returned to him. Heart lodging in his throat, trepidation beat through his veins. No, his magnificent sire had done much more than that. She'd sent him a sign, a gift—and her blessing.

Move on, she was saying. *Live again. Love again.*

It had been a long time since he'd thought about bringing a human over to join the Kynn collective. So few had seemed worthy to receive the gift.

Rachel, he believed, was worthy. A woman who gave off vibes of intense sexuality, hers was a vital life force, powerful. Just waiting to be tapped by the right man.

Determination lifted Devon's chin a notch. "I'm going to be that man."

9

Night over, shift at its end, the only thing Rachel wanted to do was go home. That, apparently, wasn't going to happen.

Frowning, she twisted her keys a second time. Hard. A weak buzz emanated from the ignition. No dash lights, no juice. No nothing. Ah shit. How totally terrific. Her first night at work, and her car had broken down right in the parking lot.

Around her the other employees were scattering posthaste.

A frustrated sigh broke from her lips. "Hell's bells, guess I'm stuck." She should have known this would happen. Lately her twenty-year-old station wagon had been giving her fits, starting with belches and moans, transmission squealing as her car rolled down the road. Right when she needed it most the old piece of junk, dubbed the "blue bastard," had finally up and died on her.

Leaning forward, Rachel propped her head on the steering wheel. A sour grimace. *Just my luck.* She'd have to call a towing service.

The idea made her wince. That alone would eat into her precious cash reserves. She didn't even want to think about repairs. Given the age of the car, the bill would probably cost more than the damn thing was worth.

Exhaustion nipped at her.

Someone tapped on her window. "Are you all right, Miss Marks?" Formal, curt, and very proper, the lightly accented voice was unmistakable.

Rachel cringed. *The gods must hate me.* It didn't occur to her they might be smiling a bit. The only thing she saw at the end of the tunnel was the oncoming train.

Since practically flipping Carnavorn the bird, she'd made a wide berth around him, praying to God he wouldn't call her into his office and fire her. To his credit, he'd given her space too. Thanking providence she'd skated through the night with her job intact, she'd hoped to escape his notice on the way out the back door.

Sitting up, she quickly brushed a few stray wisps of hair behind her ears and wiped her eyes, smudging her mascara. She didn't care. Her makeup had lost its sheen hours ago. Her nose was oily, her cheeks pale, and her mascara flecking. Hardly a beautiful sight after spending eight hours on her feet in a smoke-filled nightclub.

Not that she gave a flip nickel. Her feet hurt, her head ached, and her eyeballs felt like they were about to pop out of her skull. Oh yeah, and her fucking car had just taken a dive into the shitter. In her case, Murphy's Law was working overtime.

Rachel rolled down the window. Their gazes converged, his curious, hers wary. "I'm fine. Just a little problem. My car won't start." She dug in her purse for the cell phone stashed there. "Just need to call a tow truck, and I'll be on my way."

Devon just kept smiling in a most annoying way. "It could be a while before those fellows arrive. Why don't you let me give you a ride home?"

Remembering what had passed between them earlier, Rachel shook her head. He didn't seem to be holding a grudge. Still, it probably wouldn't be wise to be caught alone with him. Not because she didn't trust him.

Because she didn't trust herself. Lean, toned, and sculpted, the man could light her inner fires with just a touch. The first time, she'd been able to say no to his advance. Should it happen a second time, she doubted she could refuse him.

Staying out of his reach entirely would be the wisest thing to do. He had her contemplating every pleasure she could think of with a man's body—including a few she'd imagined, but never tried. A year ago, she'd have been ready, willing, and able . . .

Now, like a shy puppy abused by rough hands, she hesitated. The handsome son of a bitch with the sultry smile and sulky appeal had already slashed and burned his way through her emotions. That heartache had been devastating financially as well as emotionally.

One bitten, twice shy, babe.

Her stubborn streak reared its head. Rachel shook her head. "My car would still be stuck here. If I get it home tonight, I can arrange for it to go into the shop first thing in the morning." Her car was more trash than treasure, with a dented rear fender, more rust than paint, and a peculiar front slant on the passenger's side from a bad front-end repair.

He shrugged. "If you insist."

The quicker she handled this mess, the quicker she could go home. Alone. Aching all the way to the tips of her toes, all she wanted was a long soak in a hot tub and a cool pillow under her head.

Dialing 411, Rachel got the number of a towing service. A female voice informed her a truck could be sent. But she'd have to wait at least an hour, maybe longer.

She flipped her phone shut and tucked it away. "I've got

someone coming. It'll be an hour, maybe more. Guess I have to wait it out."

Devon leaned against her car. "I'll wait with you."

Rachel wasn't quite sure what to think—or what to do. With the nightclub shut down, the parking lot was practically a wasteland. Though well lit, it was more than a bit unsettling to be out so late at night with such a wide-open space around her. Because of its location on the outskirts of the city, the joint emptied out fast after hours.

No trouble at all if someone wanted to harass a woman alone. She glanced at Devon. Liquid desire pulsed gently between her legs. *Or if someone wanted to have his way with a willing one.*

Deciding not to take the bait, Rachel quickly shook her head to clear it. Definitely not something to be thinking about. She rubbed a hand across her stomach, attempting to ease the constriction. It didn't help. "That's generous of you, but there's really no reason for you to stay." She wished he'd take the hint and move along. Kicking the owner out of his own parking lot wasn't easy.

Devon's eyes narrowed with concern. "I can't let you sit alone—" he started to say.

Rachel remained convinced she'd do just that. She pushed down the lock—no good right now since the window was open. Not that it would stay that way much longer. "I can lock the doors until the tow truck comes. And I've got my cell phone. I'll be fine. Really."

Her words didn't budge him. "Instead of sitting there all by yourself, why don't you let me buy you a cup of coffee?" He nodded toward the highway. "There's a truck stop less than a quarter mile away. We can grab a bite to eat and be back by the time the tow truck arrives."

As if on cue, her stomach growled. No food had crossed her

lips in hours, and a jolt of coffee loaded with tons of cream and sugar would do a lot toward bringing her flagging senses back to life.

Still, she hesitated.

Rachel didn't trust men as far as she could throw them. Especially smooth-talking men with voices more decadent than buttery toffee and looks so devastating they made a woman want to weep with envy. "Really, there's no reason for me to hold you up."

Devon shrugged. "I haven't got anyplace to go—no one would miss me if I didn't show up."

How strange. She could say the same herself.

Rachel had to take a detour around that remark. No reason admitting she could evaporate into a puff of smoke and no one would miss her until the bills were due. Alone definitely sucked. But being fucked and left sucked a whole lot worse.

A coin toss to which she preferred would have her hope for alone. Alone didn't disappoint. Alone didn't lie. Alone didn't rack up charges on her credit cards and steal her laptop before taking a hike.

"I—I'll stay here."

Undeterred, Devon leaned down. Closer than he'd been in the nightclub. The subtle musk of his aftershave enhanced the scent of hot male skin. His enticing aroma seduced.

Oh God. Rachel's fingers curled around the steering wheel. Body trembling, her hormones began to run riot all over again. Willpower threatened to abandon her. "Really, I shouldn't." Then, to be polite, "But thanks for the offer."

Gaze unwavering, flickers of electricity appeared to dance in the depths of Devon's eyes. "One cup of coffee, Rachel. I promise we'll be back in plenty of time to meet the tow truck."

Nearly hypnotized, Rachel blinked hard. Damn, the man

made it hard to say no. "I . . ." Unable to continue, she licked her dry lips.

Before she could finish, Devon pressed a single finger against her mouth, shushing her. Electricity crackled between his touch and her lips. "Would you say yes if I promised not to seduce you?"

10

Rachel slid into a booth, tucking her purse between her body and the wall. Sitting down to relax after eight full hours on her feet wasn't only a blessing, it was a relief. Staying up all night would take some getting used to. Eleven o'clock used to be her bedtime. Working at Mystique meant she'd better be alert and ready to move her ass.

Devon shrugged off his coat. A white shirt worn under a silk vest hugged his broad shoulders. The dove gray shade perfectly complimented his stormy irises. Loosening his tie, he unbuttoned a few buttons, giving her a sexy peek at his chest. A hint of stubble darkened his jaw, just enough to give his elegant attire a bad-boy edge. He looked casual, laid back. Comfortable.

Tossing his coat into the booth, Devon took the side opposite her. Sliding onto the narrow seat, his leg brushed hers.

Without thinking about her reaction, she shot him a sharp glance. She cleared her throat to get his attention. "Excuse me."

He fobbed a guileless smile back. "Sorry."

She eyed him. The width of the table separated them, but it

didn't seem to be enough. Despite the steady stream of people, it felt like they were alone.

Maybe because I'm too acutely aware of his company.

Te be nice, Rachel tried to mirror his smile. "It's okay." Nervous, she rolled her eyes to the ceiling. Someone had tossed a knife in the air, and it had stuck. Since nobody had bothered to climb up and remove it, she supposed it didn't cause any harm.

She glanced around. A knife in the ceiling pretty much fit the general theme of the truck stop. Part of a popular chain, white walls with garish orange stripes ruled. You'd have to be blind to miss the blinking neon sign outside and deaf to miss the air brakes of semi trucks coming and going twenty-four hours a day.

The place accommodated people on the go. No sooner had one set of asses vacated a booth than another set occupied it—often before the dirty dishes had been cleared away. Cleanliness was negotiable, the clientele questionable, but nobody cared. Coffee was served hot, the food was edible, and the bright lights and bustle meant no hanky-panky could take place.

Hardly the kind of joint sporting immaculately attired Englishman, it was the kind of place one would expect a scantily attired barmaid to hang out at. Several of her coworkers had commandeered booths, as had some of Mystique's patrons. Drinking hours over, the night crawlers were reluctant to end their night. Though she'd worn her sweater to cover her skimpy uniform, more than one trucker's eyes found her legs. Her smoke-colored hosiery just didn't offer adequate coverage. She still felt naked.

A few people waved at Devon, hailing him. He brushed them off, instead giving her his attention. "About what happened earlier this evening—"

Trying not to wince at the memory, Rachel waved him off. "Let's just forget it."

Metal gray eyes met hers. "You sure that's what you want to do?"

Meaning was she going to sue him for being too hands on? Rachel considered. Thinking back, she had to admit the man hadn't done anything too terribly alarming. He hadn't fondled her ass or made some rude sexual remark. True, he'd touched her cheek, murmured . . . *what?*

She couldn't quite remember now. Funny, she thought she'd memorized his words. Now they seemed lost in the morass of her brain. Tired. She was so damn tired. Just keeping her eyelids propped open was an ongoing battle. She'd think about it tomorrow, just as she'd think about her body's reaction, the tremors of awareness flooding through her veins when he'd touched her. Just sitting across from him now, she felt . . .

A jaw-splitting yawn brought her back to life. Fumbling for his last words, she took up where he'd left off. "It's over. Gone. When I snapped at you, it was just nerves. First night, new job."

"You're sure that's all it was?" His deep voice vibrated unspoken innuendo.

Her heart doubled its beat. Damn it! He'd put her squarely on the spot all over again. Devon Carnavorn seemed to know nothing about pleasing an employer because the bills needed to be paid. Annoyance simmered. He'd probably been born rich and hadn't known an honest day's work in his life. From what she'd seen, he just seemed to drift around the nightclub gladhanding the patrons. If anyone did the real work, that was Rosalie Dayton. When the old lady cracked her whip, the employees jumped.

Rachel swallowed the lump building in the back of her throat. "Of course," she answered, keeping her eyes steady. "Nothing happened." The chill in her voice closed the matter.

He nodded. "Of course." Then repeated her words as if to reaffirm them. "Nothing happened."

Her brow wrinkled. "Well, nothing did happen."

He flicked a crafty grin. "Are you sure?"

Rachel ground her teeth. His flirting turned the tables on her. Just as an unflattering insult about his mother's marital status threatened to roll off her tongue, the waitress arrived.

Thank God! A break. She didn't intend to eat. A cup of coffee would do. Later, when she got home, she'd have something. The less time she had to spend with Devon, the better. She didn't know whether the man made her want to slap him silly—or kiss him.

A blush reddened her cheeks. Somehow every thought she had about Devon included sex. She coughed behind her hand to hide her embarrassment.

A busty waitress wearing tight, fashionably faded jeans and a tighter T-shirt hurried over with a couple of menus. Truck-stop logo embroidered above one massive breast, she was all masses of blond hair and smiles.

She slapped the menus down, practically ignoring Rachel to ogle Devon. Apparently a nice piece of man meat gave women a license to drool too. He seemed not to notice her hungry stare.

"Devon darling!" She bumped up against him, angling her body in a way that offered her ass. "My God, where have you been keeping yourself? Long time no see in this dump."

He shrugged and gave her rear a friendly glance. Something the waitress didn't seem to mind a bit. "Work, Jaye," he answered, addressing her by the name on her tag.

Her titter grated. Laying a hand on Devon's shoulder in a way revealing too much familiarity, Jaye smiled a hint. "And no time for play?"

"Not lately."

Jaye snapped her gum, bending forward to show her double-D tits to better advantage. As if any man could forget what those hooters looked like. "We'll have to do something about that. Real soon, babe. You know where I'm at."

Devon's gaze dropped to her luscious rack. "Always, sweetheart."

Babe? Sweetheart? The back and forth between them made Rachel want to puke. Aha. So the rumors were true. Devon liked to dally with the common ladies after all.

Eyeing the blonde, whose hips were just a tad too wide and whose makeup looked plastered on with a trowel, Rachel didn't see the appeal. If Devon liked his women busty and brassy, that would certainly send her to the sidelines. Tall, slender, with just the slightest hint of a pug to her nose, Rachel couldn't compare.

In a way it relieved. It also disappointed.

Damn.

Well, it wasn't like I intended to get involved with him, she reminded herself. Hadn't she learned her lesson after her little go-round with Dan Sawyer? Good-looking men used, abused, then kicked to the curb. A year had passed, and she still had skid marks on her rear from the roller-coaster ride her ex-boyfriend had taken her on.

Jaye whipped her pad out of her back pocket. "What'll it be, hon? The usual?"

Devon deferred to Rachel. "Just coffee," she said.

"Surely you'd like something a little more substantial than that," he countered. "We have plenty of time for a bite to eat, and the food's decent enough."

Jaye seemed to notice Rachel for the first time. Her green gaze lobbed a few daggers. Clearly she'd like to be the one sitting in the booth, and clearly she saw competition in the woman who was. "She working for you?" she asked, speaking as if Rachel weren't sitting right there and able to answer.

Devon nodded. "Her first night."

"You should eat something, honey. Busting your ass in that

place is bound to make a woman hungry." She looked to Devon again. "I know I'd wanna eat."

Rachel pursed her lips together. "Just a cup of coffee, please."

"And one for me," Devon put in.

"You going to have your usual?" Jaye asked.

Devon gave Rachel a very gentle tap to her calf with the tip of his shoe. He wasn't taking Jaye's flirting seriously, it said. She might as well relax and have something. "I'm starved, but I hate eating alone."

She caught the hint. Sexual awareness wrapped around her all over again. Might as well give him a little reply. She nudged back with the tip of her heel, running the low spike from his ankle to knee. She suppressed her smile, keeping her face serious. *There, damn it.* Two could play this game of footsie. Out of the blue, flirtation took on a whole new dimension, one she decided to indulge. *Simmer, Devon. Simmer. You can look, but you can't have.*

Opening her menu, Rachel looked over the selections. A truck stop didn't offer a lot of healthy dining. Most everything was geared to satisfy a trucker's hungry appetite. Eat one of those steaks or a platter full of Mexican food, and she'd split the seams of her uniform.

Her eyes fell on the salads. Hallelujah! The Caesar was a definite no, but she could stand a bowl of cottage cheese and pineapple. "Fruit salad."

Jaye visually measured her, puckering at the mouth in envy. "Large or small?"

Handing the menu back, Rachel smiled like a puppy eating shit. The reason Jaye didn't work at Mystique was obvious. The uniforms didn't come in her size. "Small," she answered sweetly.

Jaye took the menus. "The number three, babe?"

"With extra toast on the side. Wheat." Devon hadn't looked at his. Apparently he'd been in enough times to know it.

Scribbling on her pad, Jaye disappeared. She came back with two cups of coffee, ice water, and a monkey bowl filled with individual containers of half-and-half. She sat everything down, then added cutlery and napkins. Efficient, but no longer chatty.

"Food'll be out in a few," she informed them before buzzing off to customers who appreciated her attributes.

Just like that, they were alone again.

Not knowing what to say next, Rachel fiddled with her coffee. Adding a packet of fake sweetener, she poured in two containers of creamer. Stirring ushered the fragrant aroma of steaming hot coffee into her foggy senses. She took a long sip, relishing the taste.

Devon added nothing to his, drinking it down plain and black. "Feel better?"

She nodded. "Mmm, much." Another sip. "God, but I've been needing my caffeine."

Sipping his own coffee, he seemed satisfied. Then another nudge of his shoe connected with her ankle. "Has any man ever told you how beautiful your eyes look peeking over the rim of a coffee cup?" Longing glinted in his eyes.

Desire pummeled inside Rachel's gut. Ignoring the roar of blood in her ears, she leveled her gaze. "Don't, please."

"It's true."

She sighed and set down her mug. Her fingers remained curled around it, drawing warmth from the liquid inside. "I'll talk about anything but, Devon," she said firmly.

He tapped her ankle again. "Let's talk about you, then. How did a beautiful lady like you end up in my office?"

Grrr. Set on the path of his own agenda, he was going to do what he damn well pleased. "You know the answer."

"Your bookstore closed."

She nodded. "Yes. I loved having it. A dream of mine, you

might say." As a child, she'd spent hours with her nose in a book, living vicariously through the lives of the characters she encountered on the printed page. Then, reading was her escape from the misery of her childhood, from the parents who drank and fought as violently as they fucked.

He sipped his coffee. "Tell me about your dreams."

She grimaced. Had she known he was going to give her the third degree, she'd have stayed in her car. "They go bust. Kind of like my whole life."

Gray eyes focused on her. "Why do you think that?"

She shrugged. "Forget it. Shit happens, then you die."

Devon made a scoffing gesture with one hand. "You're too pretty to be so cynical."

She fiddled with her spoon, tapping it against her cup. "I've had a lot of practice."

"Being pretty?" he prompted with an expectant look.

Rachel shook her head. "You're doing it again."

Putting on a serious face, his smile vanished. "Sorry. Hard not to." The smile reappeared, double wattage. "I like looking at you." His good humor worked hard to make her let down her guard. She'd have to be careful. If one brick fell, she'd crumble right into his arms.

Attraction tightened her nerves. She shook off the tension, mentally arming herself against temptation. He was *not* going to break down her resistance. "I have a rule." She shook her head vigorously. "I don't mix work and play anymore."

Devon's brow rose. "Anymore? Then there was a time . . ."

Not wanting to talk about her past, she cut him off. At the moment she didn't want to talk at all. Why couldn't he just let her sit in silence and enjoy her coffee? "Did once, got burned. End of story."

"Ah. So tell me another story. Something about your life."

Raw nerves unpleasantly scraped, Rachel took a deep breath and clasped her hands together in her lap. "Got burned there too." Hoping to put him off, she checked her watch. Only five minutes had passed. Funny, it seemed much longer. The tow truck wouldn't be showing up for another forty minutes.

Forty minutes too long, she thought.

"Where *is* that waitress?" Right now doing battle with the jealous Jaye was preferable to letting Devon stroke her emotions.

Devon cleared his throat to get her attention. "I've got big shoulders if you need to cry."

Rachel felt the gentleness behind his words, the tingling awareness that this man could literally sweep her off her feet if he wished. She stared down into her coffee cup. She'd drained it, not a drop left. How ironic. Her life was as empty as her cup.

She covered her eyes with a trembling hand. "I don't cry anymore." Drawing in another deep breath, she released it carefully. Bitterness crept in. "Okay, here's the abridged version: I was born. I grew up."

Devon looked dubious. "I think I'd prefer the unabridged version."

Rachel's hand came down. Her jaw tightened. "Okay. Father drank. Mother drank. Father walked when I was seven. Mother died when I was eight. When I was twenty-one my father turned up—or rather his attorney did. Dad had died but left an insurance policy. That gave me enough to get my bookstore started. Twelve years later, I'm back on my ass. Broke." She fixed him with a pointed stare. "So when I say I prefer to be oblivious to my past, I mean it."

Devon's words came softly. "There's no refuge in oblivion. Only pain."

An unintended smile came out. "Do the English always have to trot out Shakespeare as a salve?"

He smiled, trying to put her at ease. "That was Wilde, I think." Another brush against her ankle. Slow, long, and lingering. More intimate. "Something I bet you are in bed."

Rachel didn't know whether to reach across the table and

slap him silly or groan. She eyed him warily. Having unwittingly lit an emotional fuse, she suspected Devon was trying to extinguish it before the explosion occurred. Had her life not been a freaking mess, she surely would've been tempted to take him up on his offer.

She shook her head to clear it, dismissing the fantasies he could so easily arouse. Better to keep her libido firmly in check. Devon was her boss, for God's sake. On that point alone he had to be kept at arm's length and off-limits.

Time to end his flirting. "That's something you won't ever find out, funny guy."

Hand to his heart. "You wound me."

Rachel gave a stern frown. "I might." She pointed to the ceiling. "See that knife?"

Devon's gaze found it. His sly smile faltered. "Yes." Then his chin came down again, his eyes meeting hers across the table.

Her eyes narrowed, just a bit. Just enough to let him know she meant business. "I can arrange for your dick to join it."

He made a face. "Ouch."

The arrival of their order interrupted further conversation. Deftly wielding a tray loaded to the max, Jaye set the food on the table. She'd also brought the coffeepot with her and refilled both cups. Attention turned to their appetites and the satisfaction of something they both shared: hunger.

Rachel looked at her plate. A mound of cottage cheese surrounded by fat yellow chunks of pineapple, all drizzled lightly with the syrup of the fruit. Compared to Devon's, her selection looked puny. A veritable feast awaited him: eggs, sausage patties, hash browns, a short stack, and a double serving of whole-wheat toast.

She gasped, watching him slather strawberry jam on his toast, then load up his pancakes with tons of butter and apricot-flavored syrup. "You must have a hollow leg." Eat a meal that large this late at night, and not only would she have a super case of indigestion, she'd gain ten pounds.

Devon grinned. "Can't help it, love. I like to eat." Shredding his eggs with knife and fork, he took a bite.

Rachel spooned up a bit of dull cottage cheese, not half so tasty. Tasted like a lead weight. No flavor or appeal. Still, it would chase the munchies away. Watching Devon put away his food, she suspected he fucked like he ate, with a lot of gusto and finesse. She stared at him for a minute, then said, "I don't get you."

Devon looked up from his food. "*Get* me?"

Suddenly nervous and not even knowing why, Rachel raked her hair behind one ear. "Everything about you is so contradictory. I mean, you don't look like the kind of man who'd like hanging out in a Goth club all night, or who'd be sitting in a truck stop wolfing down breakfast at almost three in the morning."

He laughed, sounding surprised. "So what should I be doing?" he countered. "Mucking about my drafty old castle, drinking tea and eating scones?"

Rachel nodded, but her thoughts were revolving. "Something like that. I mean, what is the appeal of the vampire lifestyle?"

Gaze twinkling, Devon eyed her back. "Well, the answer's very simple, Rachel."

"Oh?"

He grinned. "I'm a vampire."

11

The look on Rachel's face was priceless, almost comical. Her shapely brows rose in a question. Disbelief crammed her silence. "Excuse me," she said between spoonfuls of cottage cheese. "Did you just say you were a vampire?"

Devon hadn't meant to come right out and admit it. Somehow the words had slipped out of his mouth. *In for a penny*, he thought, *in for a pound.* "I'm absolutely serious."

Spooning up the last of her cottage cheese Rachel eyed his breakfast, half demolished from appetite. She still looked famished. "I thought vampires only drank . . ." Her face scrunched up. "Blood."

Picking at his toast, Devon chuckled. "That would be totally disgusting." He took a bite, chewed, then swallowed. "The Kynn are sexual vampires." Not quite ready to share everything about his kind, he held back on explaining that the Kynn *did* take blood, but just enough to make a connection with their chosen victim. This, too, was a part of the ritual to make a psi-connection, not to feed a disease like hunger. Later on, he'd introduce her to the rituals—but slowly. Humans had a tendency to be squeamish.

A pregnant pause ensued. A knowing glint lit the depth of her gaze. "Ah, of course." She pretended to give her forehead a smack with the palm of her hand. "Having heard the rumors about your, ah, carnal appetites, that would explain everything about you, Mister Carnavorn. I just thought you were a horny bastard.

Her willingness to play along amused him. She thought he only teased her. *If only she knew . . .*

Devon gave an exaggerated version of a fussy Englishman's shrug and disdainful sniff. "Please. My parents were legally wed. As for the horny part—I'm always interested."

"No doubt." Revived by her meal and an extra cup of coffee to fuel her waning energy, Rachel offered him a smile. This time her foot tapped his. "So what about that coffin thing I've heard about? Is it true you've got to cart around the soil from your grave?"

Trying to be diplomatic, Devon cleared his throat. "Neither one is true. Though I have known mortal death, I sleep in a bed—just like you."

That one made Rachel roll her eyes before giving him a look that said *we can't possibly be having this conversation*.

She settled back, shifting her body to tuck her legs under her. No more flirting under the table. Sipping her coffee, she appeared to turn the words over in her mind. "Mortal death . . . Now there's a new one on me." Curiosity made her ask, "So your mortal life ceased and your immortal one begins. Is that how it works?"

Every hair on Devon's head prickled with awareness. He'd never explained anything about the Kynn out loud—certainly not to an outsider. "That's right. Your sire takes away your mortal breath and replaces it with that of the collective, a very strong and powerful energy that binds the Kynn together."

Rachel's bold stare traveled through him like a jolt of electricity. "Collective?" She pretended to mull his words very seriously and deeply. "Oh my. I thought it was the Borg who had the collective. Now I find out it's the Kynn. Very useful to know."

Her words brought a reluctant grin. "I think we're a *collective* because *brethren* was already taken. Perhaps by the Lycans. I'll have to check."

Rachel laughed and her blue eyes sparkled. "So if you're a vampire," she asked, "where's your fangs, Devon? To be convinced, I need to see some serious canines here." Her own smile revealed perfect white teeth.

Devon feigned embarrassment. He snapped his fingers as if he'd forgotten something. "Damn it! I didn't get a pair. I'll have to apply to the vampire council for a set."

Rachel held up her butter knife, angling it as to get a glimpse of his reflection. "And, oh my God, a reflection. What kind of vampire are you?"

Devon gave a mock sigh. "Not a very good one, my dear." He stared at her, startled all over again by the intelligence in her eyes and the sheen of her bobbed, jet-black hair. The more he looked, the more he realized it wasn't just her resemblance to Ariel that had drawn him. Rachel had a particular spark all her own, one seeming to light her from the inside out.

She pinned him with a quizzical gaze. "So what exactly is the fascination with the vampire mystique?"

That question almost stopped Devon in his tracks. Hard to explain, but he'd give it a shot anyway. "You know the kind of people who come into the club—the hardcore Goth types lurking in the shadows striking iconic poses."

Rachel nodded. "Can't miss them."

"Why do you think they're there?"

She shook her head. "Don't know."

"Because they want a place to be, to belong. They want the fantasy to be real." He didn't mention that the people following the medieval-slash-Gothic subculture paid his bills and had made him a wealthy man many times over.

"To be vampires?"

"Of course. Think about it. There's nothing more erotic than the idea of being immortal. To many, the idea of communing with a lover in blood is a powerful aphrodisiac—erotic even."

Even as he said the words, Devon realized he wasn't adverse to the idea of giving Rachel a glimpse into the Kynn world. He felt hot blood rush straight to his groin. The idea tightened his cock deliciously. Not tonight, of course. But the opportunity would come. Of that he had no doubt.

A suggestive smile curved her lips. "Erotic?" She rolled her eyes sanctimoniously. "You would say that."

Devon sipped his coffee, cold for the lack of attention he'd given it through their conversation. "I am Kynn."

Her face turned into a question mark. "Kynn," she repeated. "Sounds like some family get-together."

Devon slowly raised his gaze until it met hers. "When mortal breath is taken, what replaces it is far more valuable than the human soul."

She puzzled over that one. "Which is?"

Hard to explain, but he'd try. "The collective is the gestalt of the Kynn as a race, a relationship of elements so unified as a whole that its properties can't be derived from the simple summation of its parts. To partake of the blood of a sire is to take in the very essence of creation hearkening back to the creator."

Rachel's eyes widened. "So that would make their point of origin—Heaven?"

He nodded. "Legend says the Kynn found their origins in the dare that the angel Lucifer had thrown out to God, a challenge that he, Lucifer, could tempt more souls into Hell than God himself could into Heaven. God accepted that challenge, casting Lucifer and his brethren out. As they fell from Heaven, not all the angels completed the transition to demons. Some hesitated, unsure which side to choose, becoming lost between the two realms, belonging neither to Heaven nor to Hell. So Earth became their realm."

Rachel grinned and finished the story. "And then they all became vampires and lived happily ever after?"

Devon had to laugh. "You're holding on to the definition of vampire as what you've seen in the movies and read in books. In reality, it's nothing like you imagine."

She hesitated. "So you are saying that vampires really do exist?" Doubt creased her forehead.

Devon didn't dare to smile, even though that's what he felt like doing. "Are you sure they don't?"

Rachel seemed to be mulling his words, and she wasn't smiling. "Of course they don't." A dreamy look filled her eyes, as if she were imagining, just imagining the possibilities. After a moment, she sighed and her dreamy gaze vanished. "If they did, I'd want to be one."

Just the words Devon wanted to hear, but no time or chance to take Rachel up on them. Yet. He'd cast his hook and caught his fish. He'd have to reel carefully to keep from losing her. If he could at least plant the idea of the Kynn in the back of her mind, perhaps she'd want to explore further.

Jaye arrived with the bill. "Can I fill you up again?" she asked, eyeing their empty coffee cups.

Rachel checked her watch, then placed her hand over her cup. "No more for me." She glanced across the table. "The tow truck will be arriving soon." Purse in hand, she slid out of the booth.

Time had zoomed by, and Devon hadn't even missed it. He'd been having too much—dare he think it?—fun. A long time since he'd spent time with anyone for the pure pleasure of their company. "We've got to get going." He glanced at the total and dug in his breast pocket. His hand came up empty. "Oh shit."

Rachel caught his muttered exclamation. "Is there a problem?"

Embarrassment flooded. "Ah, I seem to have forgotten my wallet." And he had. Even now he could picture it, still in his desk. Mind full of fantasy and eyes full of stars, he'd walked right out of the club without it.

And right now he felt like a damn fool. He didn't have a cent to his name. No cash, no credit cards. No way to pay.

"Listen, Jaye," he started to say. "You know I'm good for it."

Jaye waved him off. "Sure, hon. I can cover this one." She gave him a pat on the rear. "Maybe we can take it out in trade sometime." She winked again. "You'll owe me one."

Rachel stepped up. Still wearing her apron, she dug in the pockets and came up with a handful of bills. Her eye widened a bit as she counted through her stash. There were quite a few tens and twenties in.

She laid a twenty on the table, more than enough to cover the bill and leave a substantial tip. "I'll take care of it," she said quietly.

Devon tried to hand her back her money. Her hand felt warm and firm beneath his. "Really, that's not necessary." She'd run her ass off to earn it. No way in hell would he let his guest pay for their meal.

Reclaiming her money, Rachel tilted her head back. She looked at him through beautiful long-lashed eyes. "Just give me a ride back to my car and we'll call it even. She handed the money to Jaye. "Keep the change, please."

Jaye smiled, knowing when she'd been outfoxed. "Guess this means he owes you, girlfriend." Giving a wink, she sashayed off.

Swallowing hard, Devon moistened his lips. Damn. Most women would have been content to let matters stand as arranged. "That really wasn't necessary," he started to say.

Fixing the strap of her purse over her shoulder, Rachel cut him off. "Your company was worth the price of breakfast."

His turn to be surprised. "Oh?"

Rachel laughed. "I've never seen any man layer on the bull-shit like you do. I have to admit, you do it with style." Without waiting for him, she turned and headed up the aisle. Her hips swayed in a most enticing manner as she walked away.

A hand clapped him on the shoulder. "Better catch her, Devon," Jaye snarked. "I think she just walked off with your balls."

Indeed, she had.

No choice but to get moving.

Somehow the ride back to Mystique's parking lot went by entirely too fast. Before he knew it, they were right back where they'd begun. Rachel's old station wagon still sat, bereft and alone. The tow truck didn't seem to have made it.

Rachel groaned, slumping down in her seat and covering her face with her hands. "He's not here." She took a breath and her breasts rose and fell under the silky fabric of her uni-form. The low cut enhanced the cleft between her breasts, set-ting off a slew of erotic images in his mind. "My luck is terrible lately."

Actually, Devon relished the fact that the tow truck hadn't arrived. It gave him an excuse to offer to drive her home, just to be with her a little bit longer.

Eyes fixed on her luscious body, Devon wondered what it would be like to cup one of her breasts and gently squeeze it, stroking her erect nipple with his thumb as he leaned slowly in to . . .

Unable to resist temptation any longer, he reached out, stroking the side of her face with the lightest touch.

Rachel caught her breath, turning her head to stare into his eyes. The connection between them sizzled with pure electricity, so strong it felt as if some purely magnetic force worked to weld them together.

A wisp of bangs dropped into her eyes. "Your touch makes me feel so alive. I wish . . ." An ironic smile tugged at her lips as she dropped off into silence.

Devon brushed her hair aside. "What?"

"Nothing." Reluctance warring with longing weighted her words like lead.

Devon's fingers dropped lower, skimming the soft line of her jaw. He found her lips, tracing their moist pout. Touching her lit off an explosion of sparks in his groin. His cock leapt to throbbing readiness in his slacks. "Tell me."

Shivering, she forced an unhappy little grimace. "I haven't got any wishes left anymore."

Devon leaned in until his lips were just a few inches from her ear. He smelled the heat, the sexual need radiating from her body. A shiver of anticipation crawled down his spine. She wanted to give in, let herself go and enjoy all he had to offer. Fear kept her immobile, kept her inner walls high. Somehow he'd find a way to get through them. If he couldn't tear them down, he'd go around them.

Leaning closer, he felt the warmth of her breath. Another second and their lips would—must—meet. "I think I know your wish."

She gasped and pulled back. The tips of her fingers settled on his chin. She wasn't pushing him away, yet neither was she ready to welcome him. "Don't. You promised not to seduce me."

Devon didn't move. All his senses hummed with unfulfilled desire. He'd never wanted any woman the way he wanted Rachel. Not even Ariel had instilled such an ache of longing. He sat for a moment, relishing her touch. Wishing she would do more, knowing she wouldn't.

Not tonight, he cautioned himself. *Patience.*

He captured her hand, kissing the tips of her fingers. "Did I really say that?"

Rachel's throat worked an uneasy swallow. "Yes . . ."

"I lied."

12

Closing the door behind her, Rachel leaned against its solid strength. She had to. Keeping it shut meant she wouldn't be tempted to open it, welcome Devon inside . . .

Her mouth quirked into a smile.

And fuck him like mad.

Hearing his car roll out of the driveway and into the street, she relaxed. Good, he'd gone. Temptation had been resisted, but just barely!

To make doubly sure, Rachel peeked outside. Yep. The driveway was empty. Not a soul in sight. She checked her watch. Not that there should be anyone out and about at three forty in the morning. It still felt a little strange being out this late at night. And without a car.

Her gaze lingered on the spot where her car should be parked, but wasn't. Devon had promised to take care of it in the morning. He'd have it towed and checked into the nearest repair shop.

The bill, however, would still be hers to pick up. Even though he'd offered to take care of it and let her pay him back,

Rachel had refused. Her motto had to hold firm: Never accept favors from men. Do that, and they surely want something in return. Never failed.

Rachel locked the door, checking twice to make sure the deadbolt had caught and the chain was in its place. She sighed. Whether dressed in leather or nice silk suits, men were pigs.

"All of them, damn it."

Safe inside her own little domain, she kicked off her pumps, sure that her feet were nothing but nubbins and her shoes were full of blood. They weren't, but it still felt like it. After a night on her feet, her calves ached unmercifully, and her legs felt as huge as tree trunks. Even now she felt the pulsing of blood through her lower regions, the throb of overworked muscles.

Atrophied muscles, apparently, she thought, grimacing. God, but she felt every minute of her days here on earth. So much for sitting behind a counter on her ass for years. *I've been too lazy for too long. This is what it feels like to really work for a living.*

Speaking of working for a living, how much had she made in tips tonight? She hadn't counted her loot yet.

Too keyed up to sleep, she grabbed a wine cooler out of the fridge. She made a beeline for the living room, practically collapsing onto the sofa. Drinking this late was out of character for her, but she needed to relax, and it would help.

Twisting off the cap, she took a long sip of the blackberry-flavored drink. The fizzy wine was refreshing, bringing a bit of wakefulness to her exhausted body. She took another swallow, set it aside, and began to dig the bills and miscellaneous change out of her apron. In a very few moments, she had quite a stash lying in her lap.

She gave a low whistle. "Holy cow. I think this is more than I made in a whole week at the Book Nook." Hands half shaking from excitement, she counted her money, smoothing it out, sorting the dollar amounts into little piles. As she counted, her tongue snaked out of her mouth, tracing her upper lip.

Two hundred and seventy dollars.

"This could be good." She didn't care that she was talking to herself. She was too damn thrilled to have cleared so much easy money in one night.

Well, okay, not so easy.

She hurt like hell, but figured she would be able to bear the ache if this was the type of money she could make. Hell! Work one night, and she'd almost managed to cover the whole week. When she was paying herself a salary out of the bookstore, she'd often never brought home more than fifteen thousand dollars a year. In California, that was practically a poverty-level wage. She knew every trick about scrimping, eating cheap, driving an older car, going without any health insurance or other benefits so she could keep her business afloat.

Looking at the cash in her hands, she did a bit of mental figuring. If she worked at Mystique a year or two, she could make enough money to get out of debt and maybe even have a savings account. The prospect was an exciting one. Here, at last, was a way out of her hole.

Maybe that light at the end of the tunnel wasn't an oncoming train after all.

But did she have enough stamina to keep up with that kind of pace five nights a week? Tonight, she had been excited, eager to please, smiling, flirting. She wasn't always going to feel that way, wasn't always going to feel like laughing off being groped like a piece of meat. In that respect, she felt like a whore, giving a flash of tit and thigh as she delivered drinks. By watching the other waitresses, she'd already learned to bend extra deep, giving the customers what they wanted.

Still, the lure of money beckoned. She wouldn't have to do it forever, just long enough to get out of debt. When she was firmly on her feet, she'd quit and find a nice cushy office job, go back to pushing that pencil.

Eyes growing itchy with fatigue, Rachel put away her money. Heading back to the kitchen, she poured the rest of the wine cooler down the drain. A scratching sound at the window caused her to turn. She hurried to the window, peering through the glass into the dark street outside.

"Sleek?"

No cat. Seeing nothing, she quickly unlatched the window and slid it up. Since this was usually the cat's main entrance into the apartment, there was no screen. The night was cool, a little misty from the rain clouds that had settled upon the face of the earth like layers of soft cotton. The wind was brisk and clean, caressing her skin.

Hands braced on the windowpane, Rachel leaned out.

"Sleek?" she called again. "Here, kitty. Get your ass in here."

A presence. A pressure. What glided past her was as silent as the breeze, as subtle as a lover's touch. It briefly caressed the back of her neck, going down her back, circling her breasts, then lower, over her flat belly, between her thighs, down her legs. Closing her eyes, she gave herself to the wonderful phenomenon wrapping around her like a warm, loving embrace.

Lulled almost into sleep by the lovely feeling, an abrupt thump on the windowsill caused her eyelids to fly open, her heart almost dropping to her feet.

"Holy shit, Sleek! You scared ten years off my life." Pleasant sensations forgotten, she picked up the scrawny tomcat and set him on the floor. Filling his food and water dishes, she flipped off the kitchen light and went upstairs, unsnapping the tight crotch of her uniform as she walked.

She peeled off her clothes after reaching the bathroom. Hose and panties went into the hamper. She hung her uniform on the shower bar, where the steam from the hot water would chase away the wrinkles and odors of the smoke-filled bar. Sitting on the edge of the tub, she turned on the tap, adjusting the water until it was as hot as her skin could stand.

As it filled, she slowly eased her aching feet into its depths. Oh God, that felt so good.

Tub full, she lowered her body into the nearly scalding water, her skin soon growing red as a lobster in a pot. She lay in the water until it grew cold and her skin wrinkled like a prune.

Reluctantly getting out, she toweled herself dry, then brushed her teeth. Her contact lenses came out last. After an evening like she'd had, they felt welded to her eyeballs.

Tired from the pressures of her new job, she padded naked into the bedroom. The bed was a blur before her eyes, an inviting oasis for sleep.

The sheets were cool and inviting. Just what she needed.

Rachel slid under the covers and turned off the lamp at her bedside. Giving into the persuasions of darkness, her eyes slipped shut. Excited exhaustion gave way to the sandman's bag of magic sand.

Rachel had only been asleep a few minutes when she felt that strange presence again, the one she'd experienced when she let the cat in.

The feather-light pressure settled against her hips. Delicious warmth spread through her.

Lost in the depths of her dream, Rachel gave herself to the delicious fantasy. She could almost imagine that she was in the arms of a man. The vibrations were so intense; she had the feeling if she opened her eyes, she would find a hard male body pressed against hers.

God, yes!

The pressure moved over her skin, sliding up her sides, under her arms, over her breasts. The touch was light, sensual. An unbidden rush of sexual warmth filled her. Her nipples hardened. The strange sensation continued, feeling as if slow circles were being drawn around the pink areolas. After a moment the invisible hands sank lower. Tracing over her belly, lower still to the soft flesh between her legs.

A distinct moan floated from her parted lips. Her clit pulsed, her sex growing moist with the juices of her arousal. The light touch settled between her legs, instigating an excruciating tease. Invisible fingertips tickled her labia. Her breasts began to throb, aching with the desire to be kissed, suckled.

Rachel drew in a deep, ragged breath. Whatever was happening to her—wonderful! She trembled beneath the onslaught of sensual sensations caressing her skin. Hot excitement flooded through her. Her nerve endings tingled. Moisture pulsed between her thighs, making her hot, wet, and ready.

A faceless shadow rose before her, spreading itself over her. The air around her quivered. A delicious prickling crawled over her skin, an aura of power and blazing heat. She felt a cock pressing through her labia, entering. The invisible stab was so sharp a shock that she shuddered in immediate response. The walls spun, closing in around her.

Rachel's head rolled against the softness of her pillow. Raising her arms over her head, she grasped the headboard. The pressure pounding between her legs lunged in, withdrew a little, then plunged again until the tempo of shadow against flesh merged, a rushing sensation of sonic vibrations. The pressure quickened, deepened, sending her over the edge of pleasure and into a body-shuddering climax. Control slipped through her fingers. Her cry of pleasure caught her throat, emerging as a low, throaty moan.

Several minutes passed before the invisible pressure abated. It withdrew as it had arrived, cloaking itself in clandestine shadows. Opening her eyes, Rachel slowly let the air out of her lungs. Senses enjoyably hazed, pieces of her all too brief dream floated through her mind.

She licked dry lips. "Damn, that was intense." Had she not known she'd fallen asleep, she would've sworn someone had just made love to her. A weak laugh escaped. Impossible. She was very much alone.

Funny. She didn't *feel* alone.

Rachel turned her head, staring into the formless shadows haunting her bedroom. A shimmer of movement caught her attention. She had a feeling another presence occupied the room. The sensations bore down around her, pressing and intense. The fine hairs on the back of her neck rose.

She sat up and snapped on her bedside lamp. She squinted. Everything around her looked blurry and shapeless. She couldn't see more than a few feet in any direction without her contacts or glasses—which were in the bathroom, damn it, on the vanity shelf over the sink. God forbid she wear her glasses in public, especially in front of a man. The plain, rectangular black frames lent her no favors.

A thump landed on the bed at her feet.

Rachel squealed, then laughed. "Sleek." Seemed like the mystery intruder was only her overactive imagination.

Installing himself in his favorite place at the foot of her bed, Sleek curled into a ball. A purr of contentment soon followed.

A sigh escaped. "Glad someone's happy around here."

Rubbing her hands over her face, Rachel rolled over onto her side, hugging a pillow between her legs. What had happened a few minutes ago had awakened an incredible sexual hunger. She longed to be in the arms of a man, crushed under his weight as his cock pummeled her depth.

She touched the empty side of her bed. It would be nice to have someone to go to sleep with, to wake up beside. It had been a long time since a man's body had lain next to hers. No one occupied the blank space. Lonely was the worst disease in the world. It ate away at the heart like acid corroded.

Her mind drifted toward her new boss. A slow ribbon of desire coiled through her.

Devon Carnavorn. Even his name sounded regal.

Rachel remembered the way he'd looked at her over their meal, undressing her with his eyes. How his hand had felt, holding hers. The electric shock shooting through her body when he'd touched her. She'd never experienced anything like it before in her life.

Drawing a deep breath, she sighed. Face it. She needed a fuck. Good old in-your-face nasty sweaty sex. She easily pictured herself with Devon. No doubt he knew how to please a woman. What she wouldn't give to make love to him.

Slipping back into a drowsy torpor, Rachel slid her hands between her legs, caressing her aching sex. Her last coherent thought arrived as gentle sleep shadowed her mind. "You want this, Devon?" she whispered to her dream lover. "Seduce me."

13

Devon shrugged off his velvety bathrobe, letting it drop to the floor around his feet. Standing in his bedroom, droplets of water still beaded his skin, giving his flesh a clean, fresh sheen. Thoughts of Rachel caused that familiar warm rush of blood toward his groin. As if having a will all its own, his cock twitched. His smirk grew wider.

Ah Rachel, a lovely lithe creature to behold. Hers was a body well arranged: round, full breasts, tiny waist, and lovely curving ass cheeks. As delicate as a porcelain doll, hers was a body made to entice, tease, and please.

A shadow moved behind him and he turned, catching sight of his reflection in the full-length mirror. Light brown hair covered his arms and chest, and his penis nestled snugly in a thatch of tight pubic curls. His body was sleek, solid, deliciously muscled, the envy of other men, the desire of many women.

The Kynn were highly sexual creatures, who needed sex, craved sex as surely as other men craved air in their lungs. When he wasn't having intercourse, he thought about having sex. What he thought about now was how to get Rachel to spread her legs for him.

Reaching down, he wrapped his fingers around his growing erection. His cock pulsed in his hand, warm and velvety to his touch. Even when flaccid it was an impressive sight, filling the cut of his slacks and giving the ladies something to whisper about behind their hands. Erect, it was a magnificent length, thick and round. Closing his eyes, he stroked himself. His breathing grew ragged.

Though he had taken many lovely ladies in his time on this earth, it was the woman he had chosen to be his next mate that he fantasized about.

Rachel. Ah, she'd played her coy game with him, but behind her fresh manner and cool gaze simmered a passion yet to be tapped. He sensed it, knew it, in the way her eyes trailed over his body, lingering at his crotch. She had that certain sparkle that spoke of curiosity, wonder, and desire. Oh, she was most definitely curious.

"I'll soon have you, Rachel," he whispered. Earlier in the night he'd visited her, gaining entrance to her home when she'd let her cat inside. One of the many talents of the Kynn included the ability to move on the wind as a wraith, unseen and unheard.

Using the perfect pressure, he stroked his cock in a steady motion. Rachel's image filled his mind. His fantasy had her on her knees, looking up at him, eyes alight with anticipation. She was eager to take him, her pink tongue flicking out of her mouth to lick the precum away from the tip of his cock. The salty taste excited her, and she moaned softly, taking him inch by inch into her mouth, sucking ever so slowly to build his tension. He imagined the way he would guide her head as he fucked her warm mouth.

Devon's breathing grew harsh, labored. He rubbed his slick penis harder, giving himself no respite. He wanted Rachel, wanted her so badly he could almost see her lying naked before him, white thighs spread wide. How he longed to swirl his tongue over her pulsing clit, lapping her nectar as he flicked and sucked those delicate pink petals.

The friction on his erection grew heated, harder.

He would tease her, using first one finger and then two to prepare her. She would be excited by the sight of his engorged manhood, that angry beast of sexual conquest, and would whimper. But he would reassure her with soft whispers and softer kisses. She would taste her female spice on his lips, her supple tongue tangling with his. When he entered her in a single thrust, she would cry out, thrash her head, buck her body. Her nails would rake his flesh and she would scream his name . . .

"Mmm, nothing more lovely than watching the master pleasure himself."

Cock in hand, a smile crossed Devon's face. He turned, raking his bottom lip with his teeth. Fresh from the shower, his latest protégé, Julian Wickham, stood behind him. Skin still dewy with water, he'd wrapped a thick white towel around his narrow hips. Dark ringlets curled around his face and shoulders. As defined and taut as a Michelangelo sculpture, his lean young body rippled with strength.

"It'll be even better when I'm pleasuring myself with you." Devon smiled and slipped off his robe. "I hope you're ready for a good ass-fucking, my boy. I'm particularly hungry tonight."

Julian looked at him from under a fall of long lashes. "I'm ready to please you, lord."

Devon walked over to his young lover. Since becoming enamored with Rachel, he had no desire for any other female flesh. He wanted to make love to her and her alone. Still, hunger needed to be sated. A man would serve his purposes just fine. The sexual energies were just as strong, if not stronger, from a male.

Devon ran his hand along the cobbled plane of Julian's abdomen. "I expect you to." He trailed one hand to his hip, and then upward to feel the flat circle of Julian's nipple. His fingers traced the dusky circle. "In every way." Whether taking male or female, he was the aggressor.

The Kynn did not view same-sex coupling as a threat. Male to male or female to female, all sexual contact was welcomed, even encouraged. As a man he had the dual advantage of being able to draw his energy off either sex. Kynn females could only feed off the energies of men. Body parts had to meet and penetrate (or be penetrated) for connection to complete itself.

Schooled in prestigious but dismal English boarding schools offering only a same-sex student body, Devon had learned to appreciate the pleasures of the male form early in his sexual education. Most boys had willingly engaged in buggery by the time of adolescence.

Julian was one of his favorites, a beautiful boy with stars in his eyes and the ambition to succeed. Originally hired as a bartender at Mystique, he'd quickly ingratiated himself to Devon by revealing his willingness to barter his body to supplement his income. Less than a month later, Julian worked his way not only into Devon's bed, but into the Kynn lifestyle.

Expression heating, Julian's breath caught. His whole body vibrating, he stiffened. Heat rolled off his body in waves. "I've craved your touch," he murmured through slumberous eyes. Lust permeated the air around the ripe young stud. Core pulsing with a powerful throb of carnal eagerness, he definitely looked forward to his claiming.

Licking his lips, Devon's breathing quickened. Through a single touch he felt the rise of Julian's inner energy. The electrifying pulse nearly took his breath away. "I'm looking forward to fucking you in every way," he breathed.

Julian closed his eyes in delight as Devon worked the knotted towel away from his hips. It fell away, revealing Julian's fine, thick cock nestled among a thatch of hair as pale as that on his head. A primitive, throaty moan escaped him. He waited in sensuous suspension for the surrender he'd willingly give to his master.

Using both hands, Devon traced his fingers along the lines of Julian's sides. Leaning in, he pressed his mouth to Julian's, the beginning of a tangle of mouths and cocks as their bodies came together. Grasping Julian's hips, he guided him to the thick carpet beneath their feet. Somehow there just wasn't enough time to make it to the bed.

Julian groaned as Devon's bruising lips left his mouth to move to his chest.

Assuming the superior position, Devon captured and licked the eraser-hard nub, nipping at the tip with his teeth. "I know you like the pain." Licking his fingers, he claimed Julian's other nipple, rolling it hard.

Julian whimpered, tangling his fingers in Devon's thick hair and pressing himself closer. His cock rose, tight and pulsing with his tension. "My body was created to please you, master."

"And you do. Very much." Drawing out his tease, Devon nipped first one and then the other quivering peak, his tongue making slow, lazy circles around each. "Shall I stop?" he teased, his own voice dropping to a low, husky register.

Julian's eyes were sleepy with desire. "I want more," he whispered. "To be, to become. As you have promised." He fumbled for Devon's cock, circling the burgeoning length.

With gentle restraint, Devon caught Julian's hand and drew it away. "Your time will come soon," he said roughly.

Thus saying, Devon bent his head to graze the taut, extended peaks of Julian's nipples, teasing each in its turn without mercy or respite.

Julian trembled. "Yes, lord."

Devon ran his open palms down the flat plane of Julian's abdomen. His fingers found and traced the many small scars his feedings had left on the young man's supple skin. He looked forward to the night when he'd sire Julian fully into the Kynn realm. Only twenty-one, the boy was still too young. He needed some age, some maturity.

But first Devon needed a taste of his tight little ass.

Climbing to his feet, he walked over to the nightstand beside his bed. From the single drawer he retrieved a fresh single-edged razor blade and a tube of lubricant. He unwrapped the protective cardboard from around the blade, discarding it into a nearby wastebasket.

Julian automatically assumed the position on his hands and knees. His tender asshole beckoned, ready to be stuffed to the hilt.

Devon licked his lips. Nothing he liked more than a tight hot grip around his cock. Made no difference if the ass he plundered were male or female. Nothing could compare to the silk-encased grip of anal muscles around his rigid erection. "On your back," he ordered.

Smiling, Julian stretched out on his back. "Your wish is my command."

Lubing his palms, Devon knelt between Julian's spread thighs, well muscled and strong. He could already taste the pulse of Julian's energy in his mouth. His hand sought and found Julian's cock, thick, hard, and hot. Crown purple, ripe and ready, pearlescent drops of pre-cum seeped from the tip.

Devon stroked, a slow up and down motion. "I love it when you're so hard."

Julian moaned. His breathing quickened. "Keep jacking me like that, and I won't be long," he warned through gritted teeth.

Devon gave Julian's shaft a little twist. "You won't come until I say you can."

Julian gasped at the brief rush of pain. "Yes, lord."

Devon stroked Julian's shaft with a slow, steady motion, relishing the incredibly fierce sensations arousal engendered in both their bodies. Not having had sex in a couple of days,

Devon definitely looked forward to recharging his inner energy cells.

Wild with need, fighting the unstoppable feelings threatening to overtake him too soon, Julian dug his fingers deeply into the carpeting. Panting through slack lips, he moaned out his pleasure.

Hand working in a slow and steady motion, Devon guided Julian's legs to bend at the knee. In response Julian thrust his hips upward in anticipation of entry.

Devon eased his fingers past the crack of Julian's ass. Fingers slick with lube, he pressed into the soft warmth.

Julian's anus puckered, then opened. Body flushing with sensual heat, he fought to hold back his gasps of pleasure. "God yes," he breathed. "Go deeper."

"Mmm, my pleasure." Devon pushed his finger deeper, feeling a satisfying grip suck at his skin in response.

Julian released a soft moan. His hips rocked with abandon.

Drawing out his finger for a second, Devon returned the thrust with two. He made no effort to be slow or gentle, sensing Julian needed to be mastered.

Julian shuddered, craving a deeper, more complete fulfillment. "I want you deep inside me."

Devon swallowed hard, working to keep his own breathing even and controlled. An electric buzz tingled through him as Julian's inner muscles leapt with intense pulses of sheer sexual eagerness. The tingle of brutal pleasure was too intense to be resisted much longer. Cock rock-hard and ready, his need for orgasm knotted tight and hard in his groin.

Devon needed to make the connection. He needed to feed. Fingers sliding from Julian's moist core, his palms cupped naked buttocks. Julian's body vibrated, his anus stretching open wider to accommodate the entry of a fully erect cock.

Drawing in a sharp breath, Julian thrashed his hips against

the invasion. "Oh God! You're so big," he gasped out, half in pleasure, half in pain.

Pausing only a moment, Devon pushed until he could go no deeper. Then he pulled out, moving his hips with a deliberately measured slowness. Just as the crown of his cock appeared, he thrust back in. Hard.

Releasing a gasping groan, Julian opened to him willingly. Instinct made him raise his hips higher, an offering, a hint that he would not be easily satisfied. By the look of rapture on his face, he relished the all-consuming ache spreading through him.

An ache so sensually replicated in Devon's own body. The first connection had been made. Now the second.

Buried to the balls, Devon leaned over Julian's body. Supporting his weight on his outstretched arms, his hands bracketed Julian's shoulders. Bodies melded together, they were almost face to face.

Julian gasped and arched under him. A raw and forbidden lust roared through his gaze. Eyes sparking with fierce appetite, he writhed with a rash urgency to give every last bit. His cock throbbed against the nest between their bodies, fed by the friction of skin on skin.

Devon found the forgotten razor blade. "Where to cut?" he mused through an evil grin.

Julian automatically turned his head, baring his throat. "Here, lord." His offer was unhesitatingly given. "Drink of me through body and spirit, so that you may live."

And so he would.

Devon flicked the tip of the blade into Julian's skin. Pushed by the pulse of his heartbeat, blood immediately rose. Devon's head dipped. A moment later the honey-sweet taste of blood filled his mouth.

Devon drank. His thrusts increased in speed and strength. He pummeled Julian's ass without mercy, forcing his cock in deep, withdrawing, then thrusting again until only the physical restrictions of his body stopped him.

Julian's responses grew more heated, fevered. His fingers locked into Devon's shoulders, his hungry body crackling intensely as the energies inside his body built toward explosive pressure.

Breaking free of the body lock, Devon pushed himself back up on his knees. One hand curled around Julian's thigh, dragging him closer. The other wrapped around Julian's engorged cock, the pulse of silk-encased steel seeming to match the intense throb of his own thrusting shaft.

Clenching his teeth, Devon ordered, "Don't come yet."

Julian's hips trembled in a flurry bordering on desperation. His breath came in short, ragged gasps, underscored by his harsh pleading. "Please let me . . . !"

"No." Eyes narrowing in concentration, Devon centered his thoughts, willing his body to draw from the other man's. He jacked Julian's cock while grinding his own deep into Julian's ass.

Electric tension resonated around the perimeter of their joined bodies.

Devon felt familiar sensations fill him as his hungry body eagerly fed off Julian's life forces. His hips pistoned harder. His hand jacked harder. The throbbing force vibrated between them. Blinding in its concentration, pure unadulterated energy pulsed.

Devon closed his eyes, relishing the flood of pure power filling his senses. "Come," he grated. "Give me everything."

Obeying, Julian bellowed as the ferocity of orgasm flooded his entire being. He thrashed his head from side to side, his skin slick with sweat, air pungent with the odors of male on male sex.

Just when Devon was certain that he could reach no higher

plane of ecstasy, his second release came, so violently that he, too, screamed in the throes of magnificent primal pleasure. A quake of pleasure thundered right down the center of his spine. Pulling his hips away from Julian's ass, hot semen jetted.

Hand finding his cock, Devon milked every last pearly drop from the tip. He gasped, catching his breath, struggling to bring his breathing back to a normal level. The scent of his seed filled the air.

Side by side, both men panted while shuddering with after-shocks.

A knock on the door brought Devon's attention back to the present. He had guests coming, very important guests. The addition of a new member to the Kynn collective normally required a meeting with the chancellor of the local clan. Since Devon was chancellor, he intended to announce his intention to take a bloodmate.

Not that he'd yet told Rachel she'd been chosen . . .

"Sir?" Simpson's voice was a tad impatient. "Do you require help dressing?"

His mouth dry, Devon swept his tongue over his lips. "I'm fine," he called, putting a hint of steel in his own tone. "Certainly I am well able to dress myself."

"If you're quite sure, sir," Simpson replied. "The night's guests are beginning to arrive."

His many tensions somewhat eased by the pretty young boy at his side, Devon rose. The taste of Julian's blood still clung to his lips. He traced his mouth with his tongue. He hadn't meant to partake of his feed so early in the night, but Julian wearing nothing but a towel was a hard sight to resist. Devon would have to shower again, but quickly.

He prodded Julian. "Get dressed, you lazy boy. You've held me up long enough tonight."

Julian yawned and stretched before giving him a languid, limpid smile. "I'd rather stay naked," he pouted. Hand drifting lower, his fingers circled his cock. He gave it a long stroke.

Devon felt his own body twitch in all the right places. Bending down, he seized a handful of Julian's thick hair. Bringing the boy to his knees, he angled his hips forward.

"If you're going to stay naked," he warned. "You're going to be fucked. Repeatedly."

Crafty hazel eyes smiled. "Gladly." Julian's hands closed around Devon's cock. His lips brushed Devon's still-aching flesh, then his wet tongue followed as his talented mouth sucked down every last inch.

Hands fisting in Julian's hair, Devon cursed under his breath. His body tightened ferociously under a flood of molasses-thick lust that threatened to steal the oxygen from his lungs all over again. His hips moved with a determination that defied his brain.

Damn it, he was going to be late to his own meeting.

A low moan rolled up from his throat. Holy shit, why did Julian have to be such a talented cocksucker?

Not that he minded.

14

A soft, almost hesitant knock jerked Devon out of his thoughts. He glanced at the clock on his desk. Ten after two in the morning. He'd instructed Rosalie to send Rachel up to his office after her shift ended.

"Enter."

The door swung inward. Looking like a child about to be punished, Rachel came into his office. She carried her pumps in her hand, walking on bare feet.

A smile twitched at her lips. "You wanted to see me?" She never wavered, never let her gaze leave his. Her lips shimmered softly from a fresh slick of soft pink gloss. The pebbled tips of her breasts were clearly outlined through her sheer uniform. Just begging to be fondled, sucked.

A shot of fire electrified Devon's blood. Body temperature soaring, he almost gritted his teeth. He licked his lips, wondering how her lips would taste if he kissed her right now. Strawberry? Or a fiery hot cinnamon? His desire for Rachel, evidenced by the persistent ache in his cock, couldn't be easily denied. The wanting. The needing. It eroded his senses like acid.

Drawing on his own cloak of reserve, he beckoned her closer with his hand. "I do."

She gave a little shrug and walked to his desk. "Okay." Her lips were slightly parted, moist and succulent. "By the way, thanks for having my car towed to the shop."

"Nothing serious, I hope."

She made a futzing sound. "Damn battery cable was loose. Ten dollars to tighten it."

Devon clenched trembling hands. "Good. I'd hoped it was nothing major."

Rachel smiled ruefully. "It won't always be so simple to fix, but for now it's all good." She crossed her arms across her body, effectively shielding her breasts.

"So what did you want to talk to me about?" Her tone was casual, distant.

A distance Devon wanted to close. "I just wanted to make a little proposition." The words tumbled out of his mouth before he'd known what he'd say.

Beautifully shaped brows shot up. "A what?"

Wrong thing to say. Mind fuzzed and nervous as hell, everything seemed to be coming out backward.

Devon held up his hands. "A business proposition," he clarified. "I know you're tired, so I will be brief."

Rachel grinned sheepishly. Her steady gaze cleared. "Of course." She gestured to one of the chairs. "May I?"

He cleared his throat. So far seduction was going . . . badly. "How rude of me. Please take a seat."

Rachel sat, tugging the hem of her uniform down, slipping into her shoes. She shifted uncomfortably, attempting to hide the mark on her thigh. "Birthmark," she explained. "Ugly, isn't it?"

Her innocent words stroked along the base of his neck. Devon swallowed the sudden hitch in the back of his throat. Hers so mirrored his own that it had to be more than mere coincidence. "Not at all. I thought it a quite interesting tattoo. A lot of the girls have them."

She relaxed. "I've actually thought about having it covered. I've never found it attractive."

He stifled a moan. Oh, she didn't know the half of it. "Don't. It's unusual. Sets you apart from the others."

"I never thought of it that way. Thanks." She paused, and then asked, "So what did you plan to propose?"

Devon leaned forward, setting his elbows on his desk and lacing his fingers, his best imitation of businesslike posture.

"It's quite simple. Gina, who you know manages the waitressing staff, just handed in her resignation effective immediately. I need to replace her as soon as possible. I believe you have the necessary qualifications, so I'd like to offer you the job."

Rachel's eyes widened in disbelief. The tip of her tongue shot out, tracing the curve of her upper lip. An utterly sensual move. Desire ignited all over again.

A little laugh escaped her. "Really?"

He had to smile. The raised color in her cheeks and the way her eyes brightened as she pushed herself forward in her chair told him the offer pleased her.

He nodded. "Yes. I believe you can handle the management duties it entails. You'll work with Rosalie on scheduling and help her with the payroll, as well as supervise the girls out on the floor. Since you have owned your own business, I assume you will be able to pick up our system fairly quickly."

Rachel gulped, her slender throat contracting as she swallowed. "Of course. No problem there." She smiled, pleased.

Devon forced steadiness into his voice. "You'll start at a salary of sixty thousand, with raises and bonuses based on performance. The longer you stay with me, the more you'll make."

"Sixty thousand? Dollars?"

"Filthy American currency," he confirmed. "No pesos, or

yen. Not even francs. Good old dollar bills. A lot of them in a stack, I'm told."

Rachel blinked. Her expression conveyed what words could not; a profound sense of gratefulness. "Thank you. I really appreciate that you thought of me for the position."

Devon had to be honest. "You're the most qualified applicant I had immediately on hand," he said, trying to focus on his words and not her enticing lips. "This saves me having to put out a call through the employment agencies and sift through resumes."

She shook her head. "Talk about things taking a turn for the better."

"Looks like your luck's changed."

Her grin beguiled. "Thanks to you," she said softly.

Devon smiled ruefully and glanced at his watch. The tight rein he held on his attraction to Rachel had begun to slip away again. "I know it's late, so I should let you go home."

Eagerness lit her eyes. "What time should I come in tomorrow?"

A smile crept along his lips. "No one comes in on Sundays."

She blushed again, giggling. "Oh right. I forgot. Monday it is, then."

Devon stood. Rachel clambered to her feet as well. "Quite a view you've got here," she commented of the wall of glass.

"Take a look," he invited. "You'll be seeing the view a lot."

Rachel crossed to the security mirrors that allowed people inside the office to view the scene below without being seen themselves. "This is incredible," she enthused. "There isn't a corner I can't see."

He walked up behind her. "A security measure. We need to be able to see everything that's going on at any given time. If there's any trouble, we want to be able to handle it immediately."

"I understand." She yawned, lids dropping, rubbing her eyes. "Sorry. Guess I am a little tired. I was up late last night"

"No thanks to me." Devon lifted his hands and set them lightly on her shoulders. He massaged her neck, gently working over the soft flesh beneath his fingers. The light fruity body mist she wore tantalized his nostrils. Even after a night of working in a packed nightclub, she seemed as clean and fresh as a newborn babe.

To her credit, Rachel didn't jump under his touch or pull away with indignant words. She sighed and leaned back toward him, as if she wanted him to put his arms around her.

Devon murmured in her ear. "Feel good?" He continued to knead her shoulders, running both thumbs up the nape of her neck, making slow circles. A small tremor went through her.

"Mmm, yes. I could use a good massage right about now."

Devon circled her waist with his arms. He held her, not so tightly she couldn't pull away if she was uncomfortable. A sensation passed between them, a strange electricity seeming to crackle in the air.

His head dipped. He nuzzled a light kiss on the back of her neck, just where her short hair ended at the nape. His glance settled on the curve between her neck and shoulder. He ached to brush his lips there.

"Devon, I—"

Devon knew what she was going to say. He didn't want to hear it, either.

Spinning Rachel around, he pulled her into his arms and kissed her. She tasted like sun-warm cherries, tart and scrumptiously ripe.

Their tongues collided and fought. His tongue plunged past her lips, conquering and then claiming victory. He wanted to pleasure her in every way.

As Rachel swallowed her cry, her arms circled his waist, sliding up his back. Her fingers clutched, digging into the corded sinew of his back. Her touch was a drug in his veins. Addictive, but satisfying. He'd sell his soul to possess her.

Eager to reciprocate, Devon's hands had ideas all their own. He cupped her breasts, circling her nipples with his thumbs until they were solid and peaked. His cock strained against her belly. He backed her up against his wall of mirrors. His palms spread across her ass, spreading her open.

Her eagerness slowed. Their kiss ended.

"I—Devon . . ." His name came out breathless and mangled.

Devon traced her lips with the tip of one finger. The sensation of touching her sapped his breath all over again. Just looking at her stoked the hungry embers of need burning inside his core. "Devon what?" His voice simmered hotter than lava.

Rachel shuddered, sighing lightly into his mouth. "What am I thinking?" She lifted her hands to his chest and pushed him away.

He refused to budge.

"Don't think." He reached for her. "Just do." *Like you did last night.* Visiting her in the guise of an incubus, he'd gotten a taste of the passion simmering under her cool exterior.

"We have to stop." Rachel slipped past him. Her words were a dash of cold water.

Devon turned around. "Why?"

She turned a question on him. "Did you offer me this job so you could sleep with me?"

Their gazes locked. His eyes caught the spark, the flame of her desire. She wanted him. No doubt. Her tongue darted out quickly, moistening her lips.

Heart hammering, Devon shoved his hands into his pockets. "I don't intend to use my position as your boss to force my attentions on you." He shook his head, knowing how insincere he must sound. "My intentions as a man—"

Rachel cut him off. "I like to keep my business separate

from my pleasure." Barely audible, her voice was taut. Strained with distress . . . and lust.

Devon inhaled a ragged breath. Perspiration beaded his skin as a low-level tremor passed through him. Pulse ablaze and sparking with sheer frustration, he wanted so badly to take her that he ached. Having caught a whiff of the female sex, his cock insisted on remaining uncomfortably solid inside his slacks. Every ligament in his body remained tight, electrified wires of pure lust. "Is that how it has to be?"

Rachel hesitated, then lifted her chin. In her mind the decision had been made. "It's better that way. Less complicated." Her body disagreed. Her pupils were dilated, her nostrils flared. Her nipples still stood front and center, hard little points of yearning.

Not the words he wanted to hear. "You're right."

"Do I still work here?" she asked.

He placed a hand over his heart. "Of course. I hope you'll still want to work with an old wolf like me."

"Don't you mean an old vampire?" she asked, tweaking the confession he'd made at the truck stop. She obviously hadn't forgotten.

Devon concurred with a forced smile. The last thing he felt like doing. "Old vampire."

Rachel drew a deep breath. "Anyway, it's getting late and I should be going home."

"Running away, Miss Marks?"

She shook her head. Her gaze never wavered. "Who said I was running?"

With Devon's office door shut behind her, Rachel leaned against the wall, letting her head drop back with a soft thud against the polished paneling. It took a solid ten minutes to regulate her breathing, to stop trembling. Wow! How he'd touched her. Just thinking of it sent shivers clear into her core.

She traced her lips. She felt the tingles his kiss had aroused inside her. Her clit pulsed wildly between her legs.

"I told you I wouldn't run," she whispered. "If you want me, come on."

Though she knew she might be caught at any moment, her hand sneaked down between her legs. She rubbed through the silky material of her costume, stroking just the way she wished Devon would touch her.

Oh yes . . .

Rachel closed her eyes, enjoying the sensations, feeling her moist cunt, her panties and hose drenched with her juices. She pressed against her clit, wishing she could finger her sex deeper. Her nylon hose made that impossible.

Still, she needed a little quick relief.

She increased the pressure of her fingers, her body quivering as a long slow stream of heat coursed through her. She closed her eyes, enjoying her climax.

Hearing the sound of heavy footsteps, Rachel opened her eyes. She gathered her composure, smoothing her uniform and tugging her short skirt back into place. She took a deep breath just as Rosalie Dayton rounded the corner.

"There you are," Rosalie said. "I just got the news. Devon told me you've accepted the job. Congratulations."

Rachel smiled. "Well, thank you. I hope we'll work well together."

Rosalie rolled her eyes. "I'm thrilled to have an intelligent woman to work with and not one of Devon's floozies. Trust me when I say I get so damn tired of these fluff-haired wannabe models and actresses he parades through here so he can sleep with them."

Rachel felt her heart drop to her feet with a heavy thud. "So he sleeps with a lot of women?" Not like she hadn't heard the rumors. She had. She'd simply chosen to ignore them.

Until now.

A knowing gleam lit Rosalie's eyes. She gave an undignified snort. "Sleeping isn't what they're doing, honey. He's no more got one in the sack than he's out looking for the next." The old lady reached out and patted her arm. "But you look like a sensible girl. You've got some age on you. You don't look like the kind he can jerk around."

Straight from the horse's mouth. Could it get any plainer?

Rachel tried to keep her face neutral. Through the last three days, she'd been building new fantasies around fucking Devon—only to have them all backfire. "Thanks." *I think*.

She swallowed the lump rising in the back of her throat. Not twenty minutes before, Devon had pawed her like a prime piece of meat. Moreover, she'd been willing to let him. Thank God she hadn't followed through. If he'd said he wanted to fuck her, she wouldn't have been able to get her clothes off fast enough.

"You're welcome." An elbow nudged her in the ribs. "Congratulations again, dear." The old lady hustled off, walking with the energy of a woman half her age.

Rachel darted a glance at Devon's closed door. Success felt like a lump of coal in her Christmas stocking. She had half a mind to walk in there and toss the promotion back in his face.

Christ. Her behavior made her want to puke. She might as well have been a bitch in heat humping his leg.

Rachel had a feeling she'd narrowly avoided making a very big mistake. Thank God Devon would never know just how close she'd come to giving in. Everything about him felt so right. Yet when examined closely, she knew everything to be wrong. For a man like Devon she'd be nothing more than a brief diversion. Until the next pop tart caught his eye.

The thought tapped into her deepest fear. That not only was she cheap, but also easy. And disposable.

"Stupid stupid stupid."

Suddenly she couldn't stand being inside the nightclub.

Disregarding her closing duties, Rachel hurried down to her car. Sliding behind the wheel, she locked the doors around her.

She banged her forehead on the steering wheel. Her favorite form of self-punishment lately. Too bad she didn't do it more often. It might beat some sense into her.

"What the hell was I thinking?" Eat one meal with him and suddenly she was weaving a lovely affair in her mind. She'd best beware of Devon, a carnal, dangerous demon in the guise of an attractive man. His provocative blend of sophisticate and dark exoticism had nearly persuaded her to climb into his bed. Lust was a terrible drug, something hopeless to resist, impossible to walk away from. Her skin still tingled in all the places Devon had touched her.

Rachel raised her head, staring at red-rimmed eyes in the rearview mirror. "Stay away from that damned man. He's nothing but trouble."

Fighting back tears, she shuddered. Easy advice to give.

Hard to take when you're in love.

15

Rachel was hardly aware of the dying light outside her apartment. The skyline of the city faded quietly as the sky shifted from blue to gray and then on to a shade of somber dark soot. Lights popped on across the city's landscape. In the hours before night fell, she was once again alone.

Lost in misery, she felt as if she, too, were fading, entering a darkness from which she'd never find a way out. Instead of taking Devon up on his delicious offer, she'd turned him down flat. He'd made it clear he desired her. No doubt about that. Somehow she'd found the strength to resist him tonight—or more like it, lacked the confidence to follow her amatory desires.

Why?

Because she'd recently been burned? The buzzer sounded in the back of her mind. Not a good enough excuse.

Because she was afraid? Getting warmer.

Maybe because she wasn't good enough for a man like him? Bingo.

Rachel rubbed her eyes. "I'm tired of not being good enough," she murmured. "I'm tired of being me."

Tears stung her eyes again. "I'll be a spinster. Me and my cat, living here all alone, sharing our cat food." The idea depressed her. Was there anything more awaiting her, or was she doomed to forever feel like a fish out of water?

A knock on the door made her cringe.

She shot a nasty look toward the door and cursed. "Damn. Who the hell could that be?" No one came to see her on Sunday except the paper delivery boy. She'd already paid the rude little snot for the month.

Maybe it was the Jehovah's Witnesses, coming with Bible in hand to save her soul. She definitely didn't need that kind of saving. She also hoped it wasn't the Baptists. Their church was just a few blocks away. Not raised to follow any organized religion, she'd always been fascinated by the occult and gravitated toward Wicca, as she liked the idea of nature and its forces rather than the idea that God created man in his own image. If that was true, then God had picked a piss-poor image to re-create.

Tuck your pamphlets in the door and go away!

The doorbell rang again.

"Not now," she muttered under her breath. Since she was sitting in the dark, maybe whoever it was would assume she'd gone out and go away. She sat still, silent, holding her breath.

Another ring. And again. Someone was determined not to be ignored.

"Shit." Of course these Bible thumpers would know she was home. Her car was parked in the driveway.

Fucking genius you are, Rachel.

By the sixth ring her nerves had had enough.

Flipping on a lamp beside the couch, she headed to the front door, steeling herself to tell those self-righteous Jesus freaks to go away. Twisting the doorknob, she flung open the door.

"I told you to leave me alone!"

Seeing who stood at her door, anger slipped away. She immediately fell into silence, staring numbly at the man standing outside.

Oh great. This was just what she didn't need right now.

"Well, Rachel," Devon said slowly. "If you insist, I suppose I have no choice." Away from the club, he'd dressed casually: slacks, shirt, sport jacket. Neat and immaculate.

Rachel inwardly groaned. "W—w—what are you doing here?" she stammered, trying to regain her composure and failing. It flashed through her mind she must look an absolute fright. Eyes red from crying, face puffy, dressed in a pair of old sweats and house shoes.

Certainly not the kind of sexy beauty that would capture Carnavorn's eye at all.

"I hope you don't mind that I dropped by without calling," Devon said, "but your phone was busy."

Busy because it was off the hook. In the middle of a good depression, she didn't like answering it. "I . . . well . . . now isn't a good time." *No shit, Sherlock.*

He looked her over from head to foot. "So I see." He quirked a brow at her. "Aren't you going to invite me in?" Without waiting for a reply, he stepped over the threshold. As though he had been there a thousand times before, he crossed into the living room.

Her apartment was decorated with dark, broody colors, navy blues and browns. She just wasn't the kind of woman who went for colorful, flowery prints, acres of wide-open windows and sunshine. She preferred to keep the blinds closed, her way of keeping the outside world at bay. Her home was her sanctuary, that little piece of the world she had absolute control over. Her decoration was an eclectic mix, heavy oak furniture amid the most modern appliances.

As a hobby Rachel did needlepoint, mostly fantasy themed. Hanging on the walls, carefully matted and framed, were faeries, unicorns, beautiful sorceresses, and handsome wizards that came to life in colorful thread under her skilled needle. Most she designed herself, working from sketches she made on the material. Such a simple diversion was part of the escape that made a boring, mundane life livable.

Devon looked around, his gaze missing nothing. "Nice place you have here, Rachel. Closed within itself. Like you." He nodded approvingly. "I like it."

Trailing in his wake, Rachel digested his comments, her mind whirling with options. She couldn't very well force Devon out of her apartment, and she sure as hell couldn't call the police on her boss.

Running her fingers through her uncombed shag to smooth it, she shrugged. "Thanks. I'm glad you like it. Can I, ah, get you something to drink?"

He smiled down at her, a burst of sunshine after a long dark thunderstorm. Her knees weakened alarmingly. "Wine would be lovely, if you have it."

A second chance. This time she wouldn't fuck it up. "As a matter of fact, I do." Right now she could use a drink as well. It was bad to drink alone. Might as well have some company.

In the kitchen, she quickly splashed cool water on her face. After patting her skin dry with a dish towel, she took a bottle of white wine out of the fridge. It had cost her about three bucks.

Not the best damn stuff, probably nothing like the expensive vintages he was accustomed to drinking. Still, it was all she had.

Twisting off the cap, she filled two wineglasses. Taking them back into the living room, she offered him one.

Devon took the glass, his gaze roaming her features, settling on her eyes. "You've been crying," he observed gently. "Has something upset you?"

At his words, all the anger, frustration, and confusion of the weeks before filled her up and began to overflow. She wanted to yell, scream and shout, stomp in fury, but all she could do was watch the room turn blurry as tears pricked her eyes.

Shaking her head, she dropped to the couch. "It's nothing." She sniffed, wiping her eyes. "Just having a pity-me party."

He sipped his wine. "I think we all have those now and again."

She drew in a breath. "I've been having a lot of them since closing the bookstore. Feeling a little bit like a loser. I'm in debt to my elbows. Closing it wiped me out." Saying the words gave her no comfort. She still felt that pinching sensation deep in her chest. That ache of failure. Faced alone.

He shrugged. "It's only money, Rachel. Means nothing."

"Easy to say when you're rolling in it, Devon."

He laughed. "I've got a lot of it, yes. But it isn't something that completes my life. Money can't buy love, you know."

She shook her head, countering. "Yeah, but it can buy stuff." She swallowed her wine in a single gulp. "And stuff makes you happy." Not creditors breathing down your neck, wanting every last penny.

"I have plenty of stuff," he said slowly. "But I'm still not happy. Not by a long shot." The statement seemed absurd.

Somehow Rachel didn't think he was joking.

Silence.

She felt Devon watching her, studying her. He walked slowly toward her, a large predatory cat on the prowl.

Her body tensed in the readiness to respond when he put down his glass and sat down beside her. She had the vision he was going to wrap her in his arms and kiss her feverishly—and for a moment she wished he would grab her, throw her to the floor, and fuck her until she melted into a puddle.

"You are too beautiful to be an unhappy woman, Rachel," he said.

She sniffed, reaching for a tissue. "Yeah, and flattery will get you everywhere."

"I'm not here to flatter you." Devon linked his fingers in hers. She said nothing, only raised an eyebrow in question, looking from his hand to his face.

"I'm here to ask you a question."

Sitting up straighter, Rachel started to open her mouth. He didn't have to ask anything. She already knew.

Devon pressed a single finger across her lips. "What would you say to seeing me after hours, when we're both off work?"

A bit stunned, Rachel struggled to keep all thoughts of his proposal to herself. If he were trying to catch her at a weak moment and seduce her, well, he had certainly chosen the right time. She was vulnerable—and willing to be inveigled. Echoes of the conversation she'd had with Rosalie Dayton inevitably made their way back into her mind.

He's no more got one in the sack than he's out looking for the next, the older woman had told her.

She tried to be tactful. "I told you," she started to say, "I don't—"

Devon's incisive gaze remained fixed on her. "Mix business with pleasure?" He smiled thinly. "Yes, I know. And I want you to know that I don't sleep with my female employees either. It's a rule Rosalie makes me follow religiously."

Her throat tightened. "Then why are you here?"

Devon grinned. "To change your mind, and break a rule." He gave her a long look, the wheels in his brain seeming to turn at a furious pace. He was tense, perhaps ready to have his hopes dashed to the ground.

Her eyes narrowed. She sensed he was up to something. "And how do you intend to do that?"

"Like this."

Leaning over, Devon kissed her, his mouth lingering over hers. His hands were moving up her body, cupping her breasts, sending pleasurable chills up her spine.

Breathing choppily, Rachel pulled away. "Devon, it would be so wrong." Her lips were saying no, but her body had ideas of its own. Blood thrummed through her veins, beating against her temples at a furious pace, a roar in her ears like the surf driven by wild winds. If it pushed much harder, she was sure it would come pouring out her ears.

Devon reached out to stroke her face. "I disagree." His gaze glimmered with need. "Since the day I saw you, I have felt your body crying out to mine. I only want to please you, Rachel." A slow sexy smile turned up the corners of his full lips. "Even now, I can read your very thoughts."

Very naughty ones. She nearly forgot to breathe. "C—can you?"

He swallowed deeply, voice growing rough. "You're thinking of my touch. Of my palms resting on your hips, sliding up to cup your breasts, testing their weight in my hands." He leaned forward, whispering in her ear. "Feel that familiar tingle between your legs, the spread of warmth through your clit? You're a woman whose desires long to be freed. I can do that for you; help bring your deepest sexual fantasies into the open."

Rachel's mouth went cotton dry. Her heart almost stopped. "Oh my." She squeezed her thighs tightly together. Having Devon seducing her with his words was definitely a turn-on. She felt her sex dripping, wetting the crotch of her panties.

The expression in his eyes was impossible to resist. She tried to force herself to stand up, tell him he was being silly, but she simply could not find the words or the courage to say them. Neither could she refuse him. His words had set her mind afire.

She stifled a moan. "I want you too." This wasn't the shy Rachel Marks talking. This was a brazen hussy, knowing what she desired and going after it.

So it might very well cost her job. She could find work somewhere else. She was sure of one thing: she couldn't find another man like this to sleep with. Having sex with him was becoming an increasing hunger in her soul. The more she thought about him, the more she wanted him.

Devon cupped her face, leaning forward. "Good."

Rachel accepted the pressure of his mouth—gentle, as she had expected he would be.

Their kiss deepened, his tongue breaking the barrier of her lips to explore the depths of her mouth. He was a master. Absolutely the best kisser she'd ever experienced.

Devon pressed her back onto the soft cushions, one hand sneaking under her sweatshirt to caress the soft curves of her breast. When she didn't protest, he grew bolder, rolling her erect nipple between thumb and forefinger.

She arched herself against his rock-hard body, loving the feel of him. He was so solid, so masculine. His scent was a cloying mixture of musk and male sweat, not at all unpleasant, and more than a little enticing to her female senses. His hand left her breast, palm brushing over her flat belly to cup her Venus mound through her sweatpants. Using his middle finger, he stroked her sex.

This time she couldn't suppress her moan. "You don't know how fantastic that feels."

Devon gave her a devilish grin, changing his position and pulling her into his lap so that she straddled him. "Oh, but I do." His voice purred with seduction.

Rachel sighed softly with pleasure when he pulled her forward so he could trail his lips down her throat. Her breasts pushed against his chest, heavy and full. She hadn't bothered with a bra when she'd dressed. Her nipples were hard little points, pulsing with the anticipation of being nibbled.

Catching one of his hands, she guided it to her breast. "I like my nipple play rough," she breathed. "Nothing turns me on more than cock inside me and a hot mouth sucking me." True. The sensations traveling between breasts and clit were mind blowing. She never failed to climax.

Even more mind blowing was the fact she'd told him how to get her off. This definitely wasn't the shy old Rachel talking. Something about the man brought out her inner slut.

And she liked that.

Devon automatically rolled the tip between thumb and forefinger, tugging lightly. "I'll be sure and try it." He stopped and pulled back long enough to tug her sweatshirt over her head. Exposed skin pricked with goose bumps.

Rachel gasped when he leaned forward and took her left nipple into his mouth, teasing the hardened nub with his teeth and tongue. The exotic sensation summoned a familiar heat. Heartbeat raging in her ears, each of her soft moans stoked the fires between her thighs.

Devon's erection pressed against her crotch, surging under his slacks. His hands moved with expert ease over the curves of her back, cupping her ass as his lips meandered through the valley between her breasts. A moment later his searching mouth found her other nipple. His tongue swirled around the erect tip, driving her wild with need.

Rachel gasped, running her fingers through his thick hair, rubbing against his trapped erection. "To hell with not mixing business and pleasure," she whispered, kicking off her house shoes. "I think it's time we move this to a more appropriate venue."

His hungry gaze connected with hers. "I was hoping you would say that."

16

Devon swept Rachel into his arms, carrying her up the stairs as though she weighed no more than a sleepy child. Reaching the end of the hall, he knocked open her bedroom door with his foot. To her surprise, he bypassed the bed and headed for the bathroom. He seemed familiar with the dark room, missing nary a step.

Rachel held onto his neck, hoping to God he wouldn't fall down and kill them both. "What are we doing?"

Without missing a beat, Devon set her on her feet. "Giving you a well-deserved pampering."

"Pampering me?" Rachel fumbled for the light switch. She blinked under the resulting blaze of lights. "Not as in diapers, I hope . . ."

Devon shook his head. Leaning over the tub, he popped in the plug and turned on the water. Fiddling with the temperature, he said, "You have some odd ideas about sex if you're expecting to be diapered, Miss Marks. What I had in mind involves a nice soak, followed by a long leisurely massage."

Rachel hugged herself. "A long bath? And a massage? My god. I think I just died and went to heaven."

He glanced at her, giving a heart-stopping grin. "Despite my dubious reputation, I don't just barge in and start screwing."

She studied him a moment. A sight she never expected to see: Devon sitting on the edge of her tub, preparing to give her a bath. She couldn't help but remember her friend Frannie's wish for her: a tall, dark, and handsome man who'd sweep her off her feet.

Looks like one of her charms worked, Rachel thought.

Except this tall, dark, and handsome man came with drawbacks. "I've heard you have quite a reputation with the ladies."

Devon snorted derisively. "Be honest. You've probably heard that I fuck a lot of women."

Crossing her arms to cover her bare breasts, she eyed him. "Have you?"

He looked at her dead on. "No reason to lie to you, Rachel. I have. But it's nothing emotional. All physical."

Her smile grew thin and cynical. "And I'll be just physical too, right?"

As expected, the muscles in his jaw tightened. "No, you're more than that," he said softly. "Much more. Just give me a chance to show you."

"Why me?" she asked.

Devon gave her a sly sidelong look. "Why not?"

Rachel slowly shook her head. "Because I don't want to be just another easy fling. You know the kind. Four-F: Found, felt, fucked and forgotten."

Tub full, Devon turned off the water. Rising to his feet, he walked over to her. Fiercely turned on, a strained look of need colored his handsome face. "You're much more than an easy fling, Rachel. Just give me a chance to prove it."

Rachel gave a hint of a smile. "Convince me."

"Like this, perhaps?" Devon reached out and gently uncrossed her arms. He traced one slender finger across her left breast, first circling her areola, then pinching the erect peak.

Rachel's breath caught in her throat. A pleasant shudder rippled through her. "God yes," she breathed. "Very convincing."

"Glad you approve." Devon slid his hands to her ass, dragging her against his erect cock. His head dipped, coaxing her with a kiss as he expertly peeled her sweatpants and panties down her hips. They dropped to the floor around her feet.

A bit embarrassed to be totally naked, Rachel stepped out of the pile. Devon hadn't shed a stitch.

He smiled. "You look beautiful."

A laugh of disbelief escaped her. "Me?"

Devon turned her toward her bathroom mirror. "See for yourself."

Rachel covered her eyes with her hands. "Oh no. I look a fright."

Devon's gentle grip from behind urged her hands down. "I see a beautiful woman."

Rachel looked. A glimpse revealed two plump breasts, a flat belly, and hips flaring gently over well-muscled legs. Her eyes were wide and luminous with anticipation, her lips bee stung from his hungry kisses. Despite the redness of her eyes and tangle of her hair, for the first time she thought she looked, well, glowing.

Standing behind her, Devon's gaze connected with hers in the mirror. "Now you see what I see." His big hands settled possessively on her shoulders. "Now you see what I want."

Blushing to the roots of her hair, Rachel lowered her eyes. "I want you too," she admitted shyly.

Devon guided her toward the waiting tub. "In time," he assured her.

Stepping over the edge, Rachel sank down into the silky water. The temperature was perfect: just hot enough to give relief to her stressed muscles. His choice of a long hot soak was the perfect antidote to her emotional turmoil. The man definitely knew how to spoil a woman.

She settled back against the rim, lowering herself until the fringe of her hair met the water's edge. "Mmm. Nice." She cocked an eye toward his clothes. "Sure you don't want to take those off and join me?"

Digging for a fresh washcloth and a pile of fluffy towels, Devon shook his head. "I'd love to, but tonight is just for you." Piling the towels within easy reach, he knelt on the floor and rolled up his sleeves. "Hand me the soap, please."

Rachel handed over the plastic bottle of liquid body wash, her favorite, a lush tropical concoction.

Devon flipped open the lip and took a whiff. "Ah, there's that smell. All this time I'd envisioned some exotic perfume."

She grinned, pleased he'd noticed. "Soap and water. And an arsenal of body sprays—I love fruit scents."

"Perfect for you." Dipping the cloth in the water, he lathered it up. "Sit up, and I'll start with your back."

She leaned forward. "Long time since someone washed my back."

Beginning at the base of her neck, Devon worked the soap over her skin in small circles. "You should get someone, then."

The gentle pressure spanning her back caused a soft tugging at the nape of her neck. His touch felt deliciously sinful. "You've got the job, if you want it. Mmm. It's wonderful."

Dipping his hand into the water to rinse off the soap, he chuckled. "Thanks. Your arm, please."

She offered an arm.

"Relax. You're not supposed to be as stiff as I am."

She eyed him. "How can I relax when you're touching me?"

He mulled. "Put your mind on something else." Pause. "We never finished our conversation the other night. Why don't you tell me about your childhood?"

Erotic feelings vanished. Thinking of her childhood didn't exactly engender amorous feelings. Angry ones. Bitter ones. Certainly sad ones.

She frowned. "I did. I hate it, remember?"

Reaching for her other arm, Devon tried another tactic. "We have to get to know each other," he explained patiently.

A sullen pout. "Nothing to know," she said, the hostility in her words unmistakable.

He nibbled the tips of her damp fingers. "Let's trade facts. For everything you tell me, I'll tell you something. Deal?"

Heat pulsed all over again. Damn, he was good. "That's fair."

Devon worked the rag through each finger. "So where did you grow up?"

Rachel sighed. "State orphanage. No relatives could take me, so I grew up on my own. You?"

Moving to the end of the tub, he dipped his hand in the water and came up with a foot. "A big drafty manor in England, and then colder, draftier boarding schools."

She had to laugh. "No shit?"

His fingertips worked her toes and ankle into a white froth. "No shit."

He switched feet, repeating his soapy manipulations. "None. Now, your birthday is?"

"March seventeenth. St. Patrick's Day."

Devon grinned. "An Irish baby." Hand diving under the water, he swept the washcloth up between Rachel's legs, stopping just as he reached the juncture between her thighs.

Rachel spread her legs, a silent plea for him to go higher. "And probably not a drop of Irish in me. Yours?"

He resisted, moving up to her belly instead. He made soapy circles around her novel. The water washed the bubbles away as quickly as they formed. "July twenty-third." He inched higher toward her aching breasts.

Mesmerized by the slippery path he traced around her breasts, Rachel drew an unsteady breath. Already frayed, her sensual nerves responded to the most innocent touch. Not that the way he touched her could be confused with innocence. Each featherlike caress of his fingers drew erotic energy closer to the surface.

"How old are you?"

Devon tweaked a nipple with slippery fingers. "I have two ages: physical and Kynn. By man's age, I'm thirty-four. Counting by Kynn, I'm a hundred and forty-six years old."

Rachel didn't believe him for one second. But she liked the way he perpetuated the fantasy. Showed a sense of humor, a love of the outrageous. And creativity. She hoped he'd be as creative between the sheets as he was at spinning his elaborate myths.

She couldn't resist a bit of teasing. "Kind of old for me then, aren't you?"

He waggled a lascivious eyebrow. "The older the violin, my dear, the sweeter the music."

All sorts of feelings fluttered in her stomach. Her skin, warm and flushed, tingled. "I'd like to hear you play sometime."

Devon's smile was a promise. "You will." Rising, he repositioned himself at the end of the tub. "Now, lay your head back on the edge, if you will."

Rachel obeyed. "What are you going to do?"

Brushing her hair away from her face and off her forehead, Devon reached for the apricot scrub perched on the tub's shelf. "I promised to work you over from the tips of your toes to the top of your head."

"Wow. You are too good to be believed," she said with a grin.

Devon squirted a dollop into the palm of his hand. He smiled down at her. "I aim to please."

Rachel closed her eyes as he worked the abrasive goop around her eyes and down the bridge of her nose, then around her mouth. "Amazing how ugly a woman has to make herself before she can be attractive."

Using just the tips of his fingers, he massaged with a soft gentle motion, working the fine sandlike granules into her skin. "You'd be just as gorgeous without it."

She laughed. "You're just saying that because you have me naked and at your disposal."

Devon's fingers worked around her chin and jaw. "My dear lady, are you accusing me of impure intentions?"

Rachel cracked open an eye. "God, I sure hope so." Another sigh escaped her lips as the soothing pressure struck an exceptionally receptive spot. "You never mentioned your childhood, Devon. No fair if you don't tell me a little."

A sigh escaped him. "Privileged, but stifled. Certainly boring and staid. In my day, children were seen, but not heard."

"And?" she prodded.

His brow furrowed. "I waited in the wings for my uncle to die. Penny-pinching old bastard kept me on a tight budget. Hated that. Decided to make my own money."

"So you created Mystique?"

Devon shook his head. "I actually didn't. You might say it was inspired by a woman. Ariel."

"Beautiful name."

"Beautiful woman. Ariel introduced me to the eroticism and mystery of the Kynn. I wanted to be, to become. She sired me into the collective."

Chills crawled up Rachel's spine through the hot water. Forcing leaden eyelids open, she glanced up at Devon. "You talk like it's real."

He fixed her under a laser-beam stare. "To me, it is. Never doubt that, Rachel."

Curiosity probed. Thanks to years of working next door to a fortune-teller, she had developed more than a passing interest in the occult. The idea of sexual vampirism intrigued her. "You'll have to show me your world someday."

Reclaiming the washcloth, Devon cleaned the scrub off her face. "I intend to." He paused a beat. "Feel better?"

Rachel rubbed her hands over her face. Peeling flakes of skin had been sloughed away, leaving her cheeks as smooth as a baby's bottom. Her skin tingled, refreshed and completely cleansed. "Much. A lot better than whining in the dark."

Devon climbed to his feet and reached for a towel. Not one of the regular ones she used, all frayed and thin because she lived alone and no one cared. He'd dug out the good company towels, soft, thick, and decadent. Spreading it open, he invited her to step inside. "You weren't whining. Just needing a little time out."

"Sometimes I'd like a longer time out before reality intrudes."

Inquisitive eyes met hers. "I hope I'm not one of those intrusions," he said softly.

Rachel smiled. "Tonight you're a safety net. Something I've never had before."

Pulling the plug on the water, she stepped out of the tub. Amazing how a little water and soap could revitalize the senses. Especially when a dreamy man administered an erotic all-over wash. She'd never been so squeaky clean.

A cocoon of softness wrapped around her. Wet and dripping, enfolded in the embrace of a man she'd fantasized about: talk about a dream come true. She'd never believed in fairy tales or happy endings. Surely he'd break her heart. Had to happen.

Murphy's Law. The luck of the draw. Maybe bad Karma.

Might not last, she mused. *I'll sure as hell enjoy it while it does.*

"A man I've known barely three days has stripped me bare and bathed me," she mused aloud. "Does that make me easy?"

His gaze skimmed over her body while he considered the answer. "Eager," he corrected.

Heat crept into her face. "Not too eager, I hope."

Guiding the towel over her wet skin, Devon's brow furrowed. "Eager for me, yes. Eager for other men, no." He dried every inch. First the front, then the back. "I want you all to myself." He dropped a playful kiss everywhere he touched. He didn't miss a single inch.

Honestly! That would be a man's thought. Primitive masculine possessiveness. He might have ten dozen notches on his bedpost, and they meant nothing. If a woman had one, perhaps two, she'd be a slut.

Still, she liked the idea that he wanted her all to himself. That implied commitment.

Something she didn't dare hope for.

Not that she had time to think about it. A hard knot of need fisted in her belly when Devon's hands brushed over her hips. She shuddered at the feel of his hands on her. "Right now I think you've got every inch covered." Her voice sounded like it did in the mornings before she'd had her first cup of coffee, throaty and sensuous.

Palms resting at her waist, Devon leaned forward to nibble at her damp neck. "I've dreamed of touching you all over."

Desire beat through Rachel's veins. The pulse between her thighs grew more insistent when his hands slipped under her arms and cupped her breasts. He squeezed and rolled both her nipples.

Rachel arched back against him, losing her breath in a gasp. His cock surged against her ass. She could feel every inch of him. Every long, thick, pulsing inch. "Give it to me," she whispered.

Working his hips against hers in a slow easy motion, he nibbled her ear. If he'd just unzip his pants, he could . . .

Shaking from his own need, Devon pulled away. "I think

we'd better get into the bedroom." His muscles flexed as he swept her into his arms again.

Naked and willing, Rachel had no doubt about his destination.

Now, her nerves screamed, every inch of her aching for him to take command of her body.

17

Devon tumbled her onto the bed. His unabashed stare raked over her body, lingering over her breasts and then her sex. A smile turned up one corner of fine lips. "Rachel," he murmured. "You are exquisite."

Rachel smiled up at him, knowing she looked far from that, but glad he said the words anyway. No makeup, hair a mess, she was far from looking like a goddess of any sort. But the way he looked at her made her feel sexy, desirable, female.

She lay in a naked sprawl. The sight of him fully dressed and very aroused did nothing to keep her thoughts pure. Every picture flashing across her mind's screen involved him being just as bare and very sweaty. "I bet you say that to all your girls."

He shook his head. "At this moment, no other woman exists in this world."

To her surprise, Devon didn't immediately undress and attack her. He sat down on the edge of the bed, running his hand across her flat abdomen. He gave her a light kiss. "I promised you a massage."

Her searching hand found his very prominent erection. She

grinned. "I'd rather have sex with you." She rubbed her hand up and down his penis as well as she could through his clothes. Heat radiated, flesh surged. Definitely more than enough to fill every inch of her and then some.

Delight and desire warred across his face. A low groan slid from his throat. His gray eyes brooded, dangerously hot. "Very damn tempting."

"Then what are you waiting for?"

A quick shudder went through him before he replaced the look of desire with one more serious. He swallowed hard and met her gaze. "But I want to take it slow with you, Rachel. I want you to be comfortable with what we're doing." He gently guided her hand away.

Palms itching with the need to explore the solid planes of his back as he worked magic between her legs, Rachel rolled her eyes. "Oh, trust me. I'm damn uncomfortable, Devon. I haven't had sex in almost a year. Make me wait much longer, and I'll explode."

He cleared his throat. "Patience is a virtue," he reminded.

Rachel gritted her teeth in frustration. "A hot fuck also has its rewards."

Devon eyed her. "Why so long between lovers?" His fingertips brushed an aching nipple, then pinched lightly.

Her breath caught. Moisture pulsed between her thighs. She sucked in oxygen and tried to think. "Waiting for Prince Charming, I guess."

His grin teased. "Will the seventh Earl of Hammerston do?" His fingers plucked harder, rolling the taut nubbin.

Rachel's fingers clenched the comforter. "Perfectly."

Devon leaned over, brushing his lips against hers. "So roll over, and I'll show you how perfect I really am."

Laughing, Rachel adopted a faux English accent. She nipped at his lower lip. "A command, my lord?"

His lips teased in return. "A request, my lady." His smooth voice stroked.

"How can I resist, then?"

Rachel rolled onto her stomach, crossing her arms under her chin, wondering what he had in store for her. She felt him shift his position, move to the end of the bed. He picked up her left foot and began to stroke the curve of her arch.

Working slowly and with purpose, Devon proceeded to massage her foot. Slipping his fingers between her toes, he kneaded each one in turn. Toes done, he moved to the ball of her foot, manipulating the soft, vulnerable flesh with his thumbs before moving up to her ankle and then her calf. The insinuating warmth of his touch spread through her body, setting her blood to boiling. Letting out a tiny whimper of enjoyment, she curled her toes.

"Feel good?" His voice was as rich as pure cream, and the pressure of his fingers was strong and sure.

Rachel sighed, closing her eyes, relishing the feel of his hands. "God yes . . . it's heaven." Her blood felt thick, like rich dark honey straight from the hive. She shivered when he switched to her other foot, repeating the movements.

Pleased by her reactions, Devon purposely moved his hands up the back of her thighs. His palms brushed the insides of her legs, coming close to but not quite touching her at the point where her legs met. The light brush of his fingers against her sex felt like an electric shock, stunning her into fresh sensual awareness. Her clit pulsed, dying to be stroked, sucked.

She tried to close her legs around his hand, but he pulled away, holding off, torturing her by making her wait. "Not yet."

She moaned. "When?"

Assurance purred. "Soon."

Devon's hands moved higher, lightly cupping and rubbing her ass cheeks before settling at the base of her spine. He let his hands roam, flexing along her spine, her ribs, her shoulders, his massive hands feeling her as a blind man might.

Rachel felt his fingers brush the back of her bare neck, followed by his lips. He nibbled lightly, kissing and licking the soft skin. "Turn over," he whispered in her ear.

Anticipation building, Rachel rolled over onto her back. "With pleasure."

Devon continued the massage, taking her by the shoulders and working along her collarbone until her tense muscles began to relax. From there, his hands moved lower, over her breasts. His fingers brushed, but he didn't touch the pebble-hard tips. Next he stroked her firm, flat belly. His touch sent a hard tremor through her.

"Damn you," she mumbled through a quivering moan. "The waiting is driving me insane."

Devon ended the sensual massage by working his way down her legs, back to the tips of her toes, ending where he had started. "The wait is about over."

Finished, he stretched out beside her, supporting his weight on one elbow. His eyes dwelt on the small, excited pulse beating at the base of her throat. There was a strangely tense expression on his face, one of exhilaration mixing with wariness.

"What?" she asked, smiling.

"I was just thinking how beautiful you look," he said in a hoarse whisper.

Rachel swallowed, overwhelmed by the compliment. It touched her heart in a way he couldn't know.

Her hands rose to the nape of his neck. She caught the splendid scent of his musky aftershave as he bent toward her, his mouth claiming hers. Her lips parted willingly for the searing invasion of his tongue. He kissed her thoroughly, his lips mastering hers, his tongue promising an invasion of another kind. She tensed when his hand cupped a naked breast.

Breaking their kiss, Devon slid downward to take her nipple

in his mouth in a long suckling draw. Rachel cried out, arching up to draw him closer. God, how she wanted him inside, their bodies joined in the ultimate bliss.

As his tongue twirled around the sensitive nubbin, his free hand moved across her belly, urging without words for her to spread her legs for him. He caressed her, tracing his fingers along the swollen lips around her clit. The sensation of her own juices and the pressure almost drove her into losing complete control.

A primitive throaty gasp escaped her as she hovered on the edge of climax, fighting not to fall completely over the edge alone. "Please," she whispered, thrusting her hips upward.

"Slow down," he cautioned. "We have the night." He increased the motion of his hand. He penetrated her sex, all the while suckling her nipple.

Rachel sobbed his name, digging her feet into the mattress so that she could lift her body. Devon was working her into a frenzy, plunging one and then two fingers deep inside her. Thumb flicking her clit, he thrust into her.

Rachel felt the violent jolt as the orgasm exploded through her, her body jerking as though a mad puppeteer was pulling the strings. When it was over, she lay panting, trying to catch her breath, her body tingling all over with the lovely aftershocks. But it wasn't enough. She wanted his cock.

All of a sudden, Devon pulled away, leaving the space beside her empty as he repositioned himself between her spread legs. On his knees, he looked down at her, eyes sweeping her nakedness.

Rachel stretched her arms above her head, catching the headboard in preparation for her surrender to a good fucking even though he still had not removed a stitch of his own clothing.

"I want you inside me." The wanton ache tormenting her grew worse, threatening to overcome her senses.

Devon gave a low sexy laugh, lowering himself down over her. "Slowly now, my love. I want to wait until just the right time for us to come together. It will not be tonight . . . but soon."

His tongue traced the circumference of one rosy nipple, sending shafts of delicious torment through her. He teased each aching peak equally, then worked his way down, his hands moving possessively over her hips.

He kissed the warm surface of her rib cage, her belly, the patch of skin above her aching mound, then the insides of her thighs.

Rachel closed her eyes and sighed in sheer pleasure. She didn't know whether she wanted him to stop or go on. She only knew she was in heaven. "That feels so good."

Devon's lips seared the flat plane of her belly like fire across dry prairie grass. "I intend to please you well." Brushing his fingers through the downy hair covering her sex, he parted her labia to reveal the soft, silky rosebud of her clit. He forged a fiery route, flicking his tongue several times across her pulsing flesh.

Spears of desire shot through every inch of Rachel's body. A desperate ragged sigh was followed by the cry of, "Don't stop . . ." Hot crimson spikes shot before her closed eyes, her blood throbbing furiously, almost threatening to burst from her veins. She trembled as her own reckless hungers warred, wanting to please him as much as he was pleasing her.

Devon had total control and gave no sign of relinquishing it. His hands pressed her thighs further apart to make her more vulnerable to his ministrations, giving him free rein to lick and nibble on her throbbing clit. As the friction increased, her responses grew more and more heated.

Rachel twisted and writhed, her hands clutching at the bedspread, head tossing from side to side in ecstasy. Her hips moved with his fingers, meeting each thrust. Selfishly, she lost herself in the sweet glories of her building orgasm.

Breath catching, back arching, she jerked and shuddered. The cries of pleasure tearing from her throat were shameless, fierce. The animal needs within her, driven by his furious manipulations, sent her tumbling headlong into a final searing climax. As her pleasure peaked, her body tensed reflexively. Sensation shimmered to the pulse of blood in her veins, the beat of her heart in her ears. Her senses exploded into a harmony of blinding, spectacular color: bright then dark, then bright again, an ever-widening burst of ecstasy. Consciousness flickered as the very fabric of the world shredded into atoms.

Faintly aware, Rachel floated on the currents of the perfect climax. Time had gone completely out of focus, but she didn't care. Pure naked illumination touched her everywhere, a sparkling spiderweb of gossamer threads weaving around her. Through her.

"*Oh yes*!"

18

Yawning and stretching, Rachel rolled over onto her back, feeling the curtains of sleep continue to close in around her mind.

She closed her eyes again, tugging the covers over her head, savoring the snug little world she'd created. Warm. Safe. Who wanted to get out of bed?

Especially after last night.

Memories flooded her brain, languid, sexy images played across her mind's screen.

A sleepy smile tugged up one corner of her mouth. Curious fingertips brushed her naked skin. Finding the tips of her nipples, she traced the tender peaks. Her tongue snaked out, outlining her lips. She gently jerked the taut little pebbles, wishing Devon's mouth were there.

Oh, last night . . . Mmm, the way he touched me . . .

Without thinking, she parted her thighs, still sticky from the heat of her passion. Her hands moved over her stomach, brushing over her mound. Her sex was still moist, slick. She touched herself, tracing her silky labia, then parting the folds to rub her clit, arousing herself all over again.

Damn, I'm so horny.

Dipping a finger inside her depths, she enjoyed the sensual feelings washing through her. In her mind, Devon hovered above her, parting her legs with his, teasing her slit with the head of his engorged cock.

Wanting to touch him, needing him desperately, she rolled over on her side, reaching for his side of the bed. It was empty.

He's gone.

She looked at the empty pillow, showing not even an imprint of his head. That didn't surprise her.

Devon Carnavorn hadn't taken off more than his sport coat last night. Nor had he fucked her in the traditional sense. He'd held off having sex with her, giving her orgasm after orgasm but taking no pleasure to satisfy his own needs.

She clearly remembered every detail. How he'd felt, and how she'd felt in his arms. What would it be like to wake up next to him, feel his muscular body pressed against hers? She imagined how she'd wake him, touching his penis, feeling him grow firm in her hand. She would caress him softly, then slide down under the covers to wake him right.

But she was alone.

Typical man. Couldn't even hang around to give me a kiss good-bye.

Eager to get up, Rachel threw aside the covers. More than anything, she yearned to see her new lover, persuade him to get out of those damned clothes and into bed with her. What he had done last night was wonderful, but it wasn't enough.

She wanted more.

To hell with being just another discarded bimbo. She was an adult, single, and able to make her own choices as to whom she wanted to sleep with. So Devon would probably love her and leave her. Would that be so bad? Who said that a woman had to involve her heart in her lovemaking? Why shouldn't she seek pleasure where she wanted? It was more than a little flattering that a man like him wanted her in the first place.

She padded toward the bathroom in bare feet. *Enjoy it for what it is.*

After a quick shower, Rachel threw on her robe and made her way downstairs. In the kitchen, she fixed herself a few slices of toast and a cup of skim milk, then let Sleek outside.

She ate her breakfast on a tray in front of the television, catching up on local and world news. As usual, there were more bad things going on than good. The economy stank, the war in Iraq raged on, and there was no relief in sight. Living in a sane, peaceful world seemed impossible. It was more sink than swim.

Rachel had just stuffed the last bite into her mouth when the doorbell rang. Who the hell could that be? She brushed the crumbs off her fingers.

Opening the door, she found herself facing the absolute biggest bunch of peach roses that she'd ever seen. The floral arrangement was breathtaking.

"Miss Marks?" the delivery boy asked.

Dumbfounded, she nodded.

"These are for you." He handed over the flowers. "Sign here, please."

Setting the huge vase down, she quickly scribbled her name. "Thanks." She fished some change and a few dollar bills out of the catchall bowl on the table. "Sorry I don't have more."

The boy grinned, tipped his hat, and pocketed his tip. "Good day, ma'am."

Rachel shut the door as he departed. She looked at the flowers. A card peeked out of the fragrant mass. She opened the tiny envelope and drew it out.

Thinking about last night and wanting more, it read. It was not signed.

"Devon." She bent over the roses to take in their delicate scent, a smile parting her lips. Yes, last night was incredible. She definitely wanted more too.

19

An hour later, Rachel pulled up outside Mystique, parking in the employee section of the parking lot. Checking her makeup one more time in the rearview mirror, she picked up her purse, got out, and strode across the parking lot toward the employee entrance. A few busboys and waitresses loitering around out back taking a cigarette break silenced their conversations as she approached.

One of the busboys reached out to open the door for her. "Good day, Miss Marks." His greeting carried a cheery smile.

From behind dark glasses, Rachel's eyes searched for his name tag. For some reason she was a little bit light sensitive today. The bright day gave her more than a slight headache, a side effect of the coming flu, she supposed.

Her lips curved up. "Hi, Rusty," she returned casually. Damn. It felt good to be working, and not as a peon. She held an important position now. Keeping the wait staff in line and in order would keep her on her toes.

"You look nice today," he shyly complimented.

Rachel smiled. She looked more than nice, and she knew it.

No longer restricted to the waitress uniform, she'd dressed to kill. Taking her cue from Gina, whom she'd thought dressed a little bit too flamboyantly for the job, she'd chosen a suit the shade of charcoal gray. Slit slightly up the side, the skirt was short enough to be provocative, but not crude. She'd left a couple of buttons on her blouse undone, showing a peek of cleavage and a bit of lace from her bra.

Stopping only to grab a cup of coffee, Rachel passed through the maze of service halls, giving brief nods and a few words to the employees she encountered, and made her way to Rosalie Dayton's office. The older woman was buried under her usual barrage of paperwork.

Rosalie looked up from her reading. "Good to see you're here," she greeted, punching her adding machine. "Gina left the schedule in a mess and the waitresses' payroll undone."

Rachel sipped her coffee, heavy with cream and sugar. "Where did she go?"

Rosalie shrugged. "I don't know anything. Phone's disconnected, so no way to call. I really don't care where the hell she's gone. I still have my work to do."

Rachel set aside her cup. "Fill me in on what I do, and I'll get to work."

Rosalie gave her a grateful glance. "Good. We need to do the payroll first. People get pissed when there aren't any paychecks waiting." She handed the schedule from the last two weeks across her desk. "Total the time, and then I'll figure their pay."

Rachel glanced at the schedule. Pretty easy to figure. "I can do the pay too, if you want."

"If you can, do. It won't hurt my feelings." Rosalie motioned toward the smaller desk across from hers. "That's where you'll be working. You managers all share that space. We're getting a bigger office. Soon, I hope. That's in the works now. Until then, we have to deal with the close quarters."

Rachel nodded, taking her coffee cup and sitting down behind her new command post. "Didn't seem like Gina ever did very much." She didn't mean the remark to sound catty. Just a statement of fact.

"She didn't," Rosalie answered wryly. "Just drifted around in her own little haze. Drugs, I think. Why Devon let her get away with it so long, I don't know. The man's got a soft heart. Willing to give everyone a chance."

A smile tugged up Rachel's mouth, putting a dimple on her cheek. "Maybe because he was sleeping with her?"

Rosalie pursed her lips, half in disgust, half in envy. "He is not supposed to sleep with the help. If the rule's not been broken, it's sure as hell been bent a few times."

Rachel felt a guilty twinge in the back of her mind.

Yep. The rule's been broken, Rachel thought. "So tell me. If you had the chance, would you sleep with him?"

Caught by surprise, Rosalie coughed into her hand. "Sleep with Devon Carnavorn? Hmm. That is a hard question. Knowing that he sleeps with anything in a skirt and would fuck a snake if you held its head, would I want to be the next woman in line?" The question seemed to tantalize her, summoning memories too sweet to savor.

Rachel cleared her throat. "Well?"

"If I were forty years younger, I think I would."

Rachel's eyebrows rose. Not the answer she'd expected from the stolid old lady at all. "Even if you knew he'd probably throw you aside?"

Rosalie cocked a jaunty eyebrow. "You only live once, honey," she said sensibly. "When your youth is gone, it's gone forever. Hang on to it while you've got it. It won't ever come back."

Mind working a thousand miles a minute, Rachel nodded. "I guess it doesn't."

Rosalie was right. Rachel was seven years away from forty. Black balloons. After forty came forty-five, and then fifty. Sixty. Seventy.

I want to enjoy now.

Rosalie rolled her eyes. "It's pretty easy to see you're smitten. You two have had some kind of silent flirtation going on since minute one."

Rachel sighed, propping her elbows on the desk and balancing her chin on her hand.

"Do I look like a lovesick cow?"

Rosalie laughed out loud. No beating around the bush. "Worse."

Rachel grimaced. "Shit."

Rosalie took off her glasses, wiping them with a lacy handkerchief plucked from her ample bosom.

"If you're going to sleep with Devon, try and be discreet."

Rachel nodded. "Good advice."

Setting her glasses in place, Rosalie went back to tapping at her computer, prompting Rachel to get to work herself. She still needed to make a living.

Using a calculator found in a drawer, she tackled the waitresses' payroll. Rachel knew the correct state and federal taxes to withhold, so it was simple to arrive at the ending figures. As she added and subtracted, she paused a few minutes, tapping her pencil against the pad.

Be discreet.

Easier said than done.

20

Devon leaned against the doorframe leading into the managers' offices. He usually left immediately after the club closed, preferring to let his managers handle the mundane tasks. Tonight, he lingered.

Watching Rachel.

She sat beside Rosalie, helping prepare the money for the nightly deposit. The two woman, along with assistant manager Fred Hawks, were banding together the cash to stash in heavy canvas bank bags. Everone worked efficiently, aware of his presence, but paying him no attention.

Devon swallowed hard. Looking at Rachel, a thousand fires burst into flame inside him. Vision clouding, his pulse went into overdrive. Making love to her—completely and without restraint—was his only desire. He thought of nothing else.

He drew a deep breath and groaned silently. *Slowly*, he reminded himself. *Your time to have her will come*. Everything had changed since meeting her. Now he was planning a new life for himself—one spent with Rachel at his side.

Rosalie looked up, noticing he still lingered. She cut him a narrow glance. She clearly didn't approve of his presence. "Something you need, Devon?"

Devon squirmed, but held his place. He needed a lot, but couldn't lay his hands on it at this exact moment. Just standing a few feet away from Rachel and not being able to touch her was pure hell. He was ready to explode. "Just stopping by before I go home." He feigned disinterest. "Making sure everything's under control before I leave for the night."

The old lady snorted, seeing right through him as though he were a piece of cellophane. "Of course, Devon. Why wouldn't it be?"

Rachel lifted her head and gave him a little smile of acknowledgment. "I think we can handle it." She went back to counting the money. Casual and dismissive at the same time.

Devon's breath caught sharply in his chest. He locked his jaw against the images filtering across his mind's screen—images of Rachel, naked and aroused as he pleasured her. Work definitely conflicted with his growing tension. It took every bit of his self-control to keep from walking across that room, turning Rachel around in her chair, and capturing those cherry-red lips of hers.

Of course, he couldn't do it. Vaguely, he considered throwing propriety and convention out the window, letting his employees see him break his air of stern reserve and publicly claim the woman he desired.

No such luck.

Fred Hawks motioned for Rachel to hand him the deposit bag. "I've run the closing audit and it all balances. We are good to go."

She handed it over. "Seems easy enough."

"No rocket science needed." Fred stuffed the money into the bag and locked it. "Guess I need to get on to the bank."

Devon stopped him. "Have you told Rachel how to make the night deposits yet?"

Rosalie jerked her head up, giving him a sharp look. "No. It's only her first night as manager."

Devon made an executive decision. "She needs to know. I can show her."

Everyone looked at him as though he'd grown a second head. Doing the menial chores was not the sort of thing he usually bothered with.

Eyebrows rising over the frames of her glasses, Rosalie gave him a hard look. "Oh?" The single word spoke volumes. She clearly disapproved of Devon barging in to her domain and changing the rules.

Devon stared back. He sent a silent signal. *Not backing down*, it said. *Butt out*!

Rosalie threw up her hands and gave in. "Oh, for heaven's sake, take her."

Fred handed over the heavy bag. "Here's the dough, rich boy."

Devon hefted the deposit bag. "And getting richer." He turned to Rachel. "Don't mind riding along with me, do you?"

Rachel tensed, shoulders drawing back, her chin leveling out. She gazed primly up at him from under long, silky lashes. The barest hint of a smile lifted her lips. "Of course I don't mind."

Devon smiled inwardly, very careful to keep it from repeating on his lips. If he'd accurately read her body language, she was pleased he'd maneuvered to get her alone. There was that telltale layer of nervousness, the way her skin seemed to tremble like a cat that's suddenly been awakened from a nap. She looked a little tired, but that was to be expected after a long week of work.

"Good. Come on, then."

Outside the club, he laid a light hand on Rachel's elbow and steered her toward his car. She didn't protest at his touch, but he didn't press it either. She walked so close to him that he felt the heat of her body beside his.

"This one."

Devon made her brush by him to reach the passenger door. She pushed gracefully past him, only to have him slam the door on her before she was completely settled in. Her eyes tracked him as he rounded the front of the car, her expression impossible to make out in the shadows half covering her face.

Getting behind the wheel, he handed her the bag.

Rachel caressed the leather seat, obviously impressed by the car, a brand-new Porsche. His latest toy, it was lithe, lean, and made for speed. "Wow. Nice. This runs circles around my old car." No hint of envy in her voice, just appreciation.

Devon knew she had been pressed for money by the closing of her bookstore, but she earned a reasonable salary now. He wasn't the sort of man who would blackmail a woman, threaten her job if she didn't give in to his desires. He'd learned long ago not to sleep with a woman on his payroll.

Rachel was the sole exception—he intended to get her out of the office and into his bed as soon as was decently possible. With him, she'd never have to worry about such trivial things as lack of money.

He turned the key in the ignition and gunned the engine. It roared to life, purring smoothly as it idled. "Glad you like it." He shifted into reverse, backing out and weaving around the various cars still inhabiting the parking lot.

"I do." She turned her head away from him, looking out the window as they made the trip to the bank, watching the trendy section of the city pass by.

When he pulled up to the night deposit box at the bank, she didn't wait for him. She jumped out and used the key to open the slot and shove the bag in. Locking it, she hopped back into the car.

"That was easy enough." She was panting, lips slightly

parted, a sexy sheen of gloss still clinging to her mouth. Her breasts rose and fell under her white blouse. The hard tips of her nipples poked through the clingy material.

Devon wanted to reach over, rip the blouse right off her body, cup her breasts, and suck on those little pink nubs.

"That's about all there is to it," he said, trying to keep the hoarseness of desire out of his voice. "If you make any deposits in the future, it will always be with another person. That way you have a witness and help if you are robbed or otherwise accosted."

She flushed and looked at him, a slight knowing smile parting her lips. "Otherwise accosted?"

The space in the small car seemed to shrink even more as he became increasingly aware of Rachel. Her hands were folded primly in her lap, small and delicate, nails manicured and polished. Though she dressed professionally, he knew the body beneath her clothes to be perfect in every way.

Devon eagerly remembered exploring her body. Under his touch, she was soft, pliant, willing, even impatient. How would she react if he touched her now?

He drew in a deep breath. The scent of her subtle perfume still clung to her pale skin: light, peachy, fresh. He imagined being stretched out beside her, pressing his naked flesh to hers.

He grinned. "Otherwise accosted, as in someone trying to make love to you."

Rachel pretended innocence, widening her eyes as if scandalized. "Why, who would want to do that with little old me?" she teased in a hint of a baby's whisper.

"I do." Devon brushed his fingers down her soft cheek, over her jawline, then down her neck, letting his touch linger. He felt the soft pulse of blood through her veins. Acute awareness sizzled along every nerve ending in his body, the instantaneous sexual charge almost painful in its intensity.

Mesmerized by his touch, Rachel closed her eyes and sank

slowly back into her seat. She looked fragile, delicate, her skin so pale as to be cast in porcelain. "Then don't stop."

"About last night—" he started to say.

A slight shudder ran through her. "I know," she murmured. "You want to take it slow."

His throat tightened. "Don't you want me to?" It hurt to ask the question.

Rachel sighed. She swallowed, a delicate ridge forming at the base of her throat. How he wanted to press his lips against her throat, taste her. "I want more," she admitted slowly. "I just don't want to be left in the cold when you're finished fucking me."

Devon gave her a stark look. "You think I would do that? Walk off and leave you?"

Her hands knotted together in her lap. "I know how you are with women, Devon. Rosalie made it very clear when she said you'd screw a snake if someone would hold its head."

He wound his fingers around the nape of her neck and leaned forward, closing the distance between them. "It will be different with you," he whispered in her ear. "I want you as I have wanted no other woman." He was startled by the instant pleasure the words brought to his heart. He liked the way it felt to say them.

Rachel stubbornly dug in her heels. "Men will say anything to get in a woman's panties."

Devon had to laugh. "I had your panties off last night, remember? And I didn't go home wearing them."

She huffed, rolling her eyes toward the ceiling. "You know what I mean." Her expression grew serious. "I want you, Devon." She hesitated. "I—I just don't want it to hurt when you leave."

Devon cupped her chin, tracing her bottom lip with his thumb, feeling her heat, her softness. To touch her was to complete another part of his soul. "Who says I'm leaving?" Giving her no chance to answer, he captured her mouth with his. Her taste and scent filled his consciousness as he thrust his tongue between her soft, pliant lips.

Rachel moaned softly in the back of her throat, meeting him with her own rising passion. His tongue traced her lips, then slipped back inside her mouth. He nibbled gently on her lower lip, sucking until her mouth was wet and swollen with his kisses. He tugged on her blouse, needing to touch her bare skin.

Rachel pulled back. "Here?" A laugh of surprise escaped her. "In a bank parking lot, necking like teenagers?"

Devon hesitated, heart quickening. Nervously, he cleared his throat. "Do you want me to take you back to the club?"

"No." She reached for his hand, linking her fingers through his. "They know what you were after—so do I."

Devon looked into her eyes, caught in the heat that blazed there. His heart beat so fast she had to notice. Blood pounded in his ears, deafening him as he fought to ignore the painful sensations of his cock trapped in the confines of his slacks. "And?"

"Just drive," she purred. "We'll find a place."

"Anywhere?" he choked out, twisting the key.

Rachel nodded her assent. "Anywhere you like." She reached out, touching his thigh, sliding her hand perilously close to his throbbing cock.

Devon jumped at her unexpected touch, almost losing all control of the car. Making a quick U-turn, he came close to scraping a concrete pole as he guided the vehicle back onto the street. Steady now, or he would wreck the freaking thing.

"Careful," she warned, grinning. "Wouldn't want to ruin your nice paint job."

I don't give a damn about the paint.

21

Driving through the city, Devon pointed the car toward the freeway, heading toward the valley. Within thirty minutes, they had arrived at their destination. The city of Warren maintained one of the finest parks to be found for miles around. Immaculately groomed groves of trees encircled rolling green hills that guarded a crystal-clear lake. Along the driving paths that led through the park were little rest areas. Covered picnic tables and small, embedded barbecue grills offered a place for families to enjoy the amenities the park offered.

He passed them by, guiding the car into the more private areas densely surrounded by trees. At night, it was the perfect place to park . . . and make out. The night was clear, warm, the sky barren of the fog that haunted the larger cities. The stars twinkling in the sky were so huge that it felt as though one could reach out and touch them. Pulling onto the grass, Devon killed the engine and lights.

Rachel leaned her head back against the seat. "Mmm. Very nice." She closed her eyes and yawned. "I could almost go to sleep here."

"Don't go to sleep on me now." Getting out, Devon rounded the car. Opening the passenger door, he reached in and pulled her out, drawing her into his arms.

"Sex now," he said, kissing her hard. "Sleep later."

Out here in the middle of nowhere, he wanted to take her with no one to interrupt them but the creatures of the night. He wanted to touch every tantalizing inch of her, fuck her until she was too exhausted to move.

He kissed her again and again, his hands circling her slender waist to grasp her ass cheeks, kneading the firm flesh as he pressed her body to his. His cock throbbed, fighting to get free of his trousers. Balls heavy, he ached with need.

He fumbled with the pearly buttons on her blouse. He wasn't usually this clumsy or eager, but something about her was spurring him to hurry so he could touch her naked skin. When he could not work them fast enough, he grabbed the front and ripped the material apart.

A gasp broke from her lips. "Oh my."

A harsh breath escaped him. "I'm not waiting anymore." He stepped back, watching the mesmerizing rise and fall of her breasts. Encased in a lacy bra, those creamy twin mounds beckoned to be fondled.

Rachel's tongue flicked out, tracing the little dip of her top lip, an utterly sexy and alluring move. "Don't wait, then."

Devon's hands caught her shoulders, pulling her forward for a kiss. She accepted it willingly, not fighting when his mouth left hers, trailing over her chin and lower down her throat. Softly, gently, he nipped at her jugular, licked the vulnerable pulse, tasting her with his tongue. If he wanted to, he could easily overpower her, make the cut into her flesh, partake of her sweet blood and then her eager sex.

With great restraint, Devon held back. He wanted her to come to him willingly, make the decision to join the Kynn. When the time was right, he would tell her the truth about the mark on her thigh . . . the sigil, that magical sign proving she must belong to him alone.

"I'm not going to be gentle." His hands moved around to the small of her back, tugging her torn blouse out of her skirt so that he could slide his hands under the material and caress her skin.

Rachel moaned, pressing her body closer to his. "Don't be." Her hand had moved down past his beltline, grasping his rigid penis through his trousers. She stroked him up and down with the expertise of a woman who knew how to touch a man.

"Touch me," she whispered.

He smiled. "I am touching you."

"All of me."

Pressing her back against the car, Devon unsnapped her bra and slid it off her body with her blouse, leaving her completely naked from the waist up. Dipping his head, he closed his lips around one nipple.

Rachel tensed, her hands going to his shoulders as if she were going to push him away. Instead, she captured his head in her hands, guiding him. After a moment, he switched sides, giving the other breast equal attention. She made a soft sound: a half gasp, half laugh. Her pleasure was all that mattered to him right now.

"Devon, oh . . ." she moaned, flushing hotly. "I've been waiting for this."

"I want to please you." Anticipation ran riot through his veins, his blood pounding a strange rhythm in his temples and cock. A flame of desire shot down to his balls, making them tingle, tighten. His hands found and teased her nipples, looking so much like cherries dotting creamy mounds of vanilla pudding, good enough to eat. When she looked up at him, her eyes were full of desire. A shudder of longing crossed her face.

Devon smiled. He'd conquered her as easily as a cat lapped

up cream. His cock pulsed furiously in anticipation of her full lips.

"I want to belong to you," she breathed. "Only to you."

"I won't hurt you, Rachel," he murmured, stroking those tender tips, circling the areolas with his fingers. "I won't do anything if you tell me to stop." It was hell to spit the words out, but part of the seduction.

She gasped. "Don't stop. Please."

Smiling, he caught her around the waist. His mouth again found a hard tip. He kissed her nipples, one after the other, rolling them with his tongue.

Rachel squeezed her eyes tighter, her breathing ragged from the sensual motion of his mouth. Now he drew languid circles around her mounds with his tongue and fingers, never quite touching the sensitive tips. The vulnerable expression in her eyes was quickly replaced with a look of wanton desire.

He rubbed one breast with his palm until she released a soft gasp. He ached to open her legs and let his hand find the spot that throbbed so desperately for his touch.

Rachel's eyes lowered to the hard bulge in his trousers. Following her gaze, he took her hand, guiding it back down to his erection.

"Stroke me," he said, his voice rough with need. "Rub your hand up and down."

Rachel nodded and complied, watching him. "I'll do anything you ask me."

Devon unzipped his trousers, freeing his cock. Tight, sensitive and definitely strained. He left the top button closed. No reason to lose his pants down around his ankles. Very undignified. He didn't stop to think of Rachel's potential embarrassment over her seminudity.

Rachel wrapped her fingers around his shaft with just the right pressure. "You're, um, very rigid." She moved her hand along his length. "That must be painful."

Devon gritted his teeth. Did she know the hell she was putting him through? "Harder." His hand covered hers. "The more, the better." He started to guide her to her knees.

Rachel's back stiffened only momentarily, and then she went down, lower, her face level with his crotch. "A woman certainly wouldn't be disappointed with what's down here."

Close to losing all control, Devon grated out, "Take me in your mouth, Rachel. Suck my cock."

Placing his hands on her head, just as he'd earlier fantasized, he guided her mouth to the engorged head of his penis. She'd closed her mouth, and easing himself between her lips was like easing himself into a virgin.

Rachel playfully resisted.

He pushed harder.

Finally, she relented.

Devon slid the tip of his cock into her mouth. Her teeth scraped his private flesh, adding to the delight, a bit of pain to feed his deep-seated carnal desires.

Dipping his head back, he moved his hips gently forward, fucking her mouth. He no longer needed to guide her head.

Rachel sucked like an experienced whore, flicking her tongue over the tip, then taking him deeply until he felt the back of her throat. She wrapped one hand firmly around the shaft, using her saliva to create a slippery path. Her free hand cupped his sac, squeezing, tweaking, fingering his tender balls.

A moan escaped. "Damn you're good."

She broke contact long enough to answer. "Thanks." She grinned up at him. "I've got a lot to work with here."

Devon had almost reached his limit of self-control. If he were not careful, in a very few moments ecstasy would claim him and he would release a stream of hot, creamy semen into her waiting mouth.

He gritted his teeth. Agony, oh agony. "Glad you're happy."

He felt as if his penis were melting, a wonderful lassitude creeping up on him, dulling his brain, but sharpening his other senses. All he could think of was Rachel's willing body crushed beneath his own.

He eased away from her hungry lips and pulled Rachel to her feet. "No more waiting," he gasped, his voice harsh. His mouth sought hers in a long, hungry duel of tongues as he filled his hands with the weight of her breasts.

Her breath caught on a gasp. "*Devon.*"

Grabbing her hips, Devon lifted Rachel onto the hood of the car, trying to spread her thighs. He pushed her skirt up around her hips, cursing the pantyhose she wore. "God, why these?"

Rachel raised her head, peering down at him. "To see how determined you are."

His response arrived immediately. "Pretty damn determined."

Finding the elastic around her waist, Devon yanked the hose down her legs. He had to stop long enough to pull off her shoes, sending them flying in the process. "At last."

He ran his hands over her hips, giving her flat belly a quick kiss. He wanted to lick, suck, and taste every inch of her as she hovered in a state of peak sexual arousal. The air around her was sticky, scented from the sizzling heat of raw desire.

Devon ran his palms up her inner thighs. Delving past the coarse curls of her mound, he slid his fingers along her clit, stroking.

"Glad you finally made it," she teased.

"In the nick of time."

Devon dipped one finger inside her, swirling it. Her sex dripped with hot juice. Thumb and forefinger expertly parted her inner folds. Finding the tender nubbin, he moved his index finger in a stroking motion, beginning a sensual tease.

Rachel tipped back her head, moaning with pleasure. "Getting closer."

"Coming in." Devon slid a finger inside. Sucking muscles spasmed around his finger. Slick, warm, and very ready.

Rachel met the thrusts with increasing fervor, her wild needs increasing the pulling motions deep within her vagina. Her clit throbbed against his skin, her juices soaking his hand.

Devon bent and lapped along those tender pink petals, awakening a fierce passion in her. His cock surged, straining with a heat of its own. He stroked his penis with his free hand, pleasing himself even as he finger fucked Rachel with a body-jarring intensity, stretching her sex wider when two fingers became three.

Trembling with pent-up desire, Rachel pressed her legs together, capturing his hand snugly. She quivered violently, then peaked, her vagina pulsing greedily around his fingers.

Her body arched back when her first orgasm ripped through her, her exposed breasts heaving as she gasped for air. Her fingernail scrabbled at the hood, trying to clench the cool metal. "Damn you for making me come first."

He chuckled. "Don't worry," he murmured. "I'll make you come again and again." His fingers delved deeper.

She lay sprawled across the hood of his car, skirt pushed up around her hips. "I can't wait anymore." Wanton fierceness made her voice tremble.

Devon's own need was wild, the tempo increasing as blood pounded through his veins, deafening him. His arousal was simmering at a heat threatening to boil over like a volcano disgorging molten lava.

He had to take her, taste her, make the connection before he could claim her, experience his own climax. Already he'd gone further than he'd intended to, but he hadn't been able to resist.

Slipping his hand into his pocket, Devon withdrew a small stiletto, one whose blade rose and fell from within like the tongue of a lizard. Fitting in the palm of the hand, it was small, silent, and deadly sharp. Depressing the button released the blade.

Sliding his free hand over her breastbone, he caught her at the base of her neck. Her eyes widened in fear when she saw the knife flash in his hand.

"Devon, what—!"

His grip tightened. She started to struggle, but he was stronger. Her fear was palpable. He felt her blood pounding under her skin, her wild heartbeat driving her fear, saw the breath fluttering in her throat.

"Do not resist me, Rachel," he soothed in a soft voice.

"Please," she gasped, "Don't hurt me!"

"I will not hurt you." He loosened his grip on her neck. "Trust me so that I may bring our bodies together."

Eyes wide, lips parted, she slowly nodded, her breasts rising and falling. He could see she was excited by the danger.

"I need to taste you, take of you to feed my hunger," he whispered.

Silence.

Slowly, Rachel nodded. "Okay."

Devon brought the blade up, quickly making a small slice. Crimson seeped from the wound, trickling down her pale skin.

A small whimper escaped her throat, but she didn't resist when he slid his hands under the small of her back and lifted her into a sitting position.

He traced his tongue along her flesh, licking away the blood. Pressing his lips to the soft pulse, he drank of her, drawing her life into his body. The liquid filling his mouth was sweet and warm.

The minutes passed slowly, only the sounds of the night's creatures breaking through the wind's gentle whispering.

Devon reluctantly pulled away, careful not to get lost in the intense joy of the feed. He felt the warmth of her blood on his lips.

He looked down at her face, marveling at her beauty. Half in shadow, half in light, he could see the flush on her high cheekbones. And her mouth. Every time he looked at it, he wanted to capture it and crush it with his over and over. He could imagine that mouth pressed against his flesh, drawing his blood over her probing tongue, taking his life into her body.

When that happens we shall be one and she will truly belong to me.

He guided his mouth toward hers. "I want you to taste yourself."

Devon kissed her, slowly, deeply. When their kiss had broken, he pressed two fingers against the small cut in her neck, murmuring a few words of healing. When he drew them away, the cut had healed, leaving only a small white scar.

Licking her lips, Rachel shuddered. "That was so intense."

"Mmm, did you enjoy it?" His hunger was only half sated. There was more he needed from her.

She dragged a deep, ragged breath into her lungs. "Yes. Very much."

He tipped her chin back. "There is more. Much more I want to share with you."

Rachel laughed low in her throat, hands going down between their bodies. She wrapped her fingers around his cock, stroking up and down his length. "I hope so."

Positioned between her legs, Devon's hands slid down her body. He grabbed her by the hips, impaling her with a single hard thrust of his cock.

Tugging his shirt away from his back, Rachel's cool palms coasted over his shoulders. "I knew you'd fit."

Devon pulled out to the tip, then throttled back inside. "Tight." Hips back, another thrust. Silky muscles clenched and held. "Very nice." Her cunt was exactly as he'd imagined, undulating around him like a voracious little mouth.

Rachel's legs wound around his waist. "Nice isn't the half of it." She tapped him on the ass with her foot. "But we're not half done."

Right.

Devon settled into a leisurely canter, mashing his hips into hers with a slow deliberate grind.

As a new climax began to ripple through her body, Rachel's head dipped back. "I can't hold off much longer," she warned.

"Then don't." Devon lowered his head, expertly laving one nipple.

Instant reaction. Her cry of pleasure fueled his own desire until he couldn't tell where his body ended and hers began. Unable to breathe, unable to think, he only felt the sizzling contractions of her hungry cunt doing wonderful things all around his cock.

Devon gave one final thrust, feeling his balls draw up as if squeezed. Orgasm flooded him, a violent whirlpool of incredible force and momentum. Exploding with savage fury, he felt his loins release. Hot semen erupted, flowing into her waiting womb.

Bodies locked together at the hip, neither moved, as if to pull apart would break the magical spell of the incredible experience.

Finally, excruciatingly, Devon pulled away, arranging his clothes. The night around them was dark, quiet, peaceful.

"Rachel?"

Stretching languidly, she sat up and snuggled closer to his chest, laying her head on his shoulder like a child. "Hmm?"

"Are you awake?"

"Mmm, no." She yawned sleepily. "I just want to stay like this, forever in your arms."

Devon's throat constricted. Damn. He wanted it too. Forever.

22

Rachel wasn't prepared for the sensations overwhelming her when she sat up in bed. Her head began to spin, vision dimming, stomach rolling. She felt weak, spent, as though some creature had latched its teeth into her flesh and was sucking the very strength right out of her.

Pressing her hands to her forehead, she sank back onto the mattress. Her skin was flushed, warm, feverish. Panting, she felt her stomach lurch, bowels twisting. If she moved, she'd vomit all over herself. *Oh, shit, not now*, she thought. *I hope I'm not coming down with the flu or something*.

Head rolling on her pillow, she looked around her dim bedroom. Mercifully, the blinds were drawn, shutting out the sunlight. The light peeking around the edges hurt her eyes. Even that tiny bit of light seemed unnaturally bright.

Pressing her hands over her face, she closed her eyes. The sensations of nausea were slowly beginning to fade, her insides settling down to something resembling near normal. She had a headache, a sensation much like someone had knocked her on the side of the head with a metal bar, sending all memory flying out. With a trembling hand she reached up and rubbed her left temple. No bruise, no lump, but God, her skull felt like it was about to split in half. Her heart thumped hollowly in her chest, blood thudding through her veins like a herd of wild buffalo. Her mind was a haze, memories of the prior night mired in a murky haze.

What the hell did I do last night?

She knew she'd gone to work. That was a given. Her clothes lay discarded on the floor in a messy pile, her typical way of undressing after a hard night's work. Afterward, though, there was nothing. She couldn't remember undressing and getting into bed, much less how she'd gotten home. She wrinkled her brow in frustration, trying to recall the night.

A few vague scenes came floating up from the dark pools. Devon. Yes, now she remembered. He'd shown her where to make the night deposits. Good. On track.

Things coming back, clearer. After dropping off the money, they'd taken a drive. Trees. Grass. A clear night's sky. Devon kissing her, hard, urgently, pulling open her blouse and his hands roaming her body. The thought of their embrace sent ripples of warmth over her flesh.

Rachel shifted. Under the covers, she was as naked as a jaybird. Sleeping nude wasn't something she typically did. When she was alone, she always put on a nightgown and panties. When she was entertaining a man she slept au natural, loving the feel of her partner's flesh pressed against hers.

Did we make love last night? She searched every nook and cranny of her brain, but there was simply nothing there past a lot of heavy petting. As far as she knew, they had not gone all the way.

Well, that's too damn bad. Maybe they hadn't progressed any further because she'd become ill. Devon must have driven her home and put her into bed. At the thought of him undressing her, seeing her buck naked, a hot flush began to creep up her face, reddening her cheeks.

Oh wonderful, here she'd been naked with a handsome man and too sick to do anything with him. *Gee, my luck. What a time for the flu to hit me.*

Her stomach lurched again, this time filling her with a fresh sensation. Hunger. Perhaps a few pieces of wheat toast and hot tea would help to settle her stomach down a bit. Feeling a familiar pressure in her bladder, she slid her legs over the edge of the bed and got up. Her legs were shaky, but held her weight. She could waste all day lying in bed getting sick, or she could get on with life. Time to get up, get going. There was nothing she could do about the flu except load up on medicines. Better call in sick. No way she'd make it in today.

Eating seemed to settle her stomach. By the time she'd bitten into the second piece, she felt better. Her strength was returning, her body losing those odd "shakies" that usually preceded illness. A second piece quickly gave way to a third and then a fourth slice of toast, heavily buttered and slathered with apricot jam, along with a glass of milk and two cups of coffee, heavy with hazelnut-flavored creamer and sugar.

So much for being sick. She washed her breakfast dishes and put them away. Taking her coffee, she went back upstairs for a shower. Just as she was stripping off her bathrobe, the doorbell rang.

"Now who the hell could that be?" she cursed under her breath, putting her robe on and trekking back downstairs. Maybe it was Devon, come to check on her. If so, she'd be ready to assure him that she was perfectly fine, and invite him to join her in the shower.

Much to her disappointment it wasn't Devon.

It was Ginny. Her former employee lifted a plate of home-baked cinnamon rolls. "Since you haven't come to see me, I thought I'd come to see you," she chirruped cheerily, offering a broad smile.

Sighing inwardly, Rachel ran her fingers through her disheveled hair. "Hello, Ginny." The last person she wanted to see right this minute, but it'd be rude to send her packing.

Offering a smile that could only be called a wan parting of the lips, Rachel stepped aside. "Come in."

Ginny reached up, holding her plate in one hand, wrapping her arm around Rachel's neck in a hug.

Rachel accepted it almost grudgingly, pulling quickly away. A shiver went down her spine. God, sometimes she just absolutely didn't like being touched at all. It was as if she felt the vibes emanating off other people's bodies, going all over her skin like dirt. Perhaps her illness was making her too sensitive.

She carried the cinnamon rolls into the kitchen. "How have you been?"

Ginny followed, frowning a little, as if she'd noticed Rachel's standoffishness. "I've been fine, dear. Since the bookstore closed, I've gone to work at the Shop-N-Sack down the street from my house."

Rachel poured a cup of coffee and handed it to Ginny. "Isn't that a little hard on you, standing behind a counter all day?"

Ginny cradled her cup. "It is, but you know I like meeting new people." What she left unsaid spoke volumes. "I wish the bookstore could have stayed open."

Rachel poured a fresh cup for herself. Might as well have another. She couldn't get through the day without her caffeine boosts. By the way Ginny was acting, she didn't want to leave anytime soon. What would it hurt to give an old lady a few more minutes?

She sat down at the kitchen table, indicating a free chair. "I do, too, but it just didn't happen that way."

Ginny sat down. "Aren't you going to try one of my rolls?"

she asked, reaching for the creamer and spooning some into her coffee.

Sipping her coffee, Rachel shook her head. "I would, but I'm not hungry. I'll save them for later. Would you like one?"

"Oh no, dear, they're for you to enjoy."

"Thanks for bringing them over. I'm sure I'll love them and so will my hips."

The old woman's gaze flitted over her. "You look a little thin, dear. Have you been eating enough? You're so pale."

Rachel toyed with her spoon, eyes on her coffee, watching the steam rise from the hot liquid in her cup. "I've just got a touch of the flu, that's all. And I don't seem to see the sun anymore now that I'm working all night."

A question mark crossed the old lady's face. "All night?"

"At Mystique."

"The nightclub?"

"Yes. I'm supervisor over the waitresses and hostesses now. Just got hired a few days ago. The pay's really good. I'm going to try to be out from under the debts of the bookstore in a couple of years. Think I can do it if I put every penny over to the bills."

Ginny frowned. "I've heard that's a pretty racy place, Rachel."

Racy didn't begin to describe the half of it. "It has its moments, but I like it."

A stretch of uncomfortable silence followed.

It occurred to Rachel that because she and Ginny no longer worked together, they had nothing in common to share. Their lives had taken new directions. Her mind was no longer on the struggle to keep her store going, wondering where the money was going to come from to pay the bills.

Her luck, for a change, seemed to be turning around.

Ginny, on the other hand, was struggling to make ends meet, a woman in her sixties who had no close family to turn to or depend on.

Rachel felt sorry for Ginny. Pity, even. A position she never wanted to find herself in: old, alone, and searching for companionship.

Ginny's voice broke into her thoughts. "Heard from Dan?"

Rachel shook her head. "As in has the asshole bothered to return my laptop? No." Her words spilled out angrily. "He really screwed me over."

"I forgot that." The old lady pursed her lips, eyes sad. "He seemed so nice.

Rachel cast a narrow glance at her friend. "He wasn't a good man," she reminded. "All he did was use me and steal from me."

Ginny sipped her coffee. "That's just a shame."

Annoyed, Rachel gripped her coffee cup so hard her knuckles turned white. "Yeah. It is." Dan was in the past now, not even a blip on her radar.

Ginny looked at her for a long moment and then slowly shook her head. "I just don't want to see you end up alone." Her lower lip began to tremble. There was a slight hesitation before she finished. "Alone, like I am now."

Seeing that abject look of abandonment on the old woman's face, Rachel's anger drained away. How could she be angry with someone who was obviously so lonely that she'd seek out a former employer?

She and Ginny had never been close friends. Hell, she'd never even been to the old lady's home. What she knew of her, she knew from conversations to pass the time on slow days at work.

Rubbing her hands over her numb face, Rachel realized she was so busy being absorbed with her own problems that she'd totally ignored those of a fellow human being. How shallow could she get? She could see the reality of an old woman's loneliness sinking in slowly, by increments, a prophetic, almost frightening glimpse into her own future.

Her mind started working again, but nothing made much sense. The ache in her chest grew stronger with each passing second. How she wished she could wave her hands and make the world's problems magically disappear.

Desperately lonely people, frail emotions, tiny lives. Like hamsters running in a wheel, they were all going round and round, running down the path to nowhere. Where the hell was God? He couldn't be in his Heaven, for all was not right in the world.

"You're not alone, Ginny. You know I'll always be there for you," she heard herself saying. "I promise, just as soon—"

The doorbell cut into her words, the second time in one day.

Rachel excused herself from the table. "When did I suddenly become Miss Popular?"

A delivery boy waited. Not flowers this time. A small square package, neatly wrapped, complete with a bow on top.

From Devon.

Forgetting Ginny's presence, she tore the elaborate paper off. A jewelry box.

Rachel's heart nearly stopped. Hands shaking, barely able to breathe, she opened its lid. A necklace lay on blue crushed velvet.

She lifted it out. A pendant hung on a delicate gold chain. She recognized the strange design as being the same on the face of the signet ring Devon wore. She quickly opened the little card. *My other half*, it read mysteriously, *we are soon to be one . . .*

She read the card again. "Wow. I think I like this."

"How pretty," Ginny said from behind. "Is that from the new man in your life?"

Rachel smiled. "Yes."

"Who is he?"

Rachel admired her new treasure. "Devon Carnavorn."

Ginny's forehead puckered. "Isn't he the owner of Mystique?"

"Yes."

Ginny's mouth drew down.

"What?"

"Nothing."

Rachel frowned. "Tell me."

Ginny seemed uncomfortable. "Well, it's only gossip, mind you, but I've heard that he's quite a ladies' man, if you know what I mean."

Rachel knew. "Meaning he sleeps with a lot of women?"

"That, and I've heard a lot more. They say he has orgies at that place of his, the one on the outskirts of town—rituals of some kind too, practicing black magic."

Rachel rolled her eyes. "Oh, surely you can't believe that."

The doorbell sounded a third time, interrupting further conversation.

Four packages—large, rectangular, also beautifully wrapped.

Like a kid at Christmas, Rachel gleefully tore into them. Taking off the lid off the largest, she parted the folds of white tissue paper. A dress. Not just any dress, but one of the latest designer fashions. It came from the most expensive clothing store in town, a place she couldn't afford to even walk by, much less go inside.

Taking it out, she held it against her body. The dress was stunning, a daringly cut design that showed bosom and thigh to best advantage. Red, almost scarlet, and made of pure silk.

She picked up the envelope that came with the dress, a larger one, more direct: *You're off tonight. A car will pick you up at eight. Be ready.*

The second package was a pair of matching shoes. Just her size. The third held matching lingerie: push-up bra, daring thong panties, garter, thigh-high hose.

Wear these, the note inside said.

The fourth package was the most stunning. Inside was a mink evening cape. Pure charcoal, fashioned of the finest pelts, it must have cost a small fortune.

Although not a fan of wearing clothing made of wild animals, Rachel was flattered Devon had taken the time to choose the very best items for her.

Flowers, necklace, dress, and cape. All so overwhelming. She had to wonder if this was how Devon Carnavorn treated all his women. A bit of intuition told her that he didn't. He'd made it clear that she would be more than a cheap dalliance.

Ginny glanced over all the gifts, a sour expression crossing her face. "Looks like your young man is serious about you."

Rachel tried to make light of the many intimate gifts scattered in her living room. No doing. The thrill was too much. "I certainly hope so."

"I don't think you should accept them."

Rachel shot her friend a narrow look. "Why not?"

Ginny pointed at the pile of gifts. "It's like he's trying to own you. Dress you the way he wants you to look."

Rachel scoffed. "That's silly." She carefully rewrapped the expensive mink and put it in its box. "He's just being generous."

Ginny disagreed. "He's buying you, Rachel. Trying to make you into something you're not."

She flared, forgetting her temper. "Maybe it's something I want to be."

The moment the words were out of her mouth, Rachel regretted them. The look on Ginny's face said her words might as well have been a physical slap.

Ginny began to gather her things, putting on her jacket and pulling her purse onto her shoulder. "Thank you for the coffee, dear," she said, opening the front door.

Feeling like a total heel, Rachel hurried to make amends. "I'm sorry, Ginny. You don't have to go."

The old woman gave her a soft, almost sad smile. "But I do. I have to go to work soon."

"I'll come by," Rachel called out.

Too late.

Ginny slipped outside, closing the door behind her.

Hurrying to the window, Rachel opened the blinds in time to see Ginny disappear around the corner.

Sighing, she tiredly glanced up at the clock. Was it already going on five? She'd better hurry if she wanted to be ready by the time the car arrived to pick her up.

A little thrill went clear down her spine.

What else had Devon planned for their evening?

23

The car pulled up at eight o'clock sharp. Not just any car, but a Rolls Royce. Magnificent, silver gray and looking as if it had just rolled off the showroom floor.

A smartly uniformed chauffeur emerged, escorting her from her door to the car. "This way, please, Miss Marks."

"Thank you." Feeling every bit like royalty, Rachel clutched her expensive mink as if the pelt might come back to life and run away. Devon was certainly showing her everything he had. Taste. Charm. Money. If he intended to impress her, he'd well succeeded.

The driver opened the passenger door and helped Rachel into the cocooning depth. The car had room for six passengers behind the driver, separated by a smoky pane of privacy glass.

Rachel couldn't help but smooth her palm over the seat. Leather interior, creamy and supple as a baby's bottom. Nice. Outfitted with everything a busy executive would need to keep in touch with the outside world and be entertained within: cell phone, color television, compact disc player, and a small wet bar stocked with miniature bottles of most popular wines and whiskeys.

On the seat another present waited. A dozen roses. Light pink.

She almost pinched herself to make sure she was awake and not lost in the depths of some profligate dream. "Oh, man. I think I've died and gone to heaven."

The chauffeur buzzed in. "Did you need something, ma'am?"

Rachel quickly shook her head. "No. Everything's fine. Thank you."

"Anytime."

Settling back to enjoy the ride, she selected a single rose. Beautiful. Not a flaw on it. She lifted the flower to her nose, inhaling its heady scent. God, but she felt like a princess on her way to see her prince. What luxury.

I could get used to being pampered like this, she thought, then frowned. How long would it last? How long would it be before Devon laid his eyes on a prettier, younger woman and went after a new prize? A few weeks? A month? Six?

Would she be fortunate enough to get a year out of him?

Rachel didn't know.

One thing was certain. She planned to thoroughly enjoy the ride, go wherever it might take her. A chance like this only came along once in a lifetime.

Carpe diem.

Seize the day!

24

Rachel's heart beat with excitement when the Rolls came to a stop before a matched set of massive iron gates held in place by a six-foot-high stone fence.

Up front, the driver rolled down the window and pressed a button on the communications link. A moment later a buzzer sounded. The gates parted like the Red Sea, rolling aside to let the car and its sole passenger through.

As the car followed the drive toward the main house, she leaned forward, eager to catch a glimpse of the manor where he lived. Two years ago, Carnavorn had built the place from the ground up, allowing no cameras inside the massive stone walls guarding his private residence.

The place was rumored to have cost over nine million to build and was called Hammerston, after the estate he was reputed to own in England.

Whether it was a family title or one bought with his fortune, Rachel didn't know. She had expected to be taken to a fancy restaurant or the nightclub itself. She hadn't expected to be taken to his private residence. Outsiders were simply not allowed there. If you didn't come by invitation, you didn't come at all.

Her gaze swept the elaborately manicured gardens, lush with trees, shrubs, and early blooming spring plants. A night for whispers, for kisses, for love to blossom. Not far away stood a gazebo. Cool shadows cloaked it, silent sentinels that would not whisper of the secrets lovers might share.

The house, if you could call such an imposing edifice a house, was settled amid the vast green lawn. The sand-colored stone looked medieval, as numerous vaulted turrets were spread across the roof, lending a ferocious appearance to the otherwise composed three-story structure. One almost expected a knight in armor to come charging up on his valiant steed.

The Rolls slowed to a stop in front of the main entrance. The driver hopped out and hurried around to open the passenger door. He offered one gloved hand, helping Rachel out of the car.

With the driver's hand firmly at her arm, Rachel walked up the wide stone steps leading to the front door.

By the pressure with which he held her, it almost felt as though he were somehow trying to restrain her, keep her from running away. His silent intensity gave her an uneasy feeling. Bad enough that the butterflies in her stomach were doing loop-the-loops. Though outwardly composed, inside she was a nervous wreck.

As she crossed the last step, Rachel noticed that the elaborate iron tracery of the door displayed the coat of arms the Carnavorn family had claimed.

No knock needed to get inside.

The door swung open, guided by the formally outfitted butler. Seeing Rachel, he offered a ceremonial bow.

"Welcome, Miss Marks," the butler said, voice tinged with

an English accent. "Lord Carnavorn has been awaiting your arrival."

Without stepping inside, the unnamed driver practically propelled Rachel over the threshold. She felt as though she were the fly who'd just blundered into the spider's web.

Rachel offered a slight smile, nodding. "Thank you. I'm delighted to be here."

The butler didn't even crack a smile. "Please follow me," he said.

Rachel pressed her hand to her stomach to quell her nerves. "With pleasure."

She trailed the butler through the main foyer, a wood-paneled and flagstoned affair designed to intimidate. Passing through its voluminous depths, her gaze briefly flicked over the paintings hanging on the walls.

A passionate collector, Carnavorn had filled the manor with an impressive array of artwork—some family portraits, but also old masters like Poussin, Bourdon, and Vouet populated the walls. No doubt its furnishings were the finest to be had, a testament to his leading position in the social and financial arenas of the jet-set world.

Her high stiletto heels clicked sharply as she walked, trying not to be too eager to hurry and join Devon. She pushed her fingers through her untamed black hair.

Coming to a set of closed twin doors, the butler grandly pushed them open. Stepping aside, he allowed Rachel to proceed ahead alone.

Drawing back her shoulders, Rachel swept into the great chamber that was the formal sitting room. Her gaze ranged around. The room was spacious, comfortable, with large windows overlooking the countryside. Carpets of great beauty were spread on the floor. Each piece had obviously been carefully placed.

Her blood pressure rose when she noticed the visual decoration all depicted the same thing: people making love in various positions, a virtual Kama Sutra of statues, paintings, and other sexually oriented objects d'art.

The room was full of people.

Not people standing around having drinks and conversation, but people lounging around in various states of undress, touching each other, some making love as others sat nearby watching.

Psychedelic light wafted against the walls, floor, and ceiling, lending the room an unearthly atmosphere, like floating in space in an alien vessel. Incense hazed the air.

How many bodies there were, Rachel couldn't count.

Holy God, what have I walked into?

Rachel drew in a breath, trying not to be utterly shocked, but she couldn't stop herself from staring. Men on women, women on women, and men on men . . . Devon had not invited her on an intimate date. He'd invited her to an orgy.

Devon's guests automatically stopped what they were doing, turning their eyes toward her, lowering their voices to a whisper.

The impulse to leave immediately almost overwhelmed Rachel. She started to open her mouth to protest, but something deep inside silenced her. Instead of being repulsed, the scene before her eyes simply fascinated. She felt the sexual energy in the room, tasted it, smelled it, soaked in the whole decadent atmosphere.

Her skin felt warm, tight, her sensitive nipples rasping against the silken bra she wore. Her stomach did a funny little dance in appreciation of all the beautiful bodies stretched out around the chamber. Male and female alike, all were fine-looking people. Exquisite.

Her searching gaze moved to the center of the room.

Like a raja holding court among his concubines, Devon lazed on a couch. Two half-naked women lounged at his feet, wineglasses in hand, stroking each other, sharing deep kisses.

Seeing her, Devon lifted his dark brows. A lazy smile curled up one corner of his full mouth. He snapped his fingers, and the women at his feet moved apart, allowing him to stand. He waded through the sea of bodies.

Devon looked her over, pleased that she'd dressed as he'd wanted. "You look superb, just as I knew you would." He caught her hand, pulling her toward him. "You look good enough to eat." He cocked a devilish brow. "In every way."

Rachel said, "Thank you." She noticed he was dressed in a pair of slacks and some sort of velvet lounging jacket—with no shirt underneath.

Devon eased her closer. His hands followed the lines of her body, slipping beneath the fur wrap to caress the small of her back before squeezing her ass through the silken material of her dress. "I've been waiting to see you again."

Unable to stop herself, Rachel tensed. She traced her tongue over dry lips. "Who are these people?" Even in her wildest dreams she couldn't have imagined the rumors about Devon's private parties were true. Weren't sexual gatherings illegal in California? Perhaps that explained the high stone walls around the manor. Hard for prying eyes to see through.

Devon's gaze swept over her. His eyes looked metallic rather than gray. "Members of the collective and their mates. Sadly, our numbers have thinned. There are only a few hundred Kynn left. The Amhais—"

More confusion. "The *who*?"

Devon swept the mink off her shoulders and tossed it to the butler. "Forget my words. Tonight I want you to watch. And enjoy."

The doors closed behind her.

Rachel gulped. Warmth colored her cheekbones.

No turning back.

25

Devon tugged her hand. "Come, sit down. Join the party."

Rachel wavered. She'd never been to an orgy before. Definitely a new experience. And exciting. The idea of unbridled sexual freedom enticed. "Are you sure this is okay?"

Devon laughed. "Of course it is all right. If I didn't think you were ready, I wouldn't have brought you into the enchanted circle."

A self-conscious laugh slipped over her lips. "Isn't this more like a daisy chain?"

Catching her chin, Devon tipped her head back. "This is my world. I want you to understand it. Be a part of it. If you are uncomfortable, Rachel, I will have my driver take you home." His grip tightened a little. "But be warned. I won't ask you back."

A heavy pause filled the air.

Rachel already knew her answer before the thought formed in her mind. The idea of being banished from his life hurt too much. The way he touched her, the way he looked at her took her to the edge. A dangerous place to walk, but so exciting to experience.

She had no doubt he meant every word. She might still have her job. But not having Devon? That would be like having heart surgery without anesthesia.

Too painful to contemplate.

She looked into his eyes and saw promise there. If only she would be. If only she would become. Irresistible.

No more hesitation. No more doubt.

Rachel's lips parted. Her breath drove her raspy words. "I'll stay."

Her answer pleased him. "Excellent."

Devon took her arm and guided her through the writhing bodies. People stopped making love only long enough to smile up at her, murmuring words of welcome before going back to their activities.

Murmuring replies more nonsensical than social, Rachel couldn't remember the names. Didn't really care. Keeping her clothes on occupied her attention. More than once, strange hands reached out to stroke her, a hand caressing her leg, a thigh, her ass.

One of the women who'd been sitting at Devon's feet abandoned her partner. Pouring a glass of wine, she pressed it into Rachel's hand.

Rachel smiled politely back. "Thank you." She sipped the wine. A lovely fruity vintage rolled over her tongue. Delicious. She took another drink. Warmth spread through her stomach. Tense muscles eased a little.

Devon pulled her down beside him on the couch, a king overlooking his subjects. "Thank you, Jade."

"Always to please, my lord," Jade said with a smile.

The second woman poured him a glass. "For your thirst, lord."

Devon accepted her offering. "Many blessings, my Gia." He ran his hand over Rachel's crossed legs, sensing her unease. "Relax."

Feeling a bit like a traveler who hadn't yet learned the native language, Rachel tilted her head toward his shoulder. "I'm trying." She laughed again, nervously. "I wasn't quite expecting this."

He sipped his wine. "No one does, at first. But few see this side of my world."

Eyes wide, Rachel tried not to look at the naked people, but couldn't help herself. Their bodies were magnets that attracted her probing stare. She watched a man make delicate oral love to a woman's sex. Another pair were locked in the classic "69" position, both partners lost in the joys of mutual sex. A mesmerizing sight, one she could not seem to take her eyes off.

Rachel's hand trembled. Her body grew warm, the heat of intense arousal moistening the juncture between her thighs. "I'm flattered." She held on tighter to her wineglass, hoping her tension wouldn't shatter it.

Devon slid his arm around her. "I've been aching to touch you all day." His hand draped over her shoulder, slipping under the spaghetti strap of her dress to invade the barrier of her bra and caress her breast. The two women resumed their lovemaking at Devon and Rachel's feet, stretched out on a faux-fur rug.

Rachel's breath caught in her throat. "Oh goodness."

Devon caught her nipple and rolled the erect nubbin between thumb and forefinger. "Goodness has nothing to with it." He tweaked harder.

A spike of pure heat went straight to Rachel's core. "Keep that up, and I'll come like mad," she warned.

Devon grinned. "I know." He tweaked harder. "Just listen to the music and let it carry you."

Music?

Rachel tipped her head to one side. For the first time she noticed the strange, erotic music that was playing in the background, almost too low to be heard. An odd melody, not one hummed or sung to, but one throbbing with tones seeming to match the pulsing of blood through her veins. With the haze of the incense, the atmosphere heaved with the scent of wine and the perspiration of uninhibited animalistic intercourse.

Devon worked her nipple harder.

A vibrating moan slipped out on a whisper. "Oh God . . ."

Though Rachel hardly willed it, she found watching the people fuck turned her on. She felt no repulsion. Just total relaxation. She had been nervous about the evening, now she was calm, tranquil.

She felt warm and comfortable, watching the strange rainbow of light drift over the naked bodies like the gentle waves of the ocean. With sudden clarity, she realized she belonged here, with Devon.

Rachel uncrossed her legs and sipped her wine, leaning against his shoulder to give him free access to her body. What else did she have to do?

Nothing.

Before she knew it, her glass was being refilled. Once. Twice. Three times.

Rachel kept drinking, mesmerized by the unending sex, unaware that the minutes were passing at a slow, languid pace. She heard voices, but couldn't understand the words. They seemed so far away. Conversation faded into a comfortable silence. It could hardly be as interesting as what was going on before her eyes, anyway.

More than sex, there seemed to be some sort of strange ritual going on. More than one of the people had knives. They would make small cuts in their partner's flesh, then lick away the blood they drew.

Instead of being repulsed, Rachel watched in fascination how it appeared to heighten the sexual enjoyment of the "victim." None protested. Indeed, they seemed to welcome it, more than one helping to guide the blade. The licking, the sucking, the sight of crimson smeared against pale white skin was definitely arousing.

Devon shifted so that he was facing her. "You are a special one." He eased the strap of her dress off her shoulder. The cup followed, exposing her breast. "And I want you to be a part of my life."

Head spinning from the wine, Rachel heard herself say, "I want to be a part of it too."

Devon smiled. "Good." His mouth crushed hers. When their kiss broke, he moved his lips to her cheek, her chin, the soft pulse at the base of her neck. He was touching her in what seemed to be slow, sensuous motion.

Rachel leaned back on the cushions, hands cupping Devon's face, guiding his mouth to her taut nipple. Over his head she saw a couple dancing, naked, engrossed only in each other's bodies. So sweet. So loving. So natural.

"Join us tonight," he murmured against her skin.

She nodded, unsure of what he was talking about until she felt one of the women lying at their feet reach out and caress her leg. Though her first impulse was to pull away from the strange touch, she didn't.

Devon nodded and settled back. The woman he'd called Jade moved forward, nuzzling at Rachel's ankle with her lips.

Sliding off the stiletto heels, Jade kissed her way up Rachel's leg, trailing her tongue over the flesh-colored hose. Jade worked her way higher, expertly parting Rachel's legs and kissing her inner thighs.

Rachel gasped. The room spun. She felt frantic, but the woman was touching her in such a magical way that she didn't want her to stop. She'd never made love to another woman, had never had the desire to. Yet something about a beautiful woman serving her every sexual need appealed to her.

"You haven't existed before this night," Devon whispered in her ear. "Tonight you'll be reborn into my world."

She gazed at him, shivering at the touch of Jade's hands and lips on her skin. "Is this what you want?" she asked, trying to find the words through the misty haze starting to envelop her mind.

For an answer, he unhooked her bra, letting it drop to the floor. "Just give yourself to the sensations." He laughed, light, throaty, sexy. His eyes were afire with a passion she could not yet fathom.

"Devon . . . Oh," she started to say, but couldn't finish her sentence. The second woman, vaguely remembered as Gia, was suddenly standing before her, taking her hands and pulling her to her feet.

Gia's hands expertly slid Rachel's dress over her hips, letting it drop around her ankles.

Rachel stood naked but for the garters and hose and thin thong panties hugging her hips.

Jade pulled her down. The three women tumbled to the floor, landing on the soft furlike rug. The women stretched alongside her, caressing her body, rigid with sexual tension.

Rachel felt soft lips cover hers. Opening her mouth, she closed her eyes and relished the flavor of a long, potent, berry-flavored kiss. Jade's hands caressed her arms, her shoulders, her breasts. She welcomed every sensation.

When Jade broke their kiss, Rachel drew in a breath. The woman smiled down at her. "Do you like?" she asked.

"I've never been with a woman," she gulped.

"Then you're in for a treat," Devon said from above.

"But—" she started to say.

Gia pressed a finger across her lips. "Just lay back and enjoy." And then she brushed her lips against the sensitive hollow of Rachel's throat, her warm mouth lowering, claiming an erect nipple, sucking it with slow, tender strokes of her tongue.

Crying out, Rachel writhed with delight and agony. She was

vaguely aware of Jade unsnapping her garters, rolling her hose and then her panties down her legs and discarding them.

Like a cat on the prowl, Jade moved between her legs, stroking the insides of her thighs, hands and mouth moving upward toward her throbbing pussy.

Jade's fingertips moved in slow, gentle circles, pressing up against the moist depths of Rachel's sex. Head dipping, Jade flicked her tongue against Rachel's clit. She manipulated that sensitive little button with just the right pressure, causing a ripple of heat to roll through Rachel.

Gia made the first cut, a small slash above Rachel's right breast. She pressed her lips to the soft mound, her tongue soothing the tender cut as she savored Rachel's blood.

Lost in the lovely sensations washing over her body like a tidal pool, Rachel began to respond with an instinctive rhythm to the two women's soft touches and caresses. Her lashes fluttered, lips pouting, drawing inward as if sucking, then parting as yet another moan escaped from deep within her throat. Absolutely lost in the touch of their hands, their mouths, unable to comprehend all at once the myriad feelings rushing through her body. The kisses, the way the women were caressing her, the places they were touching . . .

All part of a dance that she'd waited to join all her life, this unknown world she'd been waiting for, to open up before her eyes. She'd only been lacking the people to show her the way. Her mind was spinning, her whole body throbbing with the passions these expert hands induced, working slowly and with purpose. She'd been sure she'd feel embarrassed, vulnerable, even a little terrified letting strange women touch her.

None of that entered her mind now. This was ecstasy!

Gia suckled at her breasts, pausing now and again to give her long, slow kisses. Between her legs, Jade delivered devastating cunnilingus, tongue flicking at Rachel's clit over and over.

Two beautiful men came over and lifted Rachel off the floor.

They carried her to the center of the room, placing her on a chaise lounge between them.

They knelt down as if in silent homage, each stroking a breast, kissing, then sucking the tender tips of her nipples.

Rachel held their heads, smiling, welcoming their attention. Everyone loved one another in tranquil acceptance. As the women had done earlier, they silently began to explore her naked flesh, making more tiny cuts, drinking her blood as a kitten lapped milk.

Mouths, hands, fingers were touching every inch of her, sliding wetly up and down her body. An incredibly physical, spiritual, and instinctive dance. Beautiful people were having incredible sex, and she was right in the middle of it all, the goddess they worshipped.

As they fed off her, Rachel felt powerful, alive, vital, the fountain of all creation itself. Nothing she'd ever experienced in her life could compare to this moment.

One of the men thrust his throbbing cock into her mouth.

Rachel took him deep, suckling at his engorged shaft.

The second man knelt between her legs, spreading her thighs wide to expose her clit. He bent, running his tongue over her tender labia, nibbling gently at the soft pink flesh.

Rachel let her legs fall open a little wider. More than anything, she needed to be fucked. The tempo of the music had changed, becoming slower, more erotic, like the beating of a human heart.

She opened her eyes and cast a look over toward Devon. She wanted him to come to her, take her in front of all these people, claim her as his own.

Gia had crawled up between his legs, unzipping his pants and wrapping her hands around his erect cock. Lowering her head, Gia licked and caressing the length of his pulsing shaft.

Devon's gaze locked with hers, unashamed to be seen by her prying eyes taking his sexual recreation. A slow, lazy smile turned up his lips.

Wanting Devon to witness her taking control of her desires, Rachel sat up and pushed the man between her legs back onto the floor. He sprawled on his back at her feet willingly, giving himself to her manipulations. A silent communication flashed between them. He was hers to use as she wanted.

Licking her lips, feeling every bit the sassy bitch in heat, she dropped gracefully to her knees, straddling his thighs with hers.

Rachel ran her hands up and down her new lover's chest, over his abdomen, lower, taking her time to thoroughly arouse him. A jutting cock rewarded her efforts. Perfect. She smiled. "Give me everything you've got."

He did. More than once

So did everyone else.

26

Coming out of the haze of sleep into a half-awake, groggy awareness of her surroundings, Rachel opened her eyes to a dim, unfamiliar room. Turning her head on her pillow, she fought the strange sense of disorientation.

Where am I?

Rachel looked around. *Not at home*.

The suite around her was an elaborate one, an attractive room, a woman's domain. The bed had a canopy of crimson with touches of gold and ivory for contrast, almost perfectly matching the heavy draperies drawn across the windows, shielding the room from almost all outside illumination. Fresh flowers overflowed the vases set on strategically positioned tables, their light fragrance filling the air.

After she'd gotten into Devon's limo, she'd lost all track of time. It was more than a little bit frightening to wake up not knowing exactly what she'd done the previous evening.

Her body tingled underneath the soft comforter and sheets.

Sitting up, Rachel let the covers fall away to reveal her nudity.

Rachel swung her legs over the edge of the bed and stood up. Her head throbbed so badly she was nearly blinded.

She held her head in her hands, wishing the agony would cease. "Just how much wine did I have to drink?" It felt like someone was pounding on her head with a hammer: thud, thud, thud. Jesus, she felt totally drained, as empty as one of the many glasses of wine she'd downed last night.

Last night.

Devon. The orgy. Making love hour after hour to strange women and men alike. Images of herself—unclothed, uninhibited, performing a sensual ballet with other twining bodies. Nothing was left to the imagination.

She'd performed every kind of sexual position possible last night. The muscles between her legs ached from being spread so wide, feeling much like her body had been dough under the hands of dozens of kneading chefs.

Drawing her hands down, she looked down on her nude body, memories of the sucking, the licking filling her head. Her pale skin was riddled with tiny cuts that covered her breasts, abdomen and thighs, red and swollen.

Rachel ran her hands over her flat belly, probing the puffy slices in her flesh with her fingertips. She wasn't really in any pain. She'd been carefully bathed, and her skin rubbed with a lightly scented oil.

Closing her eyes, she drew in a deep breath. Her olfactory senses were still clogged with the lingering odors of incense, semen, and the musky smell of her own sexual juices.

Oh no! She pressed suddenly clammy fingers against her aching temples, willing the pain to go away, willing this to be a terribly bad dream. She sat down on the edge of the bed, trying to muster the pieces of the night before into some sort of coherent sense.

Oh God, did I really do that?

Rachel made a great effort to keep calm, even though the

thoughts of what had happened to her last night made her physically ill. How could she have let Devon lead her into such debauchery? Resentment and fury filled her. Was she that easily manipulated by a man she desired? What was he doing to her? Was he trying to hurt her? Humiliate her? She pressed her hand to her mouth.

Her jaw tightened. "He certainly managed to do both."

Fighting back the panic boiling under the surface, she forced herself to stand up, search for her clothing. They lay neatly at the foot of the bed.

Grabbing them up, she wriggled into her panties and bra, cursing the frilly things, wishing now she'd worn a sweat suit and not that daringly cut dress that Devon had given her.

How could I have known? She stepped into the dress, lifting its thin straps over her shoulders, struggling to zip it and failing.

Caught in her anger, she didn't hear the door open softly behind her, nor was she aware of the soft footfalls that brought Devon to her side. She only knew that he was beside her, drawing her into his strong embrace.

"Rachel," he murmured lovingly in her ear. "I didn't mean for you to awaken alone."

Rachel pulled away. "Don't touch me! What you did to me last night was unforgivable."

She continued to dress. Foregoing the sexy garter belt and hose, she stepped into her pumps, cursing the high heels. Taking a few hurried steps, she twisted her ankle.

"Shit!" Tears stung her eyes and spilled down her face. She closed her eyes tightly, trying to convince herself that she had the strength to walk out of this place. But she was weak, oh so weak. All she wanted to do was lie down, curl up, and die.

Coming up behind her, Devon placed his hands on her shoulders. "I did nothing you didn't want, beloved."

Rachel shook off his hands, repulsed. "I drank too much

wine. I didn't know what I was doing, and you and those perverts took advantage of me." The words sounded halfway lame coming out of her mouth. She knew the minute she said them that she was lying, that she hadn't been an unwilling participant. She'd been more than willing to join them, eager even. It had been exciting to be so sexually free, so uninhibited.

Devon's eyes were darkening to a dangerous shade, a color she'd never seen before. A perilous hue. "I took advantage of nothing," he replied defensively. His unblinking gaze drifted down her slender body, visually exploring the soft curves. "You could have asked to leave at any time."

"But I couldn't," she countered. "I was . . . lost . . . in the moment." Her jaw hardened. "Raped."

Devon slid one hand under her chin, lifting her head so that he could look into her eyes. His touch was so forceful, so assured, that she let him without protest. "You can't rape the willing, my dear. And you were willing, your body crying out for sensual pleasures." A slow smile curved up the corners of his fine mouth. "I wanted to bring you into my world easily, Rachel, but there is no easy way for it to happen."

Rachel gave him a long, glacial look. His touch repulsed her. "Bring me into your world?" she repeated harshly. "Into rituals of debauchery and degradation?" You're a thief, she wanted to scream, a leech that preys on people and their sexual weaknesses. "You took something from me that can never be replaced, Devon. You took my trust."

He allowed anger to erupt. "Last night, it seemed to my eyes you were a willing participant in your so-called seduction. Were you forced to do anything you didn't wish to?"

She hesitated, momentarily lost.

Rachel steeled herself. She had to be strong. Resist. Keep her nerve. Her heart was beating against her ribs, and her stomach had twisted into knots.

For an answer, she tugged down the front of her dress, revealing a small slice between her collarbone and breast. "How can you explain this?" she demanded. "My God, they cut into my flesh, drank my blood."

When Devon's hand rose to her throat, she was sure he was going to seize her neck and strangle her. But he only traced his fingers under her jaw, along the line of her jugular.

"I too have tasted you, taken in your essences," he answered. "Remember how we made love, how I drank of you . . . took you." His voice was a mere whisper, tantalizing, summoning memories almost too intense to savor, sweeping away dense cobwebs from the darkest corners of her mind.

Myriad memories flooded her head, a torrent of longing, desire, and, ultimately, consummation. Her mind drifted back to the park. She could picture it more clearly now; how they'd parked in a cul-de-sac, had sex in the cool shadows of the night.

Rachel's trembling hand slowly rose to her neck. She didn't have to see the small scar on her throat to know it was there, that Devon had taken her blood as he'd taken her body.

Tongue snaking out to trace her lips, she easily recalled the delicious kisses he'd given her, how she had tasted her own blood on his lips after he'd drunk from the fountain of her life. Then she'd been excited, had enjoyed the forbidden nectar and found herself longing for more. With a chill, she realized she had been a part of something ritualistic.

Devon drew her into his arms, holding her captive against his hard, muscled body. "I felt how badly you ached for our bodies to join." His long fingers caressed her with a familiar tenderness, brushing over her shoulders and down to the curve of her breasts. Finding, cupping, then finally teasing her through the thin material that revealed more than it covered.

Her head dipped back. Her nipples rose at his touch. "Oh God. Stop that . . . don't . . . stop . . ." She moaned, wanting to pull away, but knowing she couldn't.

Closing her eyes, Rachel heard herself sigh as he traced his warm tongue along the side of her neck, filling her with a lulling sense of languor.

Devon's mouth came down on hers with a calculated slowness, ending her weak protests. Her lips parted blindly under his, her arms lifting and curling around his neck. He kissed her until her knees felt weak and her head spun with sensations that made all rational thinking impossible.

When his hand caught the strap of her dress and slid it down her shoulder, she didn't object. His teasingly sensual fingers nudged aside the lacy cup so he could roll the tip of her nipple between thumb and forefinger. His touch sent electric shocks through every inch of her body.

Before she knew what he was doing, he'd eased the half-zipped dress back off her body, then unhooked her bra and let it fall. The silky material pooled softly around her feet.

"You can't fight your own physical nature," he whispered, his voice deliberately provocative. The look of need, of lust, was clearly etched into his features.

With a surprising ease and swiftness, he lifted her off her feet and carried her to the tousled bed. Kicking off her shoes, she felt the ripple of his muscles under her fingers as he laid her down, then stretched out beside her.

Devon's gaze traveled with slow deliberation over her body, lingering on her breasts, then the shadowy vee of her thighs, covered only by the thin strip of silky lace. Embers of desire smoldered in the depths of his eyes. His head dipped. He began to suckle the sensitive peaks of her nipples.

Dizziness overwhelmed her. *Oh heavens, I can't believe I'm letting him do this to me again.*

Devon's hand slid between her legs, parting her thighs. He was touching her where she longed to be touched, finding and stimulating nerve endings in her clit she'd never known existed. She grew wet, warm, aching to feel his cock deep inside her sex.

"I want you, Devon," she heard herself gasp. Her body wanted him too, arching up against him. The proof of his own need pressed against her hip.

"In time, beloved," he murmured, kissing the small pulsing vein on the exposed softness of her throat.

"Please," she started to beg. "Make love to me." She couldn't believe the words were coming from her lips, but she couldn't stop.

He brushed his fingers against her cheek. "To take you, I must drink of you." His voice had slowed and deepened, taking on a mesmerizing quality.

Rachel opened her eyes, searching for his. Devon's gaze seemed darker, filled with strange shadows that veiled his eyes, keeping her from seeing what he was thinking.

"My blood?" she whispered, voice slightly atremble. "Why?"

He drew in a deep breath. "I want to bring you over into my world, Rachel. Will you give yourself to me, trust me?"

Something in his tone warned her that he wasn't teasing but deadly serious in his intention to have her blood again. The idea chilled her.

She sat up abruptly, shaking his hands off her body. "I'm into accepting a little kink in my sex, Devon, but hasn't this pseudo-bloodsucking thing gone a little too far?"

Devon touched her cheek. "It's no game, Rachel. Taking blood is how we connect with our lovers." Taking a deep breath, his voice turning dry, he continued, "Remember, I told you about my kind—the Kynn." He watched her closely, waiting for her reaction.

Hearing his words, Rachel couldn't fully comprehend them. She shook her head, disbelieving. "I thought you were joking, part of making a pass at me. My God, I never believe you were serious."

Afraid, she pushed away. His touch disturbed her now. How could she have enjoyed the feel of his lips on hers, the touch of his hands all over her body? He was no man, but a psychopath who preyed on women, using sexual desire in order to sate his unnatural hungers.

Rachel felt sure she would faint, until she willed herself to feel nothing but anger instead. Anger kept her conscious, strong, aware.

"If this is some kind of a joke, Devon, it's a sick one, and it's gone too far." Her reaction clearly caught him off guard.

Devon stiffened. He reached for her hand, seizing it, almost crushing it in his own. "I am very serious about being Kynn. The gifts I can offer are ones you choose to accept. I will not force you to cross over. You come of your own will, believing in what we are, wanting to join us."

The growl in his voice sent a shivery sensation through her. "Wanting to join you?" she repeated, disbelieving. "Whatever gave you the idea I wanted to be a vampire?"

His answer stunned. "You were meant to be one of us."

She looked at him suspiciously. "How do you know?"

"You bear a mark, one I believed impossible for another person on earth to have." His palm brushed her leg.

Rachel visually followed his touch, settling on the odd birthmark on her thigh. "This? This is no holy sign. It's just a birthmark."

A small smile touched his lips. "Believe what you will. To me it is sacrosanct. You were meant for me, to become my she-shaey, my bloodmate. I believe it's destiny's choice." He stroked her thigh.

She shivered, pulled her leg away. "You're bent." She instantly regretted her words. What was she thinking, taunting a crazy man? She sat rigidly beside him, knowing he could easily beat her senseless if he so desired. She doubted anyone would come running if she were to scream for help.

He shook his head. "I know in my heart what is true. I can feel the hungers in you, the angst you've suffered because you have never felt like you belonged among their ranks. You've always been on the outside, looking in, haven't you? Envying what you couldn't fully be a part of. I can grant you that sense of place, of belonging, that you have been missing."

His voice echoed in her ears, her head. *What I have been missing . . .*

"No." She gulped, her mouth unexpectedly dry. In a strange, unsettling way his words seemed to make sense. But that was impossible. The thing that he was claiming to be—a vampire—simply didn't exist. It went against all reason, logic, and nature itself.

Devon tugged down the collar of his shirt to reveal the small scar on his neck. He took her hand, pressing her fingers to it. "It's always hard to accept the truth of our kind, that we could exist. But I've never lied to you. I told you as much as I felt you would understand."

Rachel tried to pull her hand away, but he wouldn't release her. "You didn't tell me everything." Voice icy, a harsh laugh escaped her. "Not that it matters." She jerked harder, forcing him to let go. "I may be fucked over once, but not twice."

He cleared his throat and tried to explain. "A long time ago, I was like you. Mortal. Caught in the weaknesses of the flesh. But you can escape that box, break free of their limitations. I can give you a glimpse of true eternity. All you have to do is believe my words are true and accept what we are."

Rachel slowly slid off the bed, out of his reach. Sanity and a sense of grim purpose returned, however belatedly. She didn't appreciate being misled, no matter the purpose behind the deception. "The problem is I don't believe." A small smile touched her lips. Tears spilled down her face. "I'm sorry. I can't play this perverse game anymore."

Devon propped himself up on one elbow. "Rachel," he pleaded, reaching out for her. "Please know I would never hurt you."

She laughed, feeling as though her chest was about to burst from the bitter ache building in her heart. "If you don't want to hurt me, leave me alone. Just stay away from me. I can't live in your warped fantasy world."

Devon drew himself up sharply, angered by her words. Almost contemptuously, he threw back his head and laughed. The sound drove splinters under her skin. His steely gaze hardened, eyes narrowing ominously.

"You belong to me, Rachel," he said, letting his words drag out mockingly. "Only to me. You can run away now, but you can't escape from me forever. One day soon, I will come for you. And when I do, you will join me willingly."

Rachel quickly shook her head as if to dispel a trance. "No! You're a prisoner here in your own damned little world, but not me. I won't ever join you. Ever!"

She hurled the remarks, sharp as a dagger's blade, wishing bitterly that she could wound him, mar him as he'd scarred her. If she'd actually had a knife in her hand, she might have plunged it into his hard male body that so effortlessly besieged hers.

In the taut silence following her hysterical explosion, everything gave the impression of being suspended, even the beating of her heart.

Devon's studied pause seemed designed to throw her off balance. Through the deep chasm forming between them, she became aware that he could easily overpower her, overwhelm her senses and her body if he so wished.

"Do I frighten you that much?" he asked perceptively, a cold, cruel smile twisting his lips. Not really a smile at all, but a mockery. A blasphemy.

Courage!

Rachel hardened her heart, determined to break the strange pact they had entered into, thinking of the ugly, degrading things he'd subjected her to.

Cheeks reddening, her face burned. His mysterious, impenetrable eyes seemed to enjoy her inner struggle. The bite of steel in his tone might have killed her had it been a corporeal object. Her heart pounded wildly in her chest. Could he hear how terrified she was of him? If he came off that bed, she was sure she'd faint dead away. She simply wasn't sure she could resist his touch a third time.

Fight him, she warned herself. Fight him or he would defeat her, take her and do with her whatever he wanted. *That's what he's trying to do. Control me. Own me.*

"I don't want to hear any more. I just want to leave this evil place." She hardly recognized the brittle, hard voice as her own.

Snatching up her fallen dress, she clutched it to her body, knowing she must get away or fall prey to his desires. She had to escape, cursing him for the demon who was trying to drag her in, take her will, her very soul.

Half naked, Rachel fled the room, heading blindly down a hall, descending a long curving flight of stairs. Where she thought she was going, what was going to happen to her now, she didn't know.

27

His tall form cloaked in shadows, Devon hovered outside Rachel's apartment. No car was parked nearby, for he had not needed such a primitive conveyance, instead choosing to take the form of the invisible winds. By learning to communicate with nature, the Kynn easily manipulated the elements, traveling as a bird at wing, moving upon the air's currents as a kite.

Since Rachel had left him, he'd been in a state of agitation. Shuddering, he brought back the sinister thoughts that had troubled him since he'd opened up to her—only to have her reject him and his kind. He had believed in her acceptance so much that her anger and shock had surprised him.

He silently cursed himself. *I should have taken it slower, given her more time, explained more clearly.*

Instead, he'd tried to rush her into the collective, and in doing so he'd lost her.

Eyes burning from too little sleep, he cast another baleful glance up at her closed windows, the blinds firmly drawn shut against the outside world.

Returning home, Rachel had locked herself inside. In her

absence, he'd been trapped in some of the bleakest hours of his life since Ariel had been taken from him by the Amhais.

And now I've lost Rachel.

A colorless haze closed in around his mind. No satisfaction or joy in his heart, no sense of being alive, a being who walked the centuries as easily as most humans walked through mere days. Without a true mate, the centuries were too long, hardly worth existing through. An endless, loveless void stretching ahead.

The worst part was he'd lost her without ever really possessing her. He'd hoped she might be falling in love with him, but she'd certainly revealed otherwise. He had looked into her soul and believed she was destined to be his bloodmate, but apparently he'd made a grievous mistake.

Rachel wanted nothing to do with him.

Despair washed over him. Even now, the fact that Rachel was so close and he could not go to her frustrated him to no end. He'd even considered erasing her memories of the entire happening, easing the event out of her mind as he had the night he'd first taken her completely as his own.

But he wanted her to remember, wanted her to think about what had happened between them. Perhaps in time she would come to see the event in a different light. If not, then he would have to accept that he'd let her slip through his fingers through his own clumsy machinations.

He looked toward her windows, so firmly shut. She wouldn't even let the cat out. "I won't accept losing you, Rachel," he murmured softly. "If ever you should want me, I will be there, be it a day or a century."

Even now he felt the eternal tug of her soul on his, the hungers inside her she'd never been able to comprehend. She was angry, frustrated with the way her life had turned out. She tried to come to terms with it, tried to pretend what she felt was what every unhappy soul in this world felt.

Rachel was wrong. What she was searching for went past everyday struggles, past humanity itself. She had a hunger for more than what day-to-day living offered its humans, as he once had before his own crossing.

Devon drew a deep breath, but it failed to make him feel any stronger or better. He was tempted to cross the street, knock on her door, and beg her to give him another chance. A little voice in his head warned him this would be the wrong thing to do. He'd already risked far more than he should have by revealing his world to her—and risked even more since he'd let her walk away with her memories intact.

A lightening in the night's gloom turned Devon's bleary gaze toward the sky.

In the east, dawn peered over the edge of the earth. In another half hour the day would spread its cloak of illumination over the land, sending his kind back into the shelter of shadows in which they had to live during the daytime hours.

Devon couldn't be caught out in bright sunlight for long. Prolonged exposure could be deadly. Bathed in the sun's beams the glare was so bright, so intense, that the blood in his veins would begin to smolder, ignite as the illumination invaded every pore, crawling under his skin, burning him up like old paper in hungry flames.

Shaking his head, despondent that the night must inevitably end, Devon nevertheless knew his secret vigil must come to its completion. Tonight would not be the last time he came, though. If need be, he would come night after night, waiting, watching. Eventually, Rachel would have to come to him. For now, she'd put up an emotional barrier between them. Until it came down, he wouldn't be able to make his way into her heart.

He sighed. "If it ever comes down."

He didn't know why he should feel this way about Rachel. Only that he did. What he'd experienced making love to her had seemed so completely different from the experiences he'd had with other women.

Rachel's kisses, the way she touched him, the places she'd touched him . . . All seemed to be part of the dance their bodies knew perfectly.

Devon drew a deep breath. "I cannot make you love me, Rachel," he mumbled, his heart constricted by the pain of his loss. "But you will never forget me."

With those words, he vanished into the remnants of the diminishing darkness.

28

Rachel called in sick for a week before finally summoning up the courage to quit her job. Though she was tempted to do it over the phone, she realized skittering off like a scared puppy would do her self-respect no good. She had to go in person.

She most definitely didn't want to see Devon, so she went at a time when he usually was not present.

Driving to the nightclub, she was a little saddened that today would be the last time she'd ever lay eyes on the place. She'd really enjoyed her job, liked the people she worked with. Too bad she'd sabotaged it by letting herself get involved with Devon. She should have stuck to her rule. Don't fuck the boss. Especially if he's crazy.

She parked and got out. "I learned my lesson the hard way."

She made her way to Rosalie Dayton's office. In a few minutes she'd walk away from the best-paying job she'd ever had. She'd thought about trying to stay at Mystique, continue as if nothing had happened between her and Devon.

That would not only be uncomfortable, it would be impossible.

Right now, all she wanted to do was forget the whole damn affair. Devon wasn't entirely to blame. She'd walked right into it. Eyes wide open. He was attractive, rich, and certainly a good lover. But she doubted she could handle his peculiar lifestyle long. Sooner or later, he was going to go over the edge, and someone would be left dead. A fetish like his was dangerous.

For a few days, Rachel had considered going to the police. But she'd lost her nerve. What exactly would she tell them? What charges could they press? To an extent, she'd been a willing, consenting adult. Though a bit ashamed, she had to be honest and admit she'd enjoyed the experience.

She'd even found the idea of joining Devon an enticing one.

But one had to be sane and sensible. And she was trying to be just that. She supposed she'd feel a lot saner if the memories and longing to be with him again didn't sting at her heart like a swarm of giant bumblebees.

Rosalie pounced the moment Rachel hit the door. "About time you got back on your feet. Feeling better, I hope."

Rachel smiled wanly. "I am, thanks," she lied. "But I'm not here to work." She handed Rosalie her carefully worded letter.

A puzzled expression crossed Rosalie's face. "What's this?"

Rachel cleared her throat. "Uh, it's my resignation. I'm leaving Mystique."

The old lady paled. "When?"

Rachel swallowed hard. "Immediately."

Brow wrinkling, Rosalie took off her glasses, toying with them. "Care to say why?"

She shook her head, mouth drawing tight. "No." How could she calmly say that not only had she had slept with her boss, she'd also slept with his coterie of groupies, all of whom had sucked the blood right out of her body?

In the broad light of day, the idea of vampires—or Kynn, as Devon referred to them—was damn near impossible to accept as true fact. Had she not the scars to prove it, she would've hardly believed it. She wasn't really sure she did. The role-playing explanation seemed more viable, especially in a society where outlandish permissiveness was the new rule.

Still . . .

How to explain she'd had no memory of having sex with Devon until he'd "allowed" her to remember the event? What about the small scar on her neck? He'd taken her blood only the night before. She'd never had a scar there. Certainly she would have recalled it. One usually didn't wound one's neck and not remember it. How had she healed so fast? The cuts she'd sustained from the others had not scabbed over nearly that fast. If she went so far as to believe his words—

No, uh-uh. She just wasn't ready to bend her mind around the concept that supernatural beings walked among humans, much less that she bore some kind of sacred sign on her thigh marking her as Devon's woman. In fantasy novels such creatures had their place. But this was real life. Things were damn hard enough without having people who fancied themselves to be vampires preying on you.

And if they are, heaven help us all. Mankind hasn't got a chance.

Rosalie shrugged. The look on her face said she wasn't surprised. "Well, it's certainly not my place to pry," she finally allowed. "I will say that it's a shame you're leaving after only a few days. I thought you showed real promise for the position."

Rachel hurried to explain, feeling more than a little guilty that she was letting Rosalie down. Devon sat up in his offices high above the crowds, but Rosalie Dayton did the hands-on dirty work. "It has nothing to do with the work. I'm having a personal problem. Unfortunately, I find it would affect my ability to do my job in a capable manner."

Rosalie fiddled with her glasses. "Well, Rachel, I am certainly sorry to hear that. But I am not blind, you know. Whatever happened between you and Devon is not my concern. I am only sorry what you two engaged in so obviously ruined this job for you. If you feel you have to leave, I understand."

Relief filled Rachel. "Thank you."

Rosalie raised an iron brow and gave her a meaningful glance. "I wasn't always an old lady, you know. I know that certain, ah, attractions can turn your life upside down and make you unhappy in the process. I can see by the look on your face that you're miserable. No reason to try to stay on this job if you are."

"I am," Rachel said gratefully. "More than you know."

"You would be surprised what I do know," Rosalie commented dryly.

Had Devon told her anything?

Or did Rosalie already know about his other pursuits?

"I don't think you should clue me in," Rachel said slowly. "I just want to make a clean break."

A brief nod. "Certainly."

Rachel had one final request. "If you could write me a letter of reference, that would be great." She hurried to say, "Though I wouldn't expect you to, since I am leaving without any notice."

She doubted she could expect Devon to give her a good reference. *Oh, I'm quitting because you sucked my blood. Could I please have a letter of recommendation?*

The idea of asking made her want to giggle insanely.

Rachel kept her face straight, forcing the bizarre images that came to mind out of her head. How to explain them to her next employer? Show him the scars? Yeah right.

Rosalie nodded. "I will be glad to. Would you like it now, or shall I mail it?"

"Mail it, please," Rachel answered. "Also my final paycheck, if you don't mind. I don't expect it will be much since I've worked so little."

Rosalie did some quick figuring. "It will be, ah, adequate."

Rachel couldn't suppress her sigh. *Adequate, as in I have to go looking for a new job. Soon.*

"Thank you," she said. "I appreciate that."

"No problem," Rosalie said.

A day later, a large manila envelope arrived.

Tearing it open, Rachel pulled out the letter inside. She quickly skimmed the page. Her reference letter was prudently worded praise, considering the short amount of time she'd worked there.

Well, it's a start. Now I no longer have to have failed book-store owner at the top of my resume.

There was another envelope inside. Rachel ripped it open: her much-needed paycheck.

Looking at it, her hands started shaking. She could hardly believe her eyes.

She blinked. Had she read the damn thing correctly? Surely it couldn't be that much?

She mouthed the numbers again, counting the zeros. "One hundred and fifty thousand dollars." More than twice a year's salary. The note inside was in Devon's hand. Final paycheck, it said simply, with bonuses.

Wow. Some bonus.

Rachel sat, holding the check. She had no doubt as to what it was. A payoff. Devon was paying her off to shut her up, keep her quiet about what had happened. Only now did it occur to her she might have gotten herself an attorney and sued him for pain and suffering and whatever else the shyster might want to tack on. If done right, it could have been a lawsuit of million-dollar proportions.

She fingered the check. "This is just covering your ass, Mister Carnavorn," she mused. "No matter what you think you are, if you dabble in kink, you're going to have to pay."

One hundred and fifty thousand dollars. Was it enough for her to keep her mouth shut?

Rachel looked at it again. She could pay off her debts from the bookstore and live comfortably for a couple of years without having to worry about working if she were careful with her money.

Hmm. Yep. Enough.

Okay. So she was easy as well as cheap.

Everyone had their price, especially when they had the check in their hand, versus a costly lawsuit she might not win anyway.

Cut your losses, she counseled herself. Take the money and run. With this bit of security in her checking account, she could take her sweet time to find the job that suited her. Maybe even go back to college. Not a bad idea.

A new start.

That's exactly what she needed.

Feeling as though she'd won the lottery, and more than a little relieved that her financial problems were off her back, Rachel glanced at the clock. After three. Too late to deposit her windfall. No matter. First thing tomorrow morning she was going to cash it, putting half in savings, half in her checking account. She had no doubt as to its veracity.

Devon Carnavorn would not dare bounce a check on her.

Carefully tucking the check under the mat on the coffee table, Rachel finished going through the day's mail. Bills, of course. Some fliers for the local pizza place. More junk mail. Then the daily paper. No need to go straight to the classifieds today. She would actually have the luxury of beginning at the front page.

She skimmed over the headlines. The city council was voting on some tax ordinance. Boring. Second story. Woman shot in robbery. Normally, she would have skimmed that, too, but a name caught her eye. The Shop-N-Sack on Fifth Street. Suddenly the words seemed to leap out at her in giant, puzzlelike pieces.

Ginny Smithers, 62, shot in robbery . . . Suspect still at large . . . Victim in critical condition, rushed to Saint Peter's Medical Center . . .

That was as far as Rachel got. She could read no farther. Tears blurred her vision, stinging her cheeks. Hands going cold, her breath caught in her throat. The paper dropped from her limp fingers, pages scattering at her feet.

"Oh my God!" she mumbled through numb lips. "Not Ginny. Oh Jesus, no!"

Without further thought, Rachel snatched up her purse and keys. She didn't even bother locking the door behind her when she ran outside. "Oh Jesus, I knew it was too dangerous for an old lady to be working in a place like that."

Driving straight through several red lights, Rachel sped to the hospital, navigating through the afternoon traffic like a madwoman. It took twenty minutes to reach the hospital, another ten to circle the parking lot looking for a space in the crowded lot. When she could find no place nearby, she abandoned her car at the curb in a no parking zone.

Piss on it, she'd take the goddamned ticket.

Heels clattering on the concrete, Rachel ran into the front lobby. Hurrying to the visitor's desk, she pounded her hands on the counter to get the attention of the woman sitting behind the glass partition.

"Where's the ICU? Please, I need to be there now!"

Seeing her panic, the woman answered. "Take the elevator to the fourth floor, turn left."

Without waiting to hear any more, Rachel dashed to the elevator, elbowing past the crowd of people to push the button.

"Come on, hurry up!" she cursed under her breath, ignoring the stares of curious people.

Obviously a few understood, for they let her enter first and choose the floor she needed.

"Sorry," Rachel said, punching the fourth-floor button. "I have to get there fast."

Fourth floor, left, she repeated in her mind.

There, she practically ran over the staff trying to reach the nurses' station. "Ginny Smithers," she said to the nurses there. "Where is she?"

One of the nurses caught her arm. "Calm down, please."

Rachel shook off her hand. "I'm here to see Ginny Smithers. Please. How is she?"

A second nurse, whose name tag read "Terry," consulted her records. "I'm sorry. Only immediate family is allowed to see Ms. Smithers."

Rachel lied without thought or hesitation. "I'm her niece." She knew Ginny well enough to pass for family. Anything they needed her to answer, she could. She knew which blood pressure medicines Ginny took, what she ate to control her borderline diabetes. "Please, I have to see her. How is she?"

Satisfied by her intrusion, Terry's face softened. "I'm sorry, but she's in critical condition."

"Can I see her?"

Lips tightly pressing together, Terry hesitated. "Maybe you shouldn't. It's not hopeful."

Rachel drew a steadying breath. "I don't care. Please, I want to be with her. I can't let her be alone."

The first nurse nodded. "Go ahead."

Rachel followed Terry to a nearby room. The odors of the hospital burned into her nostrils. Antiseptics, soiled bedding, and, worst of all, the pervading smell of sick bodies. Of disease. Of death.

Ginny had room number six, behind a thick wall of glass. The privacy curtains had been pulled aside so that the nurses could monitor her every second.

Stepping up to the glass, Rachel peered inside.

Ginny lay on a hospital bed, her head swathed in bandages. Dressed in a hospital gown, all sorts of monitors were attached to her body, which now seemed so small and shriveled. Rachel dimly recalled the newspaper that said she'd been beaten, then shot in the head.

All for what? Fifty crummy bucks, which is all the store kept after hours. Who the hell was sadistic enough to attack an old woman? Surely Ginny didn't put up a fight. It wasn't in her nature. Let them walk off with the cash. It was replaceable. A human life was not.

Rachel gulped, swallowing back the bitter bile that rose to the back of her throat. "Can I go inside?"

Terry nodded. "Stay here." A moment later, she returned with a hospital gown and mask. "Put these on." She helped Rachel put them on. When she was dressed, the nurse opened the door to the room. "You can stay for twenty minutes."

"Thank you."

At the bed, Rachel looked down at her friend.

"Oh Ginny," she whispered. "I'm so sorry. I should have been here sooner."

Wiping away her tears, she reached out and took Ginny's small, cold hand in her own. Absolutely unresponsive, Ginny's body was alive only because of the machines that kept her breathing, her heart pumping. No other sound in the room save for the soft hissing of the machines. With all the monitors and blinking red lights hovering around the bed, it was like vultures. Waiting. Counting the seconds until Ginny's poor body gave up the ghost and her soul moved on.

Rachel didn't have to be a medical expert to know it was hopeless. A bullet lodged in one's head didn't usually come with a very hopeful prognosis. Even if Ginny were to survive, which seemed unlikely, she'd probably be severely disabled—a brain-damaged vegetable.

She squeezed Ginny's hand.

I wouldn't want her to live if that's the case. I wouldn't want to live myself. I'd hope someone would have the nerve to pull the plug.

Standing beside her friend, Rachel unexpectedly found herself face to face with the specter she had not closely encountered through her short life.

Death.

At her age, death was a thing people only fleetingly considered. After all, she was young, healthy. Things like car accidents, a broken leg, disease, crime—well, those things were supposed to happen to strangers. Not people you knew.

Struck full force in the face with the Reaper's scythe for the first time, she selfishly began to take a long hard look at her own mortality.

What is there to life?

Standing beside Ginny's unconscious form, hostility welled in Rachel's heart and the cynic in her came out full force, tramping through her mind like an angry bull. You're born into this shitty world to parents you can't choose. Then what? Hell, you got kicked around as a child, then thrust into a nasty world when you turned eighteen.

Not having oodles of money to fall back on, the need to work inevitably came next. Not just for her. Millions of people. Toil, toil, boil and bubble. The facing of the public hoards, pasting a false smile on your face every day, working long hours to make ends meet. Marriage? Love? Did it even really exist? Usually it was a thing twisted by the fickle human heart. Sex? Physical attraction waned as your young, firm body dropped and drooped.

Life. It was all or nothing, a never-ending attack. Physically, mentally, spiritually, and emotionally, it wore you down to a nub. And nothing was all you got in the end, slipping through the cracks like sand through your fingers. Desperate people leading tiny little lives that would only end with a hole in the ground, a too-fancy box casketing a body that would decay into worm food.

Bitter and bleak, Rachel could see no way out of the dismal fate that would someday beckon her.

Faith. Hope. Praying that everything would turn out all right. At this moment she could summon neither into her heart, nor could she fall to her knees and pray to a God she didn't believe existed. What kind of deity would allow an old woman who'd never done anyone a day's harm to be shot down like a dog?

Rachel reached out and gently stroked Ginny's chin, the only part of her face visible through the swath of bandages around her head. "I wish there was something I could do for you."

The sound of an alarm jarred Rachel out of her inward reverie. Before she was able to comprehend what had happened, a barrage of nurses and doctors were pushing her out of the room, hustling her outside.

Through the glass partition, Rachel watched them work, her hands frantically pounding against the cold window, her words incoherent to her own ears. There were hurried shouts as hands flew over Ginny's poor, frail body. Though they worked for several long minutes, the time that passed seemed to be mere seconds. And then it was over. The lines on the monitors went flat, registering zero.

As simply as that, it was over.

Ginny had died.

Rachel knew because all activity halted, heads shaking, mouths turning down into frustrated frowns. One minute alive, the next dead. No fanfare, no bells and whistles, no announcement. Nothing but a soul departing a physical shell.

Ginny Smithers had departed as quietly as she'd come into the world—hopefully, at peace.

Rachel stopped one of the first doctors who exited. "What happened?"

He shook his head. "Cardiac arrest," he said simply. "Her heart stopped beating. I'm sorry. Nothing we could do." Giving her shoulder a squeeze, he hurried off. His job was done. No reason to hang around.

"Oh." Staring in his white-coated wake, her hands dropped limply to her sides.

One of the nurses hurried to her side. "Are you her family?"

Numbly, Rachel nodded.

The nurse shoved a clipboard into her hands. "Sign here, please. Will you be taking care of final arrangements?"

Another numb nod. "Yes," she murmured. "I'll take care of everything."

Rachel shakily signed the papers, not even recognizing that she held the pen.

Holy hell, weren't they even going to allow her a few minutes to mourn? Did they need the goddamned bed so badly that they'd hustle the body out before it was even cold? Even now, two aides rushed through with a wheeled gurney that would carry the sheet-covered body to the hospital morgue.

"I'm sorry for your loss." The nurse patted her arm. "As it was, we were only sustaining her life. She was brain dead when she arrived."

"She never had a chance, did she?"

"I'm afraid not. But we did what we could to make her comfortable."

"I'm sure you did everything you could," Rachel said weakly. What the hell else could she say? When the last word was written on the page of one's life, the ending would be the same for everyone: they died.

How and when didn't matter. No one was getting out of this world alive.

29

Three hours later, Rachel walked out of the hospital. Shoulders slumped in defeat, she located her car. As expected, there was a pink slip under her windshield, a ticket for parking in a no-parking zone.

She crumpled up the ticket, cursing under her breath. *There goes one hundred and fifty dollars.* Well, at least the vehicle hadn't been towed.

Sealing herself in the safety of four doors, she rested her forehead on the steering wheel. She'd just spent the last two hours talking to the supervisor of the nursing home in Florida where Ginny's sister, Regina, lived.

Not only did Regina not have the funds to cover the expenses of a funeral, she also didn't have any way to claim Ginny's belongings. They agreed Rachel would have to be the one to pack up Ginny's apartment, selling what she could and disposing of the rest.

Dimly, Rachel remembered that Ginny had mentioned having a life insurance policy. If so, that would certainly lift a burden off her only living sibling.

Unless Ginny had left a will with other instructions, Rachel had already decided on cremation, with a graveside service. Not because it was cheaper, but because it would be simpler. Ginny had never believed in large, elaborate funerals.

"Flowers are for the living," she'd often said. "It's stupid to cut them down to put on a grave. People should give them to you while you're alive, able to enjoy them."

Rachel had to agree.

Sighing, she lifted her head and glanced up into the sky. The day was just beginning to fade, night covering the earth in its cloak of soft indigo. How restful the dark seemed, so peaceful.

Would that no one ever had to grow old and die.

Rachel's heart grew bitter, dark, and hard. Instead we live in this urban jungle, plagued by crime, ugliness, and hate, by people who would execute an old woman.

"How I hate living here," she muttered. "If there were an escape, I would take it in an instant."

If only, indeed.

Digging her keys out of her purse, Rachel started the car and put it in gear. As she navigated her way out of the parking lot, it was in her mind to go to Ginny's apartment, start sorting through her belongings.

Just as she was about to come to the exit that would take her back into the city, she suddenly changed her mind. She made a quick, illegal U-turn in traffic, heading in an entirely different direction.

She knew whom she had to see.

And she knew why.

Pulling up to Mystique, Rachel drew in a deep breath. Was she really crazy enough to be considering what Devon had offered her? Was she that desperate that she would believe what he had offered her was real?

If so, then she'd have to believe that what he had told her was indeed fact: that vampires really did exist.

"You were meant for me, to become my bloodmate," she remembered him saying about the strange mark on her left thigh. "It is destiny's choice."

Destiny's choice is my innocence lost.

A giggle broke from her throat. "Why am I even thinking of this?" she demanded to herself. "It's stupid."

Rachel thought it because she was afraid. Afraid the Reaper would someday turn his scythe her way, afraid she would die, alone and unloved, a wrinkled old shell wasting away in a nursing home, or worse, a victim of someone else's insane wrath.

"I can give you a glimpse of eternity," he'd told her. "All you have to do is accept and believe."

Could she?

Forehead wrinkling, Rachel remembered how Devon had laid open her soul, pinpointing her unhappiness. Was it because he'd truly known it himself, felt the outsider, always standing too far away to become a part of the crowd? The loneliness, the feeling of never truly belonging brought a lump to her throat, a deep ache that threatened to break her fragile heart into pieces.

He's right, she thought. *I've never belonged here, among the rest of the people.*

For the first time, she realized she did love someone. Devon. From the moment she laid eyes on him, she'd known there was something different about him, something attracting her to him in a way no other man ever had. And, like her, he stood at the periphery of the human race, because he wasn't like them, either.

Getting out of her car, Rachel hurried into the nightclub, pushing past the crowd to get inside. Wednesday night was not the busiest of the week, but there was still a fair number of people.

Hurrying past the main bar and cutting across the dance

floor, Rachel waved a hand when one of the waitresses hurried up to her.

"Where's Devon?" she asked, breathless.

Tammy shrugged. "Haven't seen him." Seeing Rachel's drawn face, she hurried to ask, "Is something wrong?"

Rachel drew a sharp breath, the words almost tumbling from her lips. "Has he been here at all tonight?"

Tammy shook her head. "As I said, I haven't seen him, but you could ask Rosalie."

Rachel shook her head. "No. This is private, something I have to talk to him about."

"Have you tried his house?"

"No, but I will. Thanks."

Sighing, Rachel patted the girl on the arm and turned away. Eternity seemed to be slipping through her fingers.

30

Exhausted, Rachel parked her car in the secluded cul-de-sac where she and Devon had first made love.

After leaving the nightclub, she'd driven around for hours, debating whether she should seek him out at home. In the end, she decided not to. Her eyes were blurry and burned from the many tears she'd shed through the day. She couldn't go home and couldn't go to Ginny's little apartment.

Somehow, coming back to the park seemed right.

Killing the engine and lights, Rachel got out. The air around her was warm, fresh. A light breeze winnowed through the trees, gently caressing her cheeks, tugging at her clothes. Crickets chirruped and the late-night birds sang their mysterious song.

Tilting back her head, she was amazed by the vastness of the sky, its seemingly endless limit. *If I could fly*, she wondered, *how far could I go before coming to the end of the universe?*

Rachel folded her arms around her body. "I wish I were free, too." She shivered, chilled to the bone with grief.

Gentle hands settled on her shoulders, pulling her to a hard body. A familiar voice whispered in her ear. "I can give you that freedom."

"Devon?" She hadn't heard another car, hadn't heard footsteps approaching from behind, yet she felt the solidity of his body. It felt so good, so familiar. She didn't want to leave his embrace. Ever. "How did you find me?"

Devon nuzzled her neck, laughing lightly. "I told you I would come for you, beloved. I was only waiting for your call."

She stood, her body trembling, sure she'd collapse if not for his strong arms circling her. "You knew I was looking for you?"

"Yes." His accented voice was low and sexy. "With every fiber of my being, I felt your need of me, your seeking . . . . You're reaching, Rachel, searching for the thing that always eludes you. I can give you that and so much more. All you have to do is believe."

Breaking free of his hold, Rachel turned to him. She looked up into his face, shadowed, serious. "I want to believe," she choked, swallowing the lump in her throat. "I want out of this ugly, evil place."

Devon smiled and brushed his fingers through the curtain of dark bangs that fell across her eyes. "I didn't want to live without you, Rachel." He took her two hands tightly between his own. "You are my soul, the half I have been missing. If you cross, you will not regret it. We will never be apart again."

31

Devon's private chambers were decorated in black and white, marble and onyx, a haven lit only by firelight and swathed in shadows. It was a haunting place, its atmosphere welcoming only those who walked the night. Heavy drapes cut off the outside world, blocking all light, muffling sound. A thick haze of incense hung in the air, a mixture of sandalwood and musk, designed to relax and to enhance erotic sensation.

Rachel trembled. Her gaze searched out every nook and cranny, flicking over the many candles, the fire burning in the hearth. "It's beautiful," she whispered, "but eerie."

Devon drew her into his arms, chasing away her shivers. "Does it frighten you?"

She nodded, burying her face in his chest. "Yes."

He kissed the top of her head. "You have nothing to fear."

"How do I know this is true?"

Devon smiled gently. His heart took on fresh speed. "You must have faith. Believe in me." A wave of warmth filled him. He couldn't believe this moment had actually arrived, the moment when Rachel would truly become more than his lover. She would become his mate, his she-shaey.

Swallowing hard, Rachel broke away from him. Crossing to the window, she drew aside the curtains, peering out into the darkness. "I'll never walk in sunlight again, will I?" Her tone was curiously distant. Every muscle in her body screamed from stress. She held herself erect, but just barely.

He walked up behind her, hands settling on her shoulders. She trembled under his touch. A tremble he hoped to soothe away. "No. Though we can move in the day, direct exposure can be deadly to our kind."

She sighed, letting the curtain drop. "Guess I won't miss it too badly. I never was a sun worshipper anyway."

Devon drew a deep breath. Might as well be honest with her.

"We have our weaknesses," he explained. "But we have many strengths as well. While others around you will grow old and die, you shall pass through the ages untouched, your youth intact. And no longer will you be an earthbound spirit. The elements are ours to command, the wind to carry us to the four corners of the Earth. We are reborn through those who once traveled the heavens at will."

More tears blurred her blue eyes. She didn't quite believe. Not yet. "It sounds unbelievable."

Devon spread his hands wide. His head started to pound. He felt queasy, sick to his stomach. If Rachel changed her mind, he wouldn't press her. The decision had to be her own. Absolutely and without regret or remorse.

"I cannot make you believe it. You must accept by faith alone."

She gave him a square look that said she questioned the idea of faith. "Did you believe?"

"I was ready to accept when Ariel came into my life. In my mind Earth had become tiresome and tedious, and Heaven did not meet expectations."

"Ariel." Rachel paced away, but had taken no more than a

few steps when she whirled around to face him. "Your sire. You told me about her."

He nodded. "Yes."

Curiosity now. The wheels in her mind were clearly turning. "And it really happened so long ago?"

Another nod. "Yes. I'm not lying when I tell you I am almost a hundred and fifty years old."

"Where is she now, your sire?"

A muscle in Devon's jaw tightened. Black anger rumbled. "She's dead." Before Rachel could voice another question, he hurried on, wanting to get the story finished. "You will find there are some who know of our kind and do not accept our right to exist on this Earth. They have made it their holy mission to destroy us. Ariel was taken from me, destroyed by those murderers like a rabid animal. We were not together long."

His words trailed off into silence.

Ariel had died so very long ago, yet the wounds etched on his heart sometimes felt as if they were inflicted only the day before. He'd often felt nothing would assuage that ache. Now he held the hope in his heart and soul that he was wrong.

The woman he'd searched for blindly through so many years stood in front of him now. Flesh, blood, and bone.

And she was willing to become his.

"I'm sorry. I shouldn't have asked." Rachel shivered, wrapping her arms around her body. "If you hadn't found me tonight, I don't know what I would have done. I can't take it anymore. I've had enough of this life." A sob broke from her throat.

Devon stroked her cheek. "Your old life is about to end. A new one will begin for you."

Blinking through fresh tears, she looked up at him. "You promise?"

Devon gazed into her deep blue eyes. The irises were fragmented with silver flecks, so reminiscent of an ocean lit by moonlight, drawing him into their depths. He felt the ache inside her, knew she silently wept for a world she could not understand because she didn't truly belong in it.

"I do."

To reassure her, he tipped back her head, giving her a soft, sweet kiss. She let out a faint gasp of surprise and pleasure when his lips trailed down her throat, his tongue rasping against the small scar on her neck. He felt the quick beating of her heart, heard the harshness of her breath. Beneath her desire, she was afraid of him, of her decision.

Devon unbuttoned the front of her blouse, his hands moving inside her clothing to caress her breasts.

Rachel pressed herself into his hands, offering the sacrifice of her body. Nearly melting when her eyes flashed up at him, the passion he beheld in her features summoned the familiar heat from low in his groin.

Not now, he warned himself. First she would cross, then he would take her. He needed to focus his energies on bringing Rachel across.

Should he lose concentration, she would be lost.

Sliding her blouse off her shoulders, Devon unzipped her skirt, helping her step out of it. Bra and panties followed, until she stood naked and vulnerable before him.

His gaze caressed every inch. "You're so beautiful."

Touching one of the scars on her abdomen, she blushed. "Even with the marks of the other feedings all over me?"

His palms curved around her hips. "You're more beautiful because you endured them so magnificently."

Picking her up, Devon carried Rachel to bed, laying her gently in the center of its softness. Settling her comfortably, he reached for a soft leather cuff attached to one of the bedposts. He encircled her left wrist with it, drawing the buckle tight.

Rachel tugged at the cuff. "What are you doing?" she asked,

tone taut. She made no attempt to fight him as he shackled her right wrist. The tightness of her jaw and firm set of her mouth betrayed her worry.

Devon stretched out beside her, propping himself up on an elbow, stroking her cheek. Under his touch, she trembled slightly. "So that you will not injure yourself when you cross."

Rachel drew a painful breath. "What's going to happen?" He could tell she was frightened even saying the words, yet she had thus far managed to remain remarkably calm.

Here he had to lie. "It will be very pleasurable for you."

Rachel relaxed a little. She gave a wan smile. "That doesn't sound too terribly bad. I can handle pleasure."

Devon's hand moved to the soft curve of her breast, fingers teasing a nipple until it grew erect under his touch. "First, I must bring you to the height of orgasm. When your energies are at their strongest, I will drink of you, take your essences into myself."

Rachel swallowed hard. "And I drink of you?"

Fighting to keep his voice steady, Devon drew a deep breath. It'd been a long time since he'd sired a new member into the collective. Some Kynn could not manage the process correctly. Make one mistake and the soul would slip away like smoke.

"Yes. When you have taken my breath and my blood, your crossing will be completed."

Rachel allowed a tiny smile. "That doesn't sound too terrible."

Devon almost had to bite his tongue to keep from screaming out that he was deceiving her, that the crossing would be painful, but well worth the experience. What he dared not tell her was that he had to take her life, her breath away, kill her so that he could resurrect her.

"Do you believe what I say is true?"

She blinked, excited and frightened, intrigued but uncertain of what lay ahead. "Yes."

"Good."

To relax her, Devon stroked her breast.

Rachel gasped. "You always touch me just right."

"Your pleasure is all mine."

Devon closed his mouth over one taut peak. Sucking, licking, teasing, he took the nipple between his teeth, then pulled it deeper into his mouth.

Rachel whimpered softly in the back of her throat. "That feels so good."

Devon nibbled at the softness of her neck, then moved to her earlobe. "It's supposed to." He flicked his tongue behind her ear, beginning a delicious tease.

Rachel moaned and lifted her hips, parting her thighs. "Touch me, please." The gleam of anticipation in her eyes was unmistakable.

"Patience."

Devon kissed and nibbled down her rib cage, over her abdomen. Rachel sucked in her breath in anticipation. He maneuvered lower. He felt the fine tremors underneath her skin. He dropped soft kisses across her belly, going lower to the soft curls covering her damp sex.

With a low groan Rachel parted her thighs. She tried to push her body against his. The cuffs held her firmly in place.

As a reward, Devon kissed the insides of her thighs. Rachel shivered. Her breath caught in her throat when he ran his finger between her spread legs. Her clit quivered against the tips of his fingers.

"Feel good?"

"Oh *yes*!"

Devon slipped one finger between the soft petals of her labia. More slippery warmth. Using thumb and forefinger, he spread her apart. His mouth claimed her clit.

Rachel's eyes shot open. "Oh my!"

She strained against the bonds holding her arms, hands flexing open and closed as pleasure washed over her body. When she couldn't pull herself loose, she whimpered and squirmed, trying to press her hips against his face.

Devon sucked even harder, making the little knob swell and pulse.

Rachel raised her hips off the bed, trying to meet his mouth. She'd reached her limits of self-control. Her body stiffened when her orgasm ripped through her, her exposed breasts heaving as she gasped for air. "I need you inside me. Please." She gasped between moans.

Licking her cream from his lips, Devon pulled away. "Not yet."

He rose to his knees, straddling Rachel's body. His knee pressed against her sex, giving her a firm pressure to rub against. Her juices left a wet spot on his trousers, the scent of her musky sex intermingling with the burning incense.

Slipping his hand under a pillow, he withdrew his small switchblade.

Rachel's eyes widened when the blade flicked out, making a soft swishing sound.

Catching her by the chin, Devon pressed the heel of his hand against her jaw to expose her neck. "I'm sorry."

Rachel had no time to scream.

In a single motion, Devon drew the blade across the soft flesh of her neck, making a small cut. Warm blood trickled over her pale white skin. He pressed his lips to the cut, drinking deeply.

Crimson life filled his mouth with warmth.

When he'd taken enough of her blood, Devon lifted his head. Her blood stained his mouth.

No time for hesitation.

Devon's mouth captured hers, allowing her to taste the blood, her blood, fusing with her female juices.

Rachel accepted his kiss greedily, sucking at his tongue, trying to take every last drop from him.

Heaven lasted only a moment.

Hell must claim its price.

Devon drew away. Reclaiming his blade, he made a quick, deep cut in his palm. "Now you must cross."

Arm trembling, Devon tipped his hand over Rachel's mouth. His blood dripped past her lips.

She drank.

Closing his hand, Devon halted the flow of his blood. When he reopened his hand, no scar marked his flesh.

Rachel had no more swallowed than her body convulsed, her head jerking sharply to one side. "Oh my god!" A mixture of fear and betrayal filled her eyes, her arms going rigid as she fought to escape the bonds holding her captive. Hands flexing open and closed, she tugged against the bonds, droplets of cold perspiration breaking out on her skin.

Guilt sliced deeply. Nothing he could do as Rachel died. He watched her closely, knowing well her agony. He'd once experienced it, too.

A scream burbled over her lips, loud and long, the agonized wail of a damned soul. "What's happening to me! It's cold . . . Oh God, so cold . . . Eating me up inside!"

Devon stroked her forehead, trying to calm her. "I am sorry." In introducing his blood to her body, he had, in essence, put a deadly virus into her system. Like acid through her veins, his blood ate through her, killing her blood cells and replacing them with an alien, inhuman mutation.

Rachel's system was beginning the metamorphoses that would take her from mortal to immortal.

Minutes passed with agonizing slowness.

Devon watched her flesh grow paler, whiter, the fall of her chest slowing as her heart stopped beating. This was the hardest part of the crossing: the self-induced asphyxiation of her body killing itself. Deprived of air, the chemistry of the blood temporarily changed. When the brain was robbed of oxygen, the victim experienced a high, euphoria, dizziness, and lowered inhibition before losing consciousness.

Rachel writhed only a few minutes more. Then she lay unmoving, dead to this world. Her last expression was one of confusion, as if she was puzzled by his deceit.

Devon let go of the breath he'd been holding.

"I always hated that part."

32

Freeing Rachel's wrists, Devon drew her limp body into his arms, lifting her into a sitting position. Brushing her damp bangs off her forehead, he tilted back her head and pressed his mouth to hers, sharing his breath with her, urging her to breathe again.

When Rachel didn't immediately respond, he feared she hadn't crossed over intact.

Devon gave her cheek a light slap, trying to penetrate her stupor. "Come on, damn it. Don't go on me now."

Rachel's eyelids fluttered. Her body heaved, taking in gulp after gulp of precious air. A low moan rasped in her throat. Her lips began to move, a weak whisper escaping her. "Devon?"

Relief filled him. "You have crossed over, beloved. It is done." He unbuttoned his shirt. Baring his chest, he made a cut just above his right nipple, then guided her lips to it. He felt her tense.

She tried to pull away, but was too weak to resist. "No . . . It hurts too bad."

Devon pressed her lips to his flesh again, urging her to drink. "It will bring no pain now. You need your strength."

Rachel hesitated, then gave in to her need, lapping at his blood, her tongue soft and warm against his skin.

Devon's fingers caressed the nape of her neck as she drank. He closed his eyes, feeling a supreme sense of peace.

When Rachel pulled away, her skin had assumed a normal, pink hue. Her eyes were bright, seeing the world around her with a new clarity.

Cradling her face between his hands, he asked, "How do you feel?"

Without a word, she touched her fingers to her lips. Drawing her hand away, she looked at the blood staining the tips. Then her hand returned to the cut he'd made in his skin. Already his blood was slowing, the wound healing. Her gaze drifted lower. A small gasp of surprise escaped her lips. A slow smile curved one corner of her mouth.

"You have a mark," she murmured. "Like mine."

He nodded. "Yes. A mark I have worn since the day of my birth."

Rachel caressed, tracing. "It's the same, but different."

Devon lifted his hand, showing her the signet ring he wore. "If you join my mark and yours, they come together to form this sign. It is a symbol of balance, of completion."

Astonishment colored her features. "Why didn't you tell me this before?"

"I didn't want you to feel manipulated," Devon said softly. "But maybe if I had told you earlier, you would have understood better. Not all Kynn wear the mark, only those chosen for a special purpose for our people."

"How?" she started to ask. "What purpose?"

Devon shook his head. "How can one question the stars in the sky or the rising of the sun that brings a new day? Some would call it the hand of God himself, though I cannot say for certain. I only know that once in a great while, we meet our true bloodmate."

A light blush crept into her cheeks, flushing and heating her skin. "Am I that to you?"

"Yes, beloved. And more."

Devon left the bed only long enough to undress. His clothes joined hers on the floor.

Naked as she, Devon retuned to bed.

Rachel greeted him with open arms. She snuggled into his embrace. "Welcome back."

Devon brushed his fingers along the curve of her breast, laying the flat of his hand on her belly. His cock was a thing alive, straining and eager to be surrounded by those luscious lips of hers.

Rachel smiled up at him, touching his face. Her eyes were shining, wide with anticipation. The nervous energy of their last encounters was gone, replaced with a comfortable sense of familiarity. Mated, they could now make love without one weakening the other.

Soon, he would have to share her with others, teach her how to sustain her new life, draw into her body the energies of mortals.

No doubt she would be an eager student.

For the present Rachel was his. And his alone.

Devon swept his hands over her lithe, naked body. Her nipples jutted. He closed his mouth over the nearest tip.

Rachel squirmed with delight. "You always get to go first."

Flicking the tender nub with his tongue, Devon moved his hand lower, parting her legs. "Isn't that the right of a husband, to enjoy his wife's body any way he wants?"

Her eyes widened. Incredulous, she stared up at him? "Husband?"

Devon laughed with delight. "What's the matter? I'm not good enough for you?"

Rachel's eyes closed briefly. She swallowed hard, fighting

myriad emotions. Too much, too soon. "This is almost unbelievable."

Devon raised one hand, gently tracing her chin, the curve of her neck. "Considering that you've just stepped into a whole new level of existence, I think a marriage proposal would be the easiest part to understand. I *want* to marry you." He paused. "That is, if you will have me." Watching her closely, he waited.

And hoped.

Rachel's eyes burst open, shining brilliant blue. She bestowed a smile glowing with joy. "Oh yes, I'll marry you."

Devon eased her toward his erection. His cock throbbed and strained. "I hope you don't mind the honeymoon coming first. I don't think I can wait another minute."

Rachel grinned. "Why wait any longer then?"

Indeed.

Blinded with heat, Devon kissed her. His mouth closed over hers, swallowing down her taste with hungry gulps. Her tongue swept in, sparking sensations that set his nerves to tingling. They feasted on each other's lips, drawing out their yearning into a long, suckling kiss.

Curling a fist into her hair, Devon barely leashed the maddening impulse to simply impale her with one deep thrust. He gently slid his erection inside her, savoring the way her tight sex welcomed his entry.

Rachel arched under him. "Damn, you're so big." Her smile deepened. "I can feel every inch of you."

"You're so lovely." Wanton fierceness made his voice tremble. "I've wanted you since the day I saw you." His hips drove harder.

Long fingernails grazed his back, his ass. Just the way he knew they would. "I'm yours, forever and always."

Devon's hips jerked. "Think you can stand me for another century or two?"

Rachel's eyes widened. "Will I really live to see centuries pass?"

He lowered his head until his lips were just inches from hers. Her gaze dewed with emotion. "That, and many more."

Myriad expressions took form across Rachel's face. Eyes clouded with incredible pleasure, she smiled up at him. "As long as we're together." Inner muscles clasped at his cock, drawing him deeper.

Thighs trembling, Devon's hips jerked. "Together forever." Feeling a surge building in his loins, his tempo increased.

Rachel responded to his thrusts with an instinctive rhythm. Her head passed back on the pillow. Her hips collided with his, taking every inch he had to offer and begging for more. Her nails scraped long red marks onto his flesh.

Devon chuckled softly and captured Rachel's hands above her head. "I knew my kitten had claws." Intending to give her a pounding and then some, he held her wrists secure.

Cheeks flushing, Rachel writhed under his weight.

Allowing no mercy, Devon thrust harder, going as deep as the limitation of their bodies would allow. His thighs rasped against hers, the sweat of lust slicking his skin. Her scent rolled into his nostrils, heady and thick with lust. The tension coiling inside his core grew. A tightening of his balls warned him that he would not be able to hold back much longer.

Without warning, a dimensional shift seemed to take place. A sense of bonding, of unique sharing fused them together. Their minds joined on some intangible level of existence, going past the physical and entering the astral. Endless skies, vast space engulfed them. Far in the distance a great glowing ball radiated energy.

The core of creation.

An aching sense of the familiar washed through Devon's senses. He felt no fear.

Devon closed his eyes, but perceived that he could see

Rachel through the brilliant colors enveloping her body. To his eyes she looked soft and transparent, glowing with tenderness. The energy caressing her seemed to flutter, pulse, and vibrate, touching his senses the way a warm summer breeze might caress the skin.

The glow of the core invaded his consciousness.

Intense. Aware.

Dual excitement grew and expanded. The energy surrounding them smoldered.

Their bodies parted, then rejoined, blending into a single unit. Touching. Surging. Responding. The bed beneath them trembled. Then a crimson spark infused the glowing core's golden lining.

Rachel went suddenly rigid. Shuddering with climax, a cry of pure primal pleasure rolled over her lips. Energy flowed through her veins, appearing to infuse her body with a rippling firelike brilliance. In that single second, Devon experienced through her the burst of consciousness attained when the soul entered the Kynn collective. The heightened awareness of the nonphysical realm overwhelmed and amazed.

Surging in and out of her depth once more, Devon gave in to his own mounting need. Orgasm dazzled, an exploding pinwheel of light and color. His cock jetted liquid electricity. Wholly receptive, Rachel's womb was his temple, her flesh the rich loam that would nourish his seed.

Afterward, they lay together. Just breathing. Just being. Somehow Devon had shifted his weight and they were side by side, entangled in each other's arms.

Devon savored every curve, every feminine angle of her, from her plump breasts to her long, lean legs. The knot of emptiness he'd carried in his heart had finally dissolved. Arousal rose all over again.

He couldn't resist touching her. His fingers brushed along her cheek, tracing her lips. "How are you doing?"

Rachel stirred under his touch. "I—I'm not sure." Her breath caught in her throat. A small shudder trembled through her body before a single tear rolled down her cheek. A strange look clouded her eyes. She quickly turned her head, trying to hide her face.

Concerned, Devon stroked her hair away from her face, smoothing the tangles with a gentle touch. The crossing was always hard. The adjustment in body, mind, and spirit was sometimes difficult to take. Everything had changed in her life. Grieving over mortality lost was normal.

"Is everything okay, honey?"

Rachel finally responded. She looked up, tears welling in her blue eyes. "I can't believe this is happening." She bit her lower lip. "It doesn't feel real. You don't feel real. It's like I'll wake up and it'll all be gone tomorrow."

Heart twisting, Devon cupped her cheek. "It's not going to end, you and I. Once a Kynn takes a mate, it is forever."

A soft smile tugged at her mouth, making him want to lay claim to her luscious lips. "Forever," she mouthed the word, drawing it out. "And a day. That's how long I want it to last. Forever and a day."

Devon dipped his head, nuzzling the soft skin of her neck. His senses were overflowing to bursting, but so was his heart. "And it shall be so, my love."

Rachel lowered her hand, brushing her palm across the smooth plane of her stomach. A shy smile turned up one corner of her mouth, like a child with a secret wish. "When you climaxed, I felt something happen inside, something I've never felt before."

He arched a single brow, grinning. "Orgasm, I hope."

She drew in a breath as if to fortify herself. "No, past that, I felt something else. Like a new energy, a new life entered me."

"In essence, one has."

Rachel shook her head, her blue eyes serious. "No, Devon.

It was something more, something else. Something only a woman would feel." Her face, already flushed, deepened a shade. "They say a woman knows when that moment happens."

Her words enticed. Curiosity filled him. "*That* moment?"

Gaze fixed on his, Rachel nodded. "That moment when she conceives." The look on her face, mirrored in her eyes, was absolutely serious.

Brows shooting up in disbelief, Devon shook his head. "The Kynn cannot reproduce." But disbelief died when he caught sight of the spark in her blue eyes. Her features were positively radiant with possibility. A woman's hopes and dreams.

Rachel lifted her hand, slowly tracing the mark on his chest, before touching the mark on her own thigh. "You said it yourself. We both bear a mark that completes the other."

Devon didn't know what to say. Everything seemed to be falling into place with frightening precision. Almost as if it had all been somehow preordained. Sucking in a deep breath, he said softly, "Our kind is on the edge of extinction. The ability to reproduce would bring new prosperity to the Kynn as a race."

Rachel's voice was hoarse and low. "I can't explain what happened, except that it was incredible." She looked at him and smiled. "But I know what I felt. Electrified, like I'd grabbed onto a hot-wire fence. The shock went all the way through my womb."

Devon didn't doubt her. In the space of mere seconds his heart was in his throat, tight with his love for this woman. Everything felt so right between them, the binding of two souls meant to be together. Forever. He never wanted this moment to end.

His gaze ranged over her, skimming her breast, then lower to her Venus mount, a sexy and seductive trail.

His body automatically tightened with fresh response. What would she look like with her belly bulging, heavy with child?

Was it true he and Rachel could somehow overcome the disease of barrenness cursing the Kynn for centuries uncounted?

He didn't know the answers to any of those questions. But he wanted to find out.

Devon held her close, caressing her, murmuring softly into her ear, "I hope you're right." Relishing the feel of her skin against his, he cupped a breast. Heavy, soft, and womanly.

Her nipple peaked when his fingers brushed over it. *Made for suckling a child.*

Anticipation gave his body fresh strength. Want exploded into desire. The blood in his head migrated to his cock. Her conviction whetted his need to delve into the possibility.

Giving him a sultry pout, Rachel's hand found the crux of his thighs. "Something happened inside me." She closed eager fingers around his length. Her touch burned into his flesh. "And it will again."

Their gazes locked, the moment suspended as a silent communication passed between them, their minds joining into one.

"Might as well try." She kissed him gently.

A jolt of need set his body on fire all over again. "We have nothing to lose."

Easing onto his back, Devon eagerly pulled Rachel on top. Might as well enjoy the view as she took her pleasure. "I'd hoped this would happen."

Rachel grinned as she straddled him. "You're insatiable," she laughed breathlessly. Her hands took control, guiding the tip of his penis toward her slick junction. "Not that I have any complaints."

Devon moaned as she seated herself to the hilt. The connection of body parts went smoothly. "If you do, my dear, you'll have to take it up with management."

Thoroughly impaled, Rachel's sweet, wet heat closed around him like a hand wearing a velvet glove. Her hips gyrated in a natural rhythm. Each undulation sent widening ripples of delight though him. Liquid friction kept them moving in sync. The sensations kept building. Higher. Hotter.

Within minutes, pleasure rose past boiling to blazing.

Rachel leaned forward. Tossing him a delighted grin, she smoothed her hands over his shoulders and chest. Warm palms teased and tweaked his flat pale nipples. A little payback. “Do you think we’re doing it right?”

Devon smiled, enjoying the rapture sparking between their bodies. He’d never felt so incredibly happy. And, dare he think it, fulfilled? His heart ached with a joy he’d never thought a man capable of attaining. The idea of becoming a father both frightened and thrilled him.

Throat tightening with emotion, his palm sought her abdomen and settled there. The contact between them shimmered, electric in its intensity. Magic as ancient as the universe itself took control. Something was definitely happening. The quaking pressure of climax built all over again.

“I don’t know,” he gasped through a groan of effort, “but we’re sure as hell going to try.”

Here's a sneak peek at Kate Douglas's latest novella, "Chanku Journey,"
in *Sexy Beast III!*

Coming soon!

1

Tia Mason stared, transfixed by the creamy white box covering her lap. After a long, silent moment, she slowly raised her head, glanced to her right, and caught her new packmate, Lisa Quinn, smiling at her. Tia took a deep breath. Let it out. Took another. With trembling hands, she slipped her fingers beneath the white satin ribbon and pushed it down the length of the box and over the end. She looked at Lisa once more, then stared at the box again.

"What's the matter? You act like you're afraid it'll bite." Lisa's teasing laughter was followed by a soft, supportive hand on Tia's forearm. "Open it, hon. It's okay."

Tia nodded as she slipped her fingers beneath the edges of the stiff cardboard lid and lifted it. A dusty hint of rose-scented sachet wafted into the air. Her first thought was how much the sweet perfume reminded her of her mother.

Then she promptly burst into tears.

She was so not ready for this. She forced the lid back on the box. The scent of the sachet lingered. "I can't do it, Lisa. I really can't do it."

"Can't do what? Marry your bonded mate, the man you've been in love with since the first time you saw him? Wear your mother's wedding gown? Say 'I do' in front of the people who love you? C'mon, hon. You should be happy, not sitting here in a puddle of tears. What's the matter?"

Tia tried to talk, couldn't, and took the tissue Lisa shoved into her hand. She blew her nose and wiped her eyes. "I have panic attacks just thinking about the wedding. What does that tell you? Putting on my mother's dress . . ." She brushed the top of the box with her fingers. "Having Dad walk me down the aisle. I mean, it all sounds perfectly normal, but everything's going to change and it's scaring the crap out of me."

Lisa snorted. Tia swung her head around and glared. "You're not taking me very seriously, are you?"

Holding up both hands, Lisa said, "Yes. Yes, I am, but it's just so funny to hear you complaining about something normal. You're a shapeshifter, for crying out loud. A fucking wolf, Tia, just like the rest of the pack. There's not anything remotely normal about any of us."

Tia glared at Lisa and then realized she suddenly felt like giggling, not crying. With a dramatic sigh, she held out her hand for another tissue, which Lisa dropped into her palm. Tia wiped her eyes again, patted the top of the box for good measure, and settled back against the arm of the couch. "Okay," she said, fighting the lingering urge to laugh hysterically, "panic attack averted. For now. I've got it under control. Dad may have to carry me down the aisle kicking and screaming, but . . ."

"You'll be fine. We'll check out the dress later if you want. Concentrate on who's coming." Lisa poured a glass of wine and handed it to Tia, obviously prepared for some heavy-duty girl talk. "It's more important, don't you think, to focus on the people who love you, not on whether you're going to make it down the aisle without tripping over your toes?"

Tia laughed. "Gee, thanks. Now you've given me a whole new

set of worries." She sipped at the chilled Pinot Grigio and began to relax. Thank goodness for Lisa. Like her mate, Tinker, she was loving and warm and so wonderfully practical. Though she hadn't known Lisa all that long, Tia felt unbelievably comfortable with her.

Just as she felt comfortable with all the others who were coming there to celebrate. Every one of them, including the often mysterious Anton Cheval. Would she and Luc have the same kind of loving relationship as Keisha and Anton? Sometimes Tia found it hard to believe Luc loved her as much as he did, as much as she loved him.

Then she'd remember their mating bond, the fact there were no secrets between them. Yes, he definitely loved her. In every way possible, at every opportunity.

She glanced at Lisa and realized that, in their own way, all of her pack members loved her, and Tia loved every one of them. The bond of Chanku was more than mere membership in a particular pack; it was a blood link among all of them, a tie that could not be broken.

She thought of Shannon, her longtime friend who was also coming west to be her maid of honor. They'd been like sisters growing up, long before either one of them suspected they were connected by more than friendship but also by their Chanku blood.

Shannon was coming out from Maine with her mate, Jacob Trent, along with Lisa's brother, Baylor. Tia took Lisa's hand and squeezed her fingers. "I just thought of Bay and it reminded me, I got a call last night from Mik Fuentes. He said they've completed their assignment in Alabama in plenty of time to get here for the wedding, so not only will Baylor be here, you'll finally get to see your sister Tala."

A huge smile spread across Lisa's face. "I can't wait to see Mary Ellen . . . er, Tala, and Bay. It's been over ten years. I still can't believe she's bonded with two men."

Tia squeezed Lisa's hand again. "Makes my bout of nerves look pretty dumb. You must be a basket case, waiting to reunite with your brother and sister."

Lisa nodded. "Excited, scared. Anxious . . . We were such a dysfunctional family."

Typical of Chanku, Tia thought. So confusing, to live as a human with the heart and mind of a wolf buried away, hidden deep in your soul. She was one of the lucky ones. She'd found the answers to all her questions in the love of one man, in the love of the pack.

Like Lisa, she'd been given the gift of an amazing birthright. Lisa was right. What was she so nervous about? Tia leaned close and kissed Lisa on the lips. "You're not dysfunctional anymore . . . and that brother of yours . . . wow! When Bay was here for those two months working while Luc got his resignation from the Secret Service all straightened out . . ." Tia fanned herself with her palm. "He is very, very hot."

"If you say so." Lisa laughed.

Lisa's dry comment and burst of laughter wiped away all of Tia's lingering nerves. For now. She slipped the lid off the box in her lap and gently shook her mother's wedding dress out of the tissue. "I can't imagine this will fit. Mom was such a tiny little thing." She held it up, barely controlling the sudden sting of tears behind her eyes. If only Camille had lived to see this day.

"Well, you're skinny all around. Just taller, I'll bet." Lisa took the white satin gown with its tiny seed pearls and held it up to Tia. "It probably touched the ground on your mom. Try it on. I think it's going to be gorgeous. I'm a decent seamstress. Trust me. I'll make it work."

Tia stood up and slipped her shirt over her head. It had better work. She'd put this off much too long—the wedding was barely two weeks away.

* * *

Shannon Murphy rolled over in bed and snuggled close against her packmate's backside. The Maine morning was crisp and cold, and Baylor Quinn radiated heat like a furnace. He slept soundly, but when she wrapped her fingers around his partially tumescent cock, he rolled his hips closer to her belly.

Even in sleep the man was more than a handful. Her fingertips barely met where they circled his girth. Still half asleep herself, Shannon rubbed her thumb lazily over the smooth flesh of the crown, touching the sensitive tip usually covered by Bay's foreskin.

Bay moaned in his sleep. The thrusting movement of his hips took on a slow but steady rhythm as Shannon rubbed lazy circles over his silky skin.

Where was Jake? She nuzzled her chin along Bay's spine and cast her thoughts for her mate. He'd been gone since long before dawn. She imagined him even now, racing along the dark trails beneath the heavy canopy of leaves with a big wolven grin on his face.

There was no answer to Shannon's questing thoughts. Instead, the mattress dipped behind her and her mate slipped beneath the covers. Jake smelled of forest and golden grass. His skin felt icy from the morning chill.

Shannon shivered when he stretched full-length along her spine. His nipples were hard little points pressing into her back. His cock, as hot as his body was cold, slipped naturally between her legs from behind and rested hard and thick against her sex.

"Were you starting without me?" he whispered.

Shannon felt the warm tickle of Jake's breath against her ear. "Thought about it. I was getting worried. I didn't expect you to be gone for so long."

"I needed the run. I've had a lot on my mind."

"I forgot to ask. Did you get the plane tickets yet for San Francisco?" Shannon tilted her hips just enough to bring his cock into perfect contact with her clit. "The wedding is just two weeks away."

That's part of what's on my mind.

Jake's switch to mindtalking hinted at more concern than mere tickets from Maine to San Francisco. *What's up?* Shannon asked.

I plan to tell Luc we're staying here permanently. Is that okay with you? He knows I've been thinking of my own pack, but . . .

You know it's okay with me, though I do want to go to the wedding. I hardly know the guys, but Tia's been my best friend for most of my life.

Wanna go on the back of my bike?

"What?" Shannon whispered fiercely as she swung her head around to look over her shoulder at Jake. He was grinning like a damned fool, even as his cock began riding slick and fast along the crease of her butt and down between her thighs. "That's got to be at least three thousand miles. I don't think so."

"Think of all that power between your legs." His voice dropped to a deeper level as he whispered the words against her neck. His lips tickled her nape. He tilted his hips and angled his cock higher until the silky crown kissed her swollen clit. Shannon moaned when he nuzzled the side of her neck and whispered in her ear. His rough, sexy voice affirmed the images filling her mind and heating her sex.

"Think of it, sweetheart . . . the rumble of that big engine throbbing, hot and solid and almost alive, the way it vibrates the warm leather over your sweet little pussy. The smells of forest and plains and the wind in your face . . ." Jake emphasizing his words with the smooth glide of his cock over her suddenly very wet sex almost took the breath from Shannon's lungs.

Almost.

She took a deep breath and reached for a bit of common

sense and control. "Right. The wind in my face and my hair tied in knots. You forget, Bay doesn't have a bike and he's going with us." Shannon let go of Bay's now fully erect cock, slipped away from Jake's, and rolled over completely. Now that she could glare directly at Jake, Shannon realized he didn't seem the least perturbed.

Bay raised up and flopped over on his left side, obviously wide awake. At least, his cock was awake. Shannon felt the thick slide of it against her buttocks and couldn't help but angle her hips just enough for him to take over Jake's smooth glide.

Bay nipped her shoulder and chuckled softly in Shannon's ear. "Sorry, sweetie. Bay does have a bike. Jake talked me into buying one yesterday. I pick it up Monday."

"I don't believe you two." She really should put her foot down, but all the time Shannon was fuming, Bay was rubbing his cock between her cheeks and Jake was meeting him in the middle, rubbing slowly between her legs.

It was hard to argue with two guys when they double teamed a girl. She knew they got off on the sensation of their sizeable penises sliding one against the other as much as they did the creamy heat between her legs. Shannon tilted her hips back against Bay's belly as his arms came around her waist and his hands found both her breasts. Crossing his arms over her chest, Bay plucked at her nipples, pinching them none too gently between callused fingers.

Not to be outdone, Jake hugged Shannon, grabbing her buttocks with his fingers, slipping them between her butt and Bay's flat belly to press against her anus. She wriggled closer, realizing Jake had managed not only to sandwich her even tighter between the two men, but that he also stroked Bay's cock with his fingertips on each thrust.

Shannon closed her eyes and absorbed the sensations, the myriad nerves tingling with each perfect sweep of Jake's fingers. She heard the rustle of crisp sheets, the steady breathing of both men, and the squishy, wet sounds of their cocks sliding against each other between her legs. When she listened very carefully, she caught the rapid beat of their hearts and the wet little click of two swollen cock heads rubbing one past the other.

She pictured the flared crowns, wet and distended now, glistening with fluids from her well-lubricated sex blended with the uncontrollable flow of pre-cum seeping from the tips. Both men were uncut. Their foreskins would be stretched back behind the swollen heads now, the skin flushed dark red, the sensitive tips exposed.

Shannon's pussy clenched as Jake's cock slipped between her slick labia with the lightest of touches. She bit back a moan. Every part of her body reacted, teased by the passage, by the smooth heat and perfect friction against her ass and her clit. Jake had found a rhythm now, pressing against her sphincter with his fingers as he thrust his cock slowly between her legs. Bay's tight grasp on her nipples made them ache, but the pain sent a constant pulse of pleasure directly to her clit.

She tightened the muscles in her sex against the hollow, needy sensation growing in the pit of her belly. Jake's fingers pressed tighter against her ass, Bay twisted her nipples, and their cocks slipped one over the other against her swollen sex.

The tension grew. She needed penetration, anything to take her over the edge. Shannon's breathing turned choppy; her eyes closed as she absorbed the pleasure. Her whole body shivered with growing arousal.

Jake's fingers penetrated her ass just as Bay pinched her nipples. Shannon jerked and screamed, her back arching as she spasmed through her first climax, shuddering and shivering, her pussy awash in a liquid orgasmic release.

Without even breaking rhythm, Jake entered her with his next stroke, burying himself all the way to the hilt on a single thrust. Shannon's muscles clenched around his cock. Her sex still rippled with aftershocks as Jake rolled over to his back and took her with him.

Bay quickly knelt between their legs and pressed the broad crown of his cock against her bottom. Still relaxed from Jake's fingers, Shannon tilted her hips to make Bay's access easier. He circled the puckered entrance with his fingers first, relaxing her even more, then pressed harder with his cock. Shannon pushed out as Bay moved forward. He was so damned big and it burned when he stretched her, slowly pressing in and out, a little farther each time as he worked beyond her tight sphincter. Once his broad crown passed beyond the loop of muscle, the pain disappeared, melding swiftly into a dark slide of pleasure. Shannon groaned as Bay entered her slowly, carefully, deeply.

Jake sighed as well. Sex-drugged, drifting in waves of sensation, Shannon opened her eyes and stared into his, into the deep amber eyes shaded in inky lashes so much like Bay's. Jake took her hands in his and stretched her arms over his head, pulling her down until her nipples rubbed the thick hair on his chest. Bay stretched out over her body and covered the backs of her hands, linking his fingers with Jake's.

Connected now, with Shannon sandwiched between them, their bodies linked but their thoughts still private, Bay slowly began moving his hips. He was the one who directed them, sliding deep inside Shannon, his erection slipping past Jake's and separated by nothing more than the thin membrane dividing her passages.

She imagined their cocks: smooth skin over muscle, swollen with blood and hard as baseball bats, slowly penetrating and retreating, one past the other deep inside her body. She tried to imagine the sensation, what her men were feeling with each pull and thrust. It was something she'd shared with both of them before.

Imagination was good, but Shannon wanted reality. She opened her mind to her lovers, slipping quietly into their thoughts and feelings, grasping at once the deep, lush sensuality of two men, lovers and friends, slowly but surely fucking each other through the woman they loved.

They didn't so much make love to Shannon as they loved each other within her body. Feeling as much like a beloved vessel as a participant, Shannon lost herself to sensation, to the coarse hair on Jake's chest scraping her tender nipples, to the hard muscles of Bay's chest and the softer, silkier hair that spread over his. She loved the way it brushed against her back, loved the small tremors she felt in his body as he fought the rising level of excitement threatening his control.

She slipped into Bay's mind, awash in his love for Jake and for herself, a pure, unquestioned love for both of them, and the hope he had to satisfy their needs and desires. She allowed herself a moment of pure sensation, the tight slide deep inside her rectum and the way her body pulled at Bay's cock, the way her muscles clenched tightly around the base of his penis like a hot, wet fist.

Bay felt it from his spine to his balls, that tight, needy pull against him, but the sensations were secondary to the solid contact between his cock and Jake's. Shannon realized she was clenching her muscles even tighter, responding to Bay's need to be closer to Jake, closer to her.

She slipped her searching thoughts free of Bay then, concentrating instead on Jake. His love was unquestionable, his pride in her almost undoing her. As caught in sensation as Bay, Jake still made love to Shannon first, to Bay second. He held on to control by a thread. Each rhythmic contraction of Shannon's sex brought him closer to the edge, but he fought it with everything he had.

Bay's cock slid past Jake's, and Jake shuddered beneath her. Shannon rubbed her taut nipples across Jake's chest and felt his pectoral muscles jerk in response. She tightened her sex, clenching both men in her velvet clasp.

Short gasps escaped them as the breath hitched in their

throats. At the same time, she sensed a silent communication pass between her lovers; she felt their muscles tense and their huge cocks, if possible, grow larger.

Jake let go of Shannon's hands, tilted his hips, and drew his knees up on either side of her, lifting her higher, dragging the full length of his cock over her clit on both retreat and entry. Bay shifted just a bit, driving deeper inside with every well-aimed thrust. Shannon felt the solid pressure against her perineum and knew their sacs pressed tightly together with each stroke, knew their trembling bodies fought the need to come.

Shannon fought it as well, even as the intensity of their loving grew, as her body shivered and her legs trembled with pleasure. Sensory overload flooded her mind. The combination of both Jake and Bay, of their arousal, of their overwhelming desire, of their love in all its myriad forms filled her thoughts, became Shannon's thoughts and she cried out with the unbelievable surge of sensations.

Her scream was the trigger, the key that sent both men into climax. Jake's thrust lifted her into Bay. Bay's cock drove deep, but he didn't hold at the point of orgasm.

Instead he thrust harder, sliding deep into her with Jake, both of them going in and out in tandem, each one filling her with their seed. Their groans enveloped her senses; their semen, hot and thick, filled her body.

Her eyes refused to focus, and her thoughts scattered. Shannon's entire body clenched in one spasmodic tremor with muscles locked, holding both men inside. Her heart pounded in her chest and sweat covered her body front and back, soaking the bedding. Hers? Bay's? Jake's?

Shannon's legs trembled beneath Bay's; her breasts, swollen and tender, throbbed in time with her racing heart. Her vision refused to clear. Little black spots wavered in front of her eyes.

Lungs heaving, she dragged in deep, ragged breaths of air. Her breasts pressed against Jake's rising and falling chest; her back felt compressed by Bay's weight. When she finally thought to open her thoughts to her men, there was a sense of surprise in both their minds, that the sex could be this good, this hot, time after time, two men with one woman.

Their woman.

Hadn't they always fantasized two women, one man?

Shannon would have smiled if she'd had the energy. Enervated, she lay there, compressed between Bay and Jake, welcoming Bay's weight, Jake's strength.

Her vision cleared slowly, the spots fading as her heart settled once again into its normal rhythm. Still she sprawled bonelessly over Jake's body, loving the feeling of both men and the knowledge they loved her, and that, after so many years searching, she'd finally found love.

Jake swept her tangled hair back from her forehead. "Anyway," he said, as if he'd not once again rocked her world, "I really think it would be an adventure to take the bike out to California. What do you say?"

Bay tilted his hips, pressing against her buttocks. His cock was no longer hard as a post, but she still felt him deep inside her. "Say yes, Shannon. Please?"

"Oh Lord, that feels good. You're cheating."

Laughing, Bay slipped free of Shannon's body and rolled to one side. He groaned. "Okay, no more undue influence." Bay swatted her on the butt, then crawled off the bed and headed for the bathroom.

Shannon sighed and tightened her vaginal muscles around Jake's cock. He'd softened a bit as well but still managed to fill her with sensation. "How will I carry enough clothes? We're supposed to have a bachelorette party for Tia, and I'll need something for the wedding and . . ."

"The bike's got big panniers, but we're going to San Francisco. They have stores. You can buy all new clothes when we get there and mail them home when it's time to leave. In fact, you can even fly home if you like and Bay and I will ride back on our own. Please, sweetie? It'll be such a cool adventure."

Laughing, Shannon lowered her head to Jake's chest. "You're willing to bribe me with a shopping trip in San Francisco? Your credit card?" He nodded. "That's cheating. I may be a wolf at heart, but it doesn't affect my shopping gene." She rubbed her nose against his chest, licked the nipple over his heart, then grumbled, "As if I have any say in the matter? Yes, we'll take the bikes to San Francisco. But I'll be damned if I sleep in a tent. Nice motels all the way, good restaurants, and stops whenever my butt gets tired or I have to pee. And backrubs. I insist on backrubs."

"Damn, woman. You drive a hard bargain." Jake lifted her chin with his hands and kissed her soundly. Shannon kissed him back and wondered what kind of fool she was.

Jake ended the kiss with a shout. "Hey! Baylor . . . we won! She said yes!"

Over three thousand miles on a motorcycle? Shannon dropped her forehead against Jake's chest. She must be nuts.

Anton Cheval checked the calendar one more time, then gazed steadily at his very pregnant mate. She stood in the doorway to his office with all the grace of an African queen: elegant, self-confident, and sexy as hell, despite the fact she was into her eighth month of pregnancy. "We're pushing it, love, flying to San Francisco for your cousin's wedding. What if you deliver early?"

Keisha laughed and Anton knew he was going to cave. So many were in awe of him, but never this lovely woman. No respect from her at all. He had to bite back a smile.

"Then you, my love, will deliver our daughter." She stepped into the room, covered his hand with hers, and placed her other palm over his heart.

He felt the damned thing skip a beat. She had no idea how

much power she held over him, how much he needed her. Anton covered her hand and pressed it against his chest. "It's not something to joke about. I'm terrified of anything happening to . . ."

"Nothing will happen. Besides, we'll have Stefan and Xandi along, and Oliver, too. I imagine he knows how to deliver babies, right?"

"Oliver is good at many things, but I'm not sure the practice of obstetrics is in his repertoire. We have two weeks. If you're still feeling this good, then we can . . ."

Keisha shook her head. "No, we don't have two weeks. We need to be there in less than a week. I am not going to miss Tia's bachelorette party, even if I can't drink those fuzzy little concoctions she loves."

Stefan and Xandi wandered into the room. Anton looked up and shrugged his shoulders. Stefan was the brother he'd never had, the son he loved, and the lover who kept him sane at times like these. "How do you feel about this trip, Stefan? I'm concerned about the girls traveling so far this late in their pregnancies. I could fly down on my own, perform the ceremony as I promised Tia and . . ."

"Not in this life you won't!" Keisha stood and glared at Anton. She reached for Xandi and the two women clasped hands.

He knew then the battle was a foregone conclusion. Stefan caught his eye, shrugged his shoulders once again, and then burst into laughter. "It is a matriarchal society, you know." He leaned over and kissed his mate. "When you mate with a Chanku bitch, she gets the balls."

Anton raised his eyes to the heavens . . . actually, to the large chandelier over the dining room table. "There are days, Stefan, when I wish I'd never divulged that bit of information."

Keisha stood up. Her body was heavy with her pregnancy, but he'd never seen her more beautiful. Nor, Anton thought, had she ever been more powerful, more sure of herself. "Your divulging information makes no difference. We are what we are. We need to leave by Thursday. Can you make arrangements so the plane is ready to go by then?"

Anton nodded, but the sense of misgiving wouldn't leave him. Xandi's pregnancy wasn't quite as far along as Keisha's, but both women were well beyond the time when doctors would normally allow them to travel. However, their doctor, one of the few familiar with the Chanku species, had found no reason to inhibit travel, at least for another few weeks.

Damned charlatan. Unfortunately, the man was brilliant and someone Anton had learned to respect.

"The plane will be ready. As will I. We leave on Thursday." He glanced over Keisha's head and caught Stefan's eyes. The bastard had a grin on his face a mile wide, but then he loved it when Anton lost a battle. Damn, if he didn't love the man, he'd kill him where he stood.

Tala held the tiny baby in her arms for one last look. The infant stared up at her, fearless, filled with trust. Her innocence made Tala think of how much she'd had to learn to trust over the past few months. How much farther she still had to go. Blinking back tears, she handed the child over to the paramedic and signaled to the two large wolves sitting patiently beside her. It was time to go home.

The Alabama police chief who'd called in the team from Pack Dynamics caught Tala before she could gather her crew and leave. "We found the kidnapper back in the swamp. Was it necessary to rip out his throat?" He glanced nervously at the wolves sitting calmly beside Tala. "I had no idea they were killers."

"So was the man who died." Tala nodded toward the helicopter lifting off with the child safely inside. Dust and leaves swirled in the golden rays of the late afternoon sun as the chopper whirled away toward Mobile. The baby would be returned to her mother: safe, unharmed, and hopefully young enough that this terrible incident would be forgotten. "The kidnapper didn't hesitate to kill the nanny. The child would have died the moment the ransom was paid. You knew it. We knew it. The bastard's killed before. This time he made a mistake when he went after my wolves with a gun. They had no choice."

The police chief shook his head. "Amazing animals. They look so calm sitting there, so intelligent. You'd never guess they killed a man not an hour ago. As tiny as you are, don't you ever worry about them? I was surprised to see they hadn't been castrated, that you worked with intact males. They can be so aggressive."

Tala immediately threw up her mental blocks. No way could she carry on an intelligent conversation with the reaction she was certain the guys had to the chief's innocent comment. Biting back laughter, she shook her head. If only the man knew . . . "No. We don't believe in neutering. We need their aggressive tendencies. They're very well trained." She patted both animals on their heads. The larger one growled. The police chief took a step back.

"I sure hope so." He held out his hand. Tala took his in a firm grasp, and they shook hands. Another crisis averted.

"We'll be going now. I have a long drive back to the airport, and my boys need some rest before the flight. You have Ulrich Mason's number if you need to reach us, and of course we'll be available should there be any hearings. I'm glad we were able to help." Tala turned and walked away with the two huge wolves following close behind. She felt the chief's gaze on her back all the way to her SUV. She'd left the rental vehicle with its darkly tinted windows parked at the side of the road.

"Okay guys. Get in." She opened the door and both animals jumped into the back seat. Tala climbed in, fastened her seat belt, and pulled out onto the pavement, heading off into the setting sun. It felt good, knowing their intervention had saved that little girl's life.

Tala glanced into the rearview mirror at the two unbelievably beautiful naked men slipping into jeans and shirts. Mik Fuentes looked up and caught her eye. The smile that spread slowly across his face made her heart beat a little faster and the muscles in her pussy clench in anticipation. He shoved his long, black hair out of his eyes and winked.

"Neutered, eh? Not this puppy."

AJ Temple pulled his knit shirt over his head and nudged Mik. "Maybe that's your problem. No balls." He winked. Tala returned his grin in the reflection in the rearview mirror. With his curling dark hair and thick black lashes around those amber eyes, he was absolutely gorgeous . . . and full of the devil.

Mik leaned back in the seat and folded his muscular arms behind his head. "You were sucking on something of mine last night, and it wasn't my cock. That piece of meat was resting comfortably deep inside our lady's lovely little pussy."

AJ laughed, but he squirmed in his seat. Tala wished she was tall enough to see more of him in the mirror because she was absolutely positive he'd gotten hard just thinking about sucking Mik's balls. Her pussy clenched in sympathy. There was something so hot about sex in a motel room with two absolutely gorgeous men.

Her men. Her bonded mates. Damn, how could she have ever gotten so lucky? Tala turned her attention toward the road west. Musing aloud, she asked, "What do you guys think of driving instead of flying home? There's a lot of country I haven't seen between here and California." *And a lot of motel rooms . . .* For a retired prostitute who'd really loved her work, roadside motels were pretty special places.

"Sounds good." Mik fastened his seatbelt and nudged AJ. "You know how it is with Tala and those seedy little motels . . ."